# The Jigsaw Maker

## Adrienne Dines

**And also by Adrienne Dines**
*Toppling Miss April*

**Other titles published by transita**

*A Proper Family Christmas* by Jane Gordon-Cumming
*After Michael* by Betty O'Rourke
*Dangerous Sports Euthanasia Society* by Christine Coleman
*Elissa's Castle* by Juliet Greenwood
*Emotional Geology* by Linda Gilliard
*Forgotten Dreams* by Doris Leadbetter
*Gang of Four* by Liz Byrski
*Neptune's Daughter* by Beryl Kingston
*Pond Lane and Paris* by Susie Vereker
*Scuba Dancing* by Nicola Slade
*Stage by Stage* by Jan Jones
*The Waiting Time* by Sara Banerji
*Tuesday Night at the Kasbah* by Patricia Kitchin
*Turning Point* by Bowering Sivers
*Uphill All the Way* by Sue Moorcroft

**transita**

To find out more about transita, our books and our authors
visit *www.transita.co.uk*

# The Jigsaw Maker

## Adrienne Dines

transita

Published by Transita
3 Newtec Place, Magdalen Road,
Oxford OX4 1RE. United Kingdom.
Tel: (01865) 204393. Fax: (01865) 248780.
email: info@transita.co.uk
http://www.transita.co.uk

British Library Cataloguing in Publication Data
A catalogue record for this book is available from the British Library

Cover design by Baseline Arts Ltd, Oxford
Produced for Transita by Deer Park Productions, Tavistock
Typeset by PDQ Typesetting, Newcastle-under-Lyme
Printed and bound by Bookmarque, Croydon

## ABOUT THE AUTHOR

Adrienne Dines was born in Dublin in 1959, which qualifies her as a 'woman of a certain age' today. She is very proud of this fact.

She graduated from Trinity College, Dublin in 1981 and moved to Weybridge, Surrey to teach in a convent school. Marriage to a BP oilman saw her packed off to Aberdeen for ten years where she taught in a variety of secondary schools, wrote poetry and speeches and gave birth to three sons. Now back in Weybridge, she is a contributor to parish and diocesan publications and a member of the American Women of Surrey Writers' Group. She is still a speech-writer – for world champion canoeists, social functions and even ordinations. Many of her speeches are delivered in verse as it affords her the freedom to 'blame it on the rhyme'.

Adrienne is also the author of *Toppling Miss April*.

ACKNOWLEDGEMENTS

I am so grateful to all the people who helped put the jigsaw together.

My family – my husband Tim and sons, Kieran, Tom and Freddy; my parents Tom and Lall Phillips and parents-in-law, Edward and Marjorie Dines; my sisters, Caroline McNiff and Margie Kennedy, and my brother Tom Phillips, are always supportive.

My friends Sue Bohane and Fiachra (Woody) Woodman proofread, and Jenny Nealon helped to juggle the pieces.

My editor Marina Oliver spotted the mistakes in time.

All at Transita Publishers – especially Nikki Read, Giles Lewis, Debbie, Helen, Ros and Fiona – who are incredibly encouraging and approachable.

The wonderful Mary Campbell and Laura Kennedy in Ireland had the enthusiasm to take The Jigsaw Maker and run with it.

The American Women of Surrey Writers' Group – Suzanne Davidovac, Mary Albanese, Tammye Huf, Kelly Gerard and Meg Gardiner who put up with six months of false starts before the pieces slotted into place!

You're all great.

# DEDICATION

For my middle son, Tom

# Rathshannan
## 2006

USUALLY WHEN SHE OPENED THE SHOP on a Monday morning a whoosh of quiet greeted her – a sort of gentle acceptance that because it was five to nine, Lizzie Flynn would be turning her key in the door. And because she took precautions, there were never surprises: no opportunist burglar broke in; no errant sparks set off a fire; nobody else got there first. Unlike today.

On the table that served as a counter there was a large cardboard box, its tissue-wrapped contents spilling out. Some of them Lizzie recognised. She stood holding the door open, unsure whether she should go for help or stay and investigate. She left the key in the lock and inched into the shop. Whoever it was was still there. She could hear shuffling in the cupboard at the back of the shop and, as she came nearer the box, marvelled at her intruder's cheek. Scattered round the table, broken bits of Lizzie's dried flower arrangements were swept into little piles, other items had been packed already – items that should have been on the shelves behind, where they always were. Bloody hell! Not only was he stealing her stock, he was packing it first. She bristled. Picking up a paperweight she crept to the cupboard.

'Good morning, Lizzie. What are you doing here so early?'

Lizzie started, amazed, as her sister backed out, arms laden. She looked dishevelled, long greying hair swept up in a careless bunch tied with a flowery scarf and her glasses askew.

'What am *I* doing here?' Lizzie glared at the mess in the shop. 'I'm not anywhere I shouldn't be at this time on a Monday.' She pointed at the table. 'This is where I come to start my week's work but it looks like I won't be able to do that today, will I? Because I can't. Because my table is covered in muck and I won't be able to do a thing till you clear it.' She stormed to the door and pulling the key out, slammed it shut. 'What are you doing here anyway?'

Anne dropped the boxes in a heap onto the table and pushed stray hair off her face. Then she stood, hands on hips and, apparently unmoved by Lizzie's anger, skimmed the shop, pausing momentarily to frown at something she saw. 'I dunno, Liz,' she said eventually. 'This place is a heap. You really must do something with it.'

Lizzie looked around the shop in amazement. What on earth was Anne talking about? Apart from the mess on the table and the spillage beneath it, the shop was as it had always been, as it was supposed to be. She started to say that but Anne was already moving towards the soap display.

'I mean, look at this!' She picked up a bar of Lily of the Valley soap and held it out, her face wrinkled as if she found it offensive. 'Who'd want to buy this? Or this?' The soap was dropped and a small tin of talc proffered.

Lizzie shrugged. 'It's talc. Lots of people buy talc.'

Anne smiled. 'They do indeed. But nobody's bought this particular talc, have they?' Her smile turned to a laugh. 'It must have been on that shelf for twenty years!'

Lizzie took the tin from her angrily. 'No, it hasn't. I don't stock out of date items and you know it.' She turned the tin upside down and searched for a 'use by' date on its base. There wasn't one. Anything that had been printed there was long faded. Lizzie felt the colour rise in her cheeks. It wasn't old, it just wasn't required at the moment. She pushed the tin back into its place on the display. 'I don't know what you're on about anyway. What does it matter to you? I stock quality items – everyone knows that.'

Anne leaned her head to one side and regarded Lizzie. There was an expression on her face that looked dangerously like sympathy. Lizzie could feel herself bristle. She hated when Anne did the big sister bit, the I-know-better-than-you bit. Eventually Anne sighed.

'That's the problem, Lizzie. You stock the best, you just don't sell any of it.' She pointed to the box on the table. 'This stuff has been here so long it's lost its edge and these – ' she pulled some postcards from the rack. The ones at the front were faded where they had been exposed. 'Who's going to buy these, for God's sake?'

In the harsh early morning light the cards did look a bit colourless but if she reduced the price, they'd be sure to sell quickly. Or maybe if she moved some of the others from the back. Lizzie crossed her arms defensively in front of her. 'It's not your business.'

Anne stuck the cards back onto the rack. 'You're quite right,' she said. 'It's not my business, it's yours.' When she turned round again her face was set. 'I am merely the supplier of home-made confectionery – which is definitely fresh and which you have not any stock of at the moment because unlike nearly everything else,' she swept the shop disdainfully, 'it sells.' She went over to the table and started to take the packed items out of the box. 'And if this is the sort of tat you want to spend your life and waste your livelihood surrounded by, go ahead. You have yourself in a rut, you've been moping about for weeks. I was only trying to help.'

As she unpacked each arrangement and placed it back on the shelf, Lizzie watched her miserably. She tried to think what to say, how to unsay, but no words came. When Anne finished, she swept the last of the dried stems into her palm and looked around. Lizzie pointed to the bin.

'Over there.'

'Thank you.'

'Anne – '

Anne turned to face her, 'Well?'

Lizzie shrugged. She looked at the arrangements back where they should be, looking neat. And faded. 'Maybe you're right.' She pointed to the shelf. 'I suppose they're looking a bit, well, dull.' She could see Anne's shoulders relax. 'Maybe I could think about replacing some of them.'

Anne shook her head. 'Lizzie, this place is like a mausoleum. You have stuff here since the year dot. You have to have a clear out and brighten the place up. Move with the times.' She held her arms out. 'It's the twenty-first century, for God's sake! The Celtic tiger is up and roaring and the tourists are flocking to hear him. And here you are.' She dropped her arms as if defeated. 'Owner of the quaintest knick-knack shop in Kilkenny and not a thing in it anyone would like to buy. It's rubbish – throw it out!'

The cheek of her! A glorified fudge maker and to listen you'd think she was marketing magnate of the century. Lizzie pulled her coat off and, flinging it on the chair, brushed past her sister angrily. The coat stayed for a minute then slid traitorously to the floor. Anne picked it up.

'Lizzie,' she said gently, as she laid the coat across the chair back. 'You know I'm right. I supply sweets to every tourist trap in the county and most of them are raking it in. They're tapping into the boom and you're living in the past.'

Enough already! 'And what's wrong with that? You got a problem with the past?'

The words were out before she had a chance to stop them. As the sisters glared at each other the air in the room froze and Lizzie could feel it on her forehead, pushing back her hair and making her scalp tingle. She held Anne's eyes as long as she could before she turned away and lifted the empty box onto the floor. Then she took a key from her pocket and, unlocking the drawer of her desk, pulled out her accounts book and opened it. As she made a show of running her fingers down the column she heard Anne cross the room and open the door quietly. As she shut it behind her the air shifted and rustled the dried flowers on the shelf. They scratched against each other and for a moment Lizzie could have sworn they were whispering together. Whispering about her. She kept her head down and tried to focus on the figures on the page in front.

Suddenly, the shop door was flung open and Lizzie braced herself for Anne's retaliatory tirade. She took a deep breath and lifted her head to face the music.

A man was standing in the doorway. With the light behind him she couldn't see his face – just the silhouette of a tall, thin figure with a greatcoat. As he bent his head to come into the shop, the hairs on the back of her head stood on end. So familiar. But his face as he came towards her was a stranger's. She put her pen down. When he reached the table he swung a leather satchel off his shoulder and laid it carefully on the floor beside him.

'Are you Lizzie Flynn?'

'I am.'

His face cleared and he smiled broadly. 'Thank goodness! Then I'm in the right place.' He held his hand out to her. 'I've been looking for you. I'm Jim Nealon. I'm the Jigsaw Maker.'

\*

Lizzie's first inclination was to shake the proffered hand politely, explain that she did not do business with peddlers and then send him on his way. She didn't want to have him there if Anne came back. She couldn't afford to lose the moment. Anne wasn't fiery like her – Anne simmered. And she could sulk for Ireland if given the opportunity.

But he didn't give her the chance. He picked up his satchel and laid it on the table as if he feared whatever was inside might break. He undid the buckles and started to unpack some boxes. They were brick sized and covered in brown paper, thick and flecked with lighter colours, tied with raffia.

'They don't look like jigsaws,' Lizzie said. 'Where are the pictures?' She picked one up and turned it over. 'How do you know how it's supposed to turn out?'

Jim smiled. 'We never do.'

She put the box back on the table. 'How very cryptic. Now, if you'll excuse me, I'm not really in the market for new stock.'

He put the box he was holding down and looked around the shop. 'That's a pity,' he said. 'I thought this was perfect for you – something new, something different.'

For goodness sake, what's with the need to ring changes all of a sudden? She opened her mouth to tell him that she had no intention of buying anything from him, new or not, when the flash of Anne's green Polo passed the window. Inside she caught a glimpse her sister, leaning forward on the steering wheel as she always did, singing to herself. Not a care in the world. Lizzie bit her lip.

'Are you all right?' His voice was gentle. 'If you're too busy, I'll pack up and go away.'

She turned back to see him pick up one of the boxes and start to re-pack.

'No,' she said. 'I'm not busy. Let me see.'

He handed it to her.

Lizzie untied the raffia and one end of the box eased open. She tipped the contents onto a space on the table and spread them out. The pieces were beautiful, tiny, intricately shaped. The backs of them were wood, in this case beech, finely cut so that they were more like buttons than jigsaw pieces and on the fronts varying shades from black to white. Lizzie held one out to him, puzzled. 'What is it?'

Jim took the piece from her and turned it over. 'This side's beech – I didn't plunder it.' He showed her the other side. 'And this is where the beech is from.' He smiled at her confusion. 'Look here.' From the envelope he took some papers. One was a photograph and the other hand-written sheets. He handed the photograph to her.

'It's lovely, where is it?' She took it over to the window to have a better look. It was a black and white picture of an old house, once fine but now rundown, the ivy and roses overgrown. 'It must have been wonderful in its day.'

'It was – here, read this.' He handed her the other pieces of paper.

Lizzie read. *'Balmullen House, Kildangan, Co Kildare, once the residence of...* oh, the full history. What a nice touch. So you provide the picture and the background and...'

'No, read on.'

Lizzie scanned the rest of the page. The handwriting was slanted and old-fashioned. After the initial introduction, the writer identified herself as Mel Sheedy, the daughter of the last housekeeper to have served in the house. For paragraph after paragraph she told of her childhood, the parties, the work and the hardship. It was like being there.

'It's not just a history,' Jim said. 'It's real life. You don't just know what it looks like now; you get a feel for what it was like in its heyday. It's a personal memory.'

'I see. I like that.' Lizzie looked at the picture again. 'But why black and white? That makes it so much harder to put together.'

Jim picked up a few pieces and rolled them in his palms. 'Yes, but so much more rewarding. He held them out. 'What colour are your memories, Lizzie?'

She wasn't expecting that question. It hit her like a wet slap and she could feel it shatter and drip onto her shoulder where it spread and dried in purple stains. She shook her head to clear the image. 'I don't know. Multi-coloured, I suppose.' She could hear her voice, hard.

Jim didn't seem to notice. 'Okay, so look at the photograph and then shut your eyes and imagine that you're Mel. Describe the house, the front of it.'

Lizzie did as she was told and to her surprise the picture sprang into her mind almost straight away. She could see the long drive up to the front and she could hear the sound of carriage wheels on gravel as they slowed to a halt. She saw herself getting out and standing at the front door. There was a breeze and the air was full of the smell of the roses on the trellis to one side and the steady hum of bees.

'You can feel it, can't you?' Jim whispered.

Lizzie nodded.

'Ha!' Jim dropped the pieces back onto the table. 'There you are then! It's personal.' He started to scoop them back into the box. 'I took the photograph, you know. It was a beautiful summer's day and the air was clear and all the colours vivid. But they were just the colours of that day. If I had gone the following day, the sky would have been overcast and grey and it would have been a different picture altogether.' He turned and looked at her. 'You see? A coloured picture would have pinned it down, made it particular to one moment in time.' He folded the letter and slid it back into the envelope. 'But this house doesn't belong to one particular day. When you read Mel's memories they're of lots of days – happy, busy, dull – real life days.' He tied the package up again. 'That's what I hope to do in Rathshannan.'

Lizzie sat down and shook her head. 'Well, I think they're beautiful, I really do. But I can't for the life of me see why you'd want to make jigsaws of Rathshannan. It's probably the least exciting village in the whole of County Kilkenny. Nothing ever happens here.' There was a heat in her cheeks. She held up her hand. 'Honestly. In almost every other place there's something to visit. We're not like that. We're just a place to rest your head en route from one exciting day out to another.'

Jim leaned forward on the table, and placed his palms on either side of the jigsaw he had just repackaged. 'And is that what people want who come to visit a place, do you think? Do you think they want excitement?'

Lizzie shrugged. 'I suppose so.'

Jim shook his head. 'No, they don't, they go to theme parks for that. In country places like this they want memories. They want to understand about a place, feel part of it, even identify with it. Why do you think so many Americans come to Ireland summer after summer? They're looking for their roots, that's why. They don't just want to see the grand buildings, the churches and castles – that's other people's history. They want to see the other places too, the hidden places, the places they might have lived in.' He pushed the box towards her. 'They want to read stories like Mel's and make those memories their own. And then, after they've gone home, they want to sit by the fire, or at the kitchen table and put the pieces of their memories together. And they don't want those memories confined to one particular day either. I give them the outline in black and white and they make whatever colour of it they please.' He looked so intense. 'Don't you see? They want to colour it for themselves – in their own heads. That makes it theirs.' He sat back and was silent.

For a minute Lizzie wasn't quite sure what to say to him. He was deadly serious.

'I see. And are they all on wood... your puzzles?'

Jim was businesslike again. He pulled another couple of boxes out. 'Yep, look here.' He turned the boxes on their ends and showed her some tiny writing in the corner of each. On the one she had seen was written *Balmullen on Beech*. Another said *Clary Bridge on Rowan*.

'I didn't plunder the wood. I wasn't joking about that. It's one of the conditions of the puzzle. It has to be cut from a piece of wood local to the particular scene. In the case of Balmullen, there had been a storm a couple of years before I went there and some of the trees in the grounds were damaged. I managed to salvage some bigger branches and turned the wood till I had pieces suitable.'

'So all the wood is native to the memory?'

'Yes, and that's what I hope to do here. This village may not be exciting in the usual sense but it's old and friendly and has lots of wonderful buildings full of memories that people could share – and lots of trees to work on.' He smiled. 'And you, of course.'

'What do I come under – living memory or dead wood?'

Jim laughed. 'I'm told there isn't a thing about Rathshannan, past or present, you don't know. Definitely living memory.'

Lizzie pointed to the boxes. There were rowans, oaks, yew and sycamore but there was mostly beech. 'And all of it native, you say. Don't you ever cheat?'

'Sometimes.' He smoothed the paper on the box he was holding. 'But I much prefer to get it right.' He smiled at her.

Lizzie smiled back. Even back in their boxes, the wooden jigsaw pieces gave off a smell. It pervaded the usual scents of candles, soap and talc. Old soap, unsold talc. The wood smelt fresh and clean. Lizzie looked at the rows of dried herb arrangements on the counter above the desk. Then she reached over.

'Do you know what, Jim? It's a great idea and I think we might be in business.' She took his hand and shook it warmly. 'Welcome to Rathshannan, Jigsaw Man.'

*

By eleven o'clock that morning the day's excitement was over. A strong wind brought grey clouds that hovered for a while then unleashed a drizzle that stayed all day. Lizzie watched the deserted street and sighed. If there was a good downpour people would wait till it was over then come out in the air afterwards to celebrate its end, potter around and maybe buy themselves something to celebrate their release. Or else they'd don macs and grab umbrellas and go for it, armed with a sense of purpose and a certain opening to any conversation they might get the opportunity to start. *Dreadful weather, isn't it?*

Drizzle was a different matter. Nobody ventured out in drizzle, it was too insidious, 'wettin' rain'. By two in the afternoon she gave up all hope of a customer and, fuelled with thoughts of the morning's conversations, made up her mind. While Anne was not completely right about the state of her shop, there was a hint of truth in her observations and it wouldn't harm anyone if she were to make a few alterations. She would move the seasonal stock into the window and clear a few shelves behind the counter for the new. She wracked her brain trying to recall Jim's definition of his jigsaws – *harnessing one person's memories so that another could feel part of them* – something like that. And her role was to write the history of the scene. That should be easy. She smiled as she predicted the places he would choose to photograph.

One was bound to be the old church in Kilfane, Norman built, with its tombstones engraved with effigies of knights. No American tourist would have anything like that at home. Neither could she imagine the water fountain at the cross-roads being in their experience. It was so old nobody knew when it was built or who had built it, though there were legends that stretched back hundreds of years. Thinking about it, Lizzie could feel a tingle of excitement. Writing about these ancient places, with their lore and mysteries, would be the perfect task for her and a bonus that she would get commission on each sold. As she packed and sealed the boxes to store in the cupboard against the time they might be fashionable again, she determined to stay a step ahead of her intriguing new friend. If the rain didn't let up, she'd close early and go home and make some notes in preparation. He would definitely be impressed.

Lizzie stopped. Oh, you foolish old woman! Without realising it, she had paused and was running her fingers through her hair as if to release curls she never had. She almost laughed aloud. What has gotten into you, Lizzie Flynn? You haven't taken a notion of the Jigsaw Maker, have you? For a start he's at least a decade too young and while that mightn't be an issue if the decade in question was between twenty and thirty, Lizzie was getting on for fifty. Skinny busy Lizzie, spinster of the parish, with her out-of-date shop with its out-of-date stock.

'Well that's fine,' she said aloud to the empty shelves above her counter. 'Someone has to keep all the pieces together, keep things ticking over so that it doesn't all come apart. Someone had to take responsibility.'

In the quiet of the shop with the pattering of drizzle on the windows, Lizzie's voice distorted and came back to her ears sounding different. It sounded like her mother berating her. *Someone has to take responsibility.* She looked at Anne's empty basket and flushed with shame. Anne was trying to help and if she hadn't, then maybe Lizzie wouldn't have been so receptive to the propositions of a perfect stranger and wouldn't now be looking forward to a new venture.

Jigsaws.

*

It was two weeks before the Jigsaw Maker reappeared. Lizzie surprised herself by not worrying about his absence in the slightest. Usually, if a delivery was supposed to be there at nine, and didn't arrive till ten past, the delivery man got short shrift – heavy traffic on the Kilkenny road or not. And if someone, by dint of a comment made, led her to believe that he would turn up in a week and didn't, he'd suffer for expectations created. Lizzie Flynn did not tolerate unpredictability.

Jim Nealon was so enthusiastic, Lizzie expected him to turn up by the end of the week. The weather cleared by Wednesday and there were blue skies. The light was good for taking photographs. Every day as she sat at her table scouring catalogues she watched the door out of the corner of her eye, waiting for an unkempt figure with a leather satchel to appear.

And now he hadn't returned and Lizzie didn't mind at all. Even if he never did, his initial visit, coming so soon after her conflict with Anne, sparked something off in her. Together and separately, both had pinpointed a rut she'd let herself slide into. Life was uneventful, humdrum, and that was such a safe place to be. With her fiftieth in view, Lizzie could feel the burden of safety grow heavy and stifling. Wouldn't it be nice to break out a bit, take a risk for once in her adult life? As she turned the pages of the catalogues, bizarre items, the ones she usually ignored, were the ones to which she paid most attention. Maybe she should fill her shelves with them, have a refit, even close up for a while and reopen with a whole new look.

'Hello.'

She hadn't even heard the door open. Some cards were knocked off the display as Jim came into the shop; knocking things with his satchel as he passed.

'Sorry, I was always clumsy.'

Lizzie raised an eyebrow. 'That doesn't seem likely – your jigsaw pieces are so precise.'

'Ah yes, but have you tried putting them together?' The corners of his eyes creased with merriment as he took an A4 sized envelope out of his bag. He laid the envelope on the table. 'They mightn't fit.'

Lizzie took the envelope and opened the flap. 'Great,' she said, 'now he tells me. A jigsaw maker whose pieces don't fit – that should be popular.' She motioned him to sit down. 'You look very pleased with yourself.'

Jim was still smiling. 'To tell you the truth, I'm delighted. This village of yours is a treasure trove of the most beautiful, evocative places. You can walk around a corner and there it is, living history, humming with atmosphere.'

Lizzie sniffed. 'History, yes; living, no; humming; maybe.' She pulled some photographs out of the envelope and laid them on the table without looking at them closely. 'I bet I can guess what these are.'

He smiled but said nothing.

Lizzie slid her reading glasses onto her nose and picked up the first picture. For a minute she stared at it then slid the next one from behind and laid it on top, then the next. She didn't say a word until she had digested every detail then handed them back to him and exhaled slowly.

'I don't understand,' she said eventually.

'Understand what?'

'These,' she gestured at the photos. 'I don't understand what these are.'

He spread the three pictures out and leaned over them. 'Rathshannan,' he said. 'These are, to my mind, some of the most evocative images of this village. Anyone could look at one of these and recognise it. Take this,' he picked up the top picture. It was of the village school – or rather the old village school which had shut its doors to pupils two seasons ago. Talk was that some developer had it now and was planning to turn it into apartments – posh weekend retreats for city-weary high earners. 'How many National Schools in the country look like this?'

'Most of them probably. The old ones anyway.'

'Exactly. They were everywhere once but now they're an endangered species. Soon they'll be ripped down, soaped up, changed. And what good will they be to us then?'

Lizzie felt cross. Whether at being wrong in her predictions or because she couldn't see what he was getting at, she wasn't sure.

'Jim,' she said, 'I don't see what good they are to us now. I thought you were going to come back with the old church on the Thomastown road or the fountain at the crossroads. They're unique.'

'You can get photographs with those places on, everyone goes there. But nobody belongs. It's just history. This is different; this is personal. If the people who buy our jigsaws haven't been to one of these schools themselves, their fathers and mothers will have. They'll have walked up a path like that,' he prodded the path on the photograph, 'rushed in a door like that. It'll be a part of their past in a way that old Norman effigies never could.'

Lizzie picked up the picture and looked at it. 'You're right, of course, but I don't see what you want me to do for you. I can tell you when the school was founded, how many pupils went there, who were the nuns who ran the place and when it closed, but apart from that, nothing exciting happened there at all.'

Jim shrugged. 'Depends on what you call exciting. For someone looking to confirm their identity – as so many of our tourists are – it's the most ordinary things that are the most exciting. Being part of the everyday humdrum is the goal.'

Lizzie yawned and stretched. 'Oh dear. Well, you've got your expert there. Humdrum is my middle name.' She picked up the other pictures as well and fanned them out in her hands. 'Go on then. Tell me exactly what I am to do.'

Jim took the first picture from her. 'You were a pupil here, circa...?'

Lizzie felt herself blush. 'The sixties, if you must know.'

'Perfect.' He turned the picture over and pulled a pen from his pocket. 'So let's imagine that Lizzie Flynn is back in

Rathshannan National School in... say 1969, and that's where you start.' He wrote some notes on the back of the photo. 'Take this home with you and look at it, think about it for a few days, really get into the scene and then write me up all you can recall about that particular year in that school. Everything, the big events, the outings, the ordinary. I want to be able to read it afterwards and really feel that I was there.' He pointed to the other two photos. 'Maybe we should leave these for the time being. They might be distracting.'

Lizzie held on to them. 'No, let me have these too.' She looked at them again and smiled. 'Funny you should have picked 1969.' She could hear the shake in her voice and hoped that he couldn't. 'That was quite an eventful year.'

He sat watching her, saying nothing.

'Really,' she said. 'I spent eight years in that school and the only year anything happened was that one. The only year, in fact that everything happened.' She was silent then and he sat watching her. 'So, 1969, Rathshannan National School. I can't think where to begin.'

Jim took one of the jigsaws from his satchel. 'When Mel wrote the story of Balmullen House, she told me she just shut her eyes and let the years pass away. And when she opened them again, she wrote without stopping as if what she was writing was what she was seeing in front of her. Maybe that might work for you.'

'It might.'

'Great!' Jim stood up and slung the bag over his shoulder, 'I'll leave you to it so and get to work on superimposing this image onto wood. I've got the most beautiful pieces to work on.'

'Really? Sourced, cut and turned to perfection in a fortnight? You are a quick worker, Jim Nealon.'

Jim grinned. 'And you're a sharp one, Lizzie Flynn.' And then he was gone.

Watching as he walked past the window and on up the street, Lizzie shivered then berated herself. Honestly, she was practically flirting! In the distance, she could see him climb into an old Land Rover, like himself unkempt and bordering on scruffy. She waited till it disappeared from view. It wasn't even as if she found him attractive – he wasn't – he was just relaxed, like someone you'd known forever and from whom there'd be no point in keeping secrets. Not that she had any secrets to keep. She looked at the picture.

Not from the Rathshannan National School in 1969 anyway.

*

'You are not going to believe what those twins have gone and done – bloody hell! What's happened here? Have you been burgled?' Teresa Callaghan dumped her bags beside the counter and fell into the chair.

Lizzie laughed. 'I decided it was high time I had a clear out. I'm thinking of carrying some new lines – more crafty things, more exclusive.'

Teresa raised an eyebrow. 'Oh yea? Lizzie Flynn breaking out? What's all that about?'

Lizzie closed her account book and slid it into the drawer. 'Fancied brightening up, that's all. So, tell me, what have the twins gone and done that has you so upset?'

Teresa sniffed and it was clear she'd been crying. 'Tattoos,' she said eventually. 'They took themselves into Kilkenny and found some *gombeen* man with a needle and ink who did tattoos on the both of them.'

'But they're only fifteen. Is that legal?'

'I don't know. Whatever it is, it's a bloody disgrace. You should see the state of Kylie's arm.' She leaned forward and rolled up her sleeve. 'It's infected, of course.' With her palm cupped she indicated a swelling the size of a tennis ball. 'And up to here. There's probably God knows how much disease swilling around in there – enough to infect a continent by the look of it. And Jason's not a lot better – fecking eejit.'

'Whose idea was it?'

Teresa raised her eyes to Heaven. 'You know what that pair are like – thick as thieves. Both claim full responsibility and that the other had to be coerced. He says a fellow in school had it done and she says she saw it advertised at a concert and so they each decided it would be a good idea.'

'Oh dear.' Lizzie felt a rush of sympathy for Teresa with her wayward twins. They'd been a handful since birth and the strain of their high spirits and sleeplessness had eventually sent their father into bed in a quieter household. 'How big is the damage?'

Teresa picked up the stapler and held it sideways on. 'This. When the swelling goes down and the pus is all squeezed out, it will apparently read *We are the future.* Some future – only two fecking functional arms between them!'

Lizzie smiled. 'Poor Teresa, I don't know how you cope.'

Teresa sniffed. 'I don't, Lizzie, and that's being honest with you. They're wild and I can't keep control of them at all. And do you know the worst of it?'

Lizzie shook her head.

'Their bloody father – he and his slut are expecting! Mam was over that way visiting and one of the women there told her about it. Apparently he's going around the place with his hand on her big fat belly, telling the world what a great fellow he is and how much he's looking forward to being a father! Being a father – can you believe the cheek of it. Where does he think the twins came from – the bloody fairies? It's not right.'

Now she was crying openly and Lizzie put her arms around her. 'It's not fair, you're right. He's a shit and the twins aren't being much better, giving you all this grief.'

In her arms Teresa stiffened. 'There's nothing wrong with the twins, Lizzie Flynn, if you don't mind.'

'I didn't – '

'Well don't. I have enough grief from my mother without criticism from you as well.'

Lizzie sighed. Teresa was impossible. She could spend hours on the dreadful escapades of her offspring and how difficult they were but as soon as you agreed with her, she was up in arms. 'I'll put the kettle on.'

By the time she came back with two mugs, Teresa seemed a bit calmer. She had tipped the Balmullen jigsaw onto the table and was fingering the pieces. 'These are lovely, like fine buttons.'

Lizzie pushed the mug towards her. 'That's exactly what I thought. They're a new line.' Recalling Jim's words as accurately as she could she told Teresa about the plan.

'It sounds great. Does he do any other stuff?'

'Like what?'

'Coasters, family photos, that sort of thing. My cousin has place mats with pictures of her kids on them. If your man is a photographer and he's good with the wood as well, maybe he could do that too, earn a bit of money while he cuts his fancy jigsaws.' She turned the piece over in her hands. 'I mean, this can't be very cost-effective, can it? How long do you think it would take a fellow to do a puzzle like this? And he's planning to sell it for how much?'

Lizzie took the piece from her and examined it. Teresa was right. It was beautifully turned. Where he cut the shapes he had smoothed the edges and drawn a fine line in black or white or shades of grey, depending on where the piece was to fit. It was a labour of love.

'They won't be cheap. He reckons if they sell, he might do the preliminary work then send it off somewhere to be finished.' She tapped the side of her nose. 'He has connections, you know.'

Teresa frowned. 'Who is he anyway? Do you think he's above board?'

'Teresa Callaghan! What a suspicious mind you have!' Lizzie was smiling but she didn't feel amused. Why would

Jim not be above board? Of course he was above board. He was a jigsaw maker.

Teresa shrugged. 'Maybe. It's just that these really are beautiful – he's obviously good at what he does so why does he choose to do it here and why now?'

'I don't know.' Lizzie drained her mug, disregarding the scalding on her tongue. Teresa's provincial mindedness was getting up her nose. 'Maybe he likes the countryside; maybe he likes the air; maybe – '

'I've got it!' Teresa slammed her mug triumphantly on the counter, slopping tea over the jigsaw. 'He's a down and out artist, looking for a rich wife. He's done his research and found out that in the sleepy village of Rathshannan there lives a rich bachelor woman, with a small shop and farmland to let. He's come here looking for you! A sugar Mammy!' Her eyes were bright with merriment.

Lizzie laughed. 'I don't think so somehow. Anyway, Anne's the sugar mammy. I'm hardly a catch at this stage – he's years too young for me.'

Teresa was enjoying herself now. 'I don't know. The older the fiddle and all that. Anyway, why did he want *you* to write up the spiel for each? Couldn't one of the old nuns have done it just as well?'

Lizzie lifted the mug and started to wipe the spots of tea off the jigsaw pieces. 'You'd better ask him that.' Through the window she could hear the rumble of Jim's Land Rover. Yesterday she'd mentioned that she'd be getting in a supply of Anne's home-made fudge and his eyes lit up as he confessed to a sweet tooth. He passed the window now and was approaching the shop door. 'Here he is.'

As he paused, hand on handle to examine the rack she'd hung outside with the papers on, Teresa squinted and then turned to Lizzie. 'Why didn't you tell me? He's bloody gorgeous! He's like Clint Eastwood only with more flesh and no orang-utan!'

Lizzie smiled. 'I suppose he is – I hadn't noticed.'

Teresa pushed her hair off her face. 'In that case, you're not joking, Lizzie – you *are* past it.'

'Thanks!'

'And he's not married, did you say?'

'I don't know.'

'Well, for the love of God, would you find out?' Teresa picked up her bag and opening her coat so that her ample bosom would be apparent to anyone she might run into in a doorway, she winked. 'I'm off!' And rushing to the door in order to facilitate a collision, she walked straight into Jim as he came in.

'Oh!' she said. 'I didn't see you there.'

Jim held out his arms to steady her. 'My fault, I didn't realise anyone was coming out. You okay?'

Teresa batted her eyelashes. 'I'm sure I'll recover.' She looked at Lizzie hopefully as if she might be invited to stay but Lizzie was still mopping the spilt tea off the table and she obviously decided it was better not to hang around while he discovered someone had been careless with his handiwork.

'Bye then Lizzie.' Her voice had risen at least an octave.

'Bye, Teresa. Hope the twins are better soon!'

Teresa shot her a glare that said *Bitch* and Lizzie tried not to laugh. The door was shut with a bang. Jim looked from one to the other, bemused.

'Friend of yours?'

'When she's after something.' Lizzie dried off the last of the spill. 'Ah no, that's just me being nasty. Actually she's grand – has a rough time of it with two demon twins, teenagers.'

Jim winced theatrically.

'You know about teenagers, then?'

'Who doesn't?' Jim leaned over the basket on the counter and ran his fingers down the selection of neatly packaged bags of fudge that Anne left in earlier. There were seven different flavours and he was taking his time deciding. 'These look lovely.'

'They are, wickedly lovely.'

He picked one up and examined the bag carefully. 'And they're made... '

'Locally. My sister is the mastermind. She provides the recipes and the expertise and local women do the stirring.' She took the bag from his hand and gave him a piece. 'Here, try before you buy, the secret's in the stirring.'

'I'm sure you're right.' Jim put the sweet in his mouth and closed his eyes. While it dissolved he was silent and Lizzie waited for him to speak again. Teresa was right, he was a handsome man, in an untidy, lived-in sort of way. His dark hair fell over his forehead and she fought the impulse to push it back behind his ear. To touch it.

'Perfect.'

Lizzie started as she realised that Jim's eyes were open and he was looking at her. She felt the blushes and turned away. 'So you like it then?'

'Absolutely! It's exactly as I remember – ' he fished in the bag for another piece, 'it's proper fudge made the way it should be. I suppose it's an old recipe?'

'Could be.'

He took another piece. 'I used to get a bag, every year on my birthday. Don't know where my mother got it but there was always a little note in it, a love note.'

'Aah, sweet.'

Jim grinned at the teasing. 'Right so,' he rummaged in his pocket and pulled out two notes. 'How much can I get for this?'

Lizzie took the notes. 'Practically all of it, ten bags. You'll be sick, rot your teeth and suck your way through life if you're careful.' She handed him a carrier bag. 'Here, take your pick.'

Jim chose a variety. 'You sound just like my mother.' He was laughing.

Lizzie's face burned. His bloody mother! Great. She wasn't that old, and comparing her with his mother would do little to endear him. That was for sure.

*

'I was right – I knew I was,' Teresa announced the following morning.

'And good morning to you too.' Lizzie didn't look up. Sister Moira from the National School had requested an array of ribbons, small baskets and decorative paints for their school harvest display and she wanted them by lunchtime.

'Here, I'll give you a hand.' Teresa left her coat on the chair and rolled up her sleeves. 'These are nice.' She held the ribbon up to the light. 'Is it for the school?'

'Um.'

Teresa sniffed. 'I remember when my two did things like this. They were lovely then, innocent.'

Lizzie looked up and smiled. In her memory there was never a time when the Callaghan twins could accurately be described as innocent.

'We used to make bows around the baskets, like this,' and taking a length of ribbon she wrapped it round and tied it loosely in a soft bow at the front. Then she held it up. 'There, what do you think?'

'It's lovely.' Lizzie took the basket from her. 'I can never do bows properly, the knot's always too tight. How did you do that?'

Teresa showed her but no matter how often Lizzie tried, she could not get it right. In the end she undid her efforts and handed the ribbon over. 'I give up. I bow to your superior ability to get knotted. I'm too tight myself.'

'You said it.' Teresa was grinning. 'So tell me, what's the latest on your man?'

'Ah ha! The purpose of the visit. Well, I'm sorry to disappoint you but there is no latest and he is not my man.'

'Wish he was mine.' Teresa was smoothing the ribbon between her fingers. 'I could really do with a good man in my life just now. Especially with Gerry's slut expecting.' She sighed and put the ribbon down. 'Not that I want him back or anything but life's so unfair. He's the one who walked out; he's the one who broke his marriage vows; he's the one who abandoned his kids. And now he's the one with the partner, the new baby on the way and by all accounts, a grand new flat over looking the river!'

'He's never – the new ones?'

'Yea.'

Lizzie pushed her work to one side and stood, hands on hips. 'That stinks, it really does. What are you going to do about it?'

Teresa shrugged. 'What can I do? Obviously I hope the baby's fine but, God forgive me, I hope its mother has the most unmerciful piles after the birth that no amount of creaming or sitting on ice packets will shrink... '

Lizzie smiled.

'And I hope its father is shat on, spat on and puked over at every possible opportunity – and especially when he has his best shirt on – for at least the first three years. After which I hope they have triplets.' She banged the table. 'And that's how I feel about it!'

Lizzie nodded. 'I see – you don't really mind then.'

'No.'

'And there was I thinking you might have a vindictive streak in you.'

Teresa made a face. 'How could you – bad-minded old woman that you are.'

Lizzie smiled but the comment stung. 'I'm not that old, you know, I'm not fifty yet.'

'Okay then, just bad-minded. When's your significant birthday anyway?'

'A couple of years.'

'We should have a party.'

Lizzie shook her head. 'You can if you like. I don't intend to.'

'Why not? You're hardly going to keep it a secret. Everyone round here knows you anyway and so there'd be little point in trying to knock off a few years at this stage.'

'Not everyone knows.'

Teresa opened her mouth but as a thought struck her she closed it again and a sly gleam came into her eyes. She sucked in her cheeks and nodded slowly. Lizzie could feel the irritation growing.

'What?' she said at last. 'What's so amusing?'

Teresa shrugged. 'I didn't come down in the last shower. I know why you want to keep your approaching decade a secret. *We* all know how old you are but someone new around here mightn't.' She nudged the jigsaw box on the edge of the table.

Lizzie reddened. 'Teresa Callaghan, you talk a lot of bull. Jim Nealon is at least a decade younger than I am and while you may be desperate to have a man in your life I am perfectly happy thank you. I am neither dependent nor depended on and that suits me just fine.'

Teresa looked sceptical. 'And what about keeping warm at night?'

Lizzie reached over and took two floppy corduroy bags off the shelf. They were filled with something that rustled and gave off a faint smell of lavender. She handed one to Teresa. 'I use these. Filled with wheat and scented with aroma therapeutic oils, they are heated in the microwave for three minutes and retain their heat for ages. They don't snore, take up too much space, smell disgusting after a night in the pub and they don't – ' she patted the top of hers, 'get you pregnant and abandon you when your twins are nine months old.'

Teresa dropped the bag she was holding. She looked as if she had just been slapped.

'Thanks, Lizzie. I needed that.' She picked up her coat and without bothering to put it on, left the shop.

Lizzie watched her walk up the street, stiff and defensive, and her cheeks burned with shame. What on earth had come over her? She looked around her empty shop, and the basket on the table caught her eye. The wheat bag had crushed Teresa's lovely bow as she dropped it. Lizzie picked the bag up and put it back on the shelf. The calming scent of lavender seemed to be mocking her. Didn't work that time, did it? She tried to fix the bow where it was creased but as she smoothed it, she pulled the knot too tight and it was ruined. Damn! She could do nothing right. Beside it on the table, Anne's last few bags of fudge reminded her that she hadn't made peace with her sister yet either. And she had been squiffy with Jim after he made the remark about her sounding like his mother – a perfectly innocent remark that anyone could make who was being preached at. She could feel tears threatening. I'm losing it, she thought, losing my marbles and throwing away everyone else's. She flopped back into her chair and fought the temptation to cry like a baby. I am nearly fifty years old and I don't belong to anyone and nobody belongs to me. And other people don't like me because I am turning into a caustic old woman.

She held her hands out and looked at them. The palms were smooth – testament to a life with all the appliances, the washing machines, dishwashers – but age had squeezed its mark onto the back. Where once the dimples dented plump fingers, now her knuckles were lined and creased. Her mother's engagement ring was on the fourth finger of her right hand but her left hand was unmarked. Untouched.

A shiver ran down her spine and she felt ashamed. She stood up and moved the school pile into the middle. She'd get this lot ready and drop it in to Sister Moira at lunchtime. If that didn't take too long she'd go around to see Anne and apologise for her surliness – blame an impending menopause or something. Then she'd go and see Teresa. With all the talk of bows and beaus Teresa had never managed to reveal what it was she had been right about.

This time Lizzie would listen and keep her own nasty mouth shut.

*

Sister Moira was delighted with her collection of paraphernalia – baskets, ribbons, stickers and things that sparkled. She pulled some pages of sticky-back farmyard pictures out of the box and held them up.

'Now you know what'll happen, don't you?' She put the pages to one side. 'All the boys will want to cut things out, just so that they can stab one another with the scissors when my back is turned and the girls will pull the fluff off the feathers and stick them to their ear lobes – jewelled princesses by three-thirty.'

Lizzie laughed. 'Is it worth the bother?'

'It is really. With a bit of careful rearrangement our harvest display will look fine by the time the Mammies and Daddies arrive to see it. And anyway, if I'm being honest, it isn't for the glorification of autumn that I do it at all.' She swept the bits back into the box and put it aside. 'When it's all finished, the colours make a lovely backdrop for the school photos next week. They have to be ordered and delivered in time for the Christmas cards. Piles of fruit and bread and little colourful baskets look a lot nicer than anaemic school walls or a curly-sided map of Ireland.' She pointed to the huge map that dominated the far wall.

'You ought to get a new one. I'd swear that was in use when I went to the old school.' Lizzie pulled the edges of the map and tried to flatten them.

'It probably was.' Sister Moira waved a hand. 'If you look closely you'll see that most of the furniture was salvaged too. The powers that be have promised to get some new tables – but always next year.' She went to one of the desks and opened its lid. 'Look here, there are names on this that go back years; the hinges are rusty; and whatever unfortunate child has to sit on the seat will end up with splinters in her backside if she slides off it too quickly.'

Lizzie nodded. 'Ah yes, I remember it well. Splinters in your knickers – that's when you find out who your friends are.'

'Lizzie Flynn! You're a bit fruity today!'

'Sorry,' Lizzie smiled. She looked around the classroom which, though it was not the classroom of her childhood, had the same feel about it, the same smell. A thought struck her. 'Moira, is it just furniture from the old school that you have, are there any old photographs?'

'From when?'

'My time, the sixties, the olden days?'

'We have actually.' She closed the desk lid and beckoned to Lizzie to follow her. 'We threw out a lot of paperwork when we moved over but someone suggested we keep class photos, in the faint hope that one of our past pupils might achieve great fame in the future and we might acquire great fortune selling their photograph.' Fiddling with her keys she opened the store cupboard at the end of the corridor. 'Needless to say we are still in possession of a heap of yellowed pictures that usually nobody wants to look at and not even space in the cupboard for a pencil.' She indicated a pile of dusty boxes on the shelf and passed it to Lizzie. 'Here,' she said, 'stored carefully between sheets of dust for years and all of a sudden they're in great demand. Do you want to have a look at them? They're all organised in class years and it goes back to the thirties.' She smiled at Lizzie. 'At what stage were you wishing to see yourself? What was your best year?'

Lizzie scanned the labels. 'It's not vanity, I'll have you know. I'm doing research. Have you any photos from 1969?'

Moira rubbed the dust off the labels and peered at the writing. 'Let me see. They're not in order at the minute because someone else was asking about photos recently and Sister Helen had a rummage.' She turned and smiled. 'A very short, unsuccessful one actually because there are as many spiders as anything else in here and Helen is terrified of anything with more legs than herself. I think she told him she couldn't find any and spent the rest of the day grappling with her guilt.' She started to pull a box out. 'Here you go, 1960 to 1969.' She peeled off the drying sellotape and lifted the lid. 'Aren't you the spring chicken – some of these are in colour!'

Lizzie took the box from her. 'Thank you and why wouldn't they be?' Mindful of her recent sharpness with Anne and Teresa, she smiled. 'Is there something people are trying to tell me? This is the fourth time recently I have been reminded that I am out-of-date, ageing or generally past my prime.'

'Never. You could take them away if you like and bring them back in a decade or two.'

Lizzie took the box. 'Thanks – don't you want to tell Helen we have them?'

'No, don't worry. I don't think it was important. Just some fellow wanted to know if we had information about the old National School and asked if there were photographs. Helen said he didn't seem too bothered when she said there weren't and he went away.'

The box felt heavy in her arms. 'A fellow? A past pupil, was he?'

'No.' Moira pulled a handkerchief out of her pocket and gave the top of the box a cursory wipe. 'An English fellow. He's staying somewhere locally I think, some sort of an artist.'

'A photographer?'

'Could be.'

More than could be – Lizzie smiled. 'I know the fellow. He's doing a series of local photographs, pretty scenes to make into jigsaws. He's a jigsaw maker. I'm helping him with the background.'

'Ah ha! Hence the research.'

Lizzie nodded. 'He took a gorgeous shot of the old school. He was probably looking for some pictures taken from the same angle when the school was still open so that so that he could see if it had changed much in appearance – capture the authentic flavour.'

Moira shook the dust from her handkerchief. 'Um, now, are you all right with those? Don't rush back with them, it's a grand excuse to give that cupboard a clean out. All I need now is a few bold children in need of punishment who can be assigned the job of sorting and dusting for a few hours and then I won't have to do it myself.'

'You're a wicked woman, Sister Moira.'

Moira smiled. 'I am, thank God – it gets the chores done very quickly. Here, let me get the door for you. Oh! And your cheque, for the display material... ' seeing Lizzie about to protest she held up a hand, 'which you will accept or I will never ask you for anything again.' She disappeared into the classroom and came back with a cheque that she folded and slipped into Lizzie's bag. 'There you are – are you all right now?'

'I'm always right,' Lizzie smiled.

Sister Moira held open the car door for her. 'Nearly always,' she said.

Lizzie slid the box onto the passenger seat and went around to open her door. 'What am I wrong about?'

'Your man,' Moira called as the bell went and there was the sound of children thundering into lines in the playground.

'What about him?'

'Helen said he was quite specific. Asked if there were photographs of a particular year – '

'1969?'

'That's right. And it wasn't photographs of the school he wanted. He didn't ask about the building,' she waved as she went back inside, 'so you were wrong in your supposition. Your jigsaw maker wanted photographs of the children.'

*

There was a blue mini-van parked in the yard outside Anne's when Lizzie pulled up. Inside, Matt Devine had the seat tipped back, the window open and was snoring soundly. Lizzie crept up and watched his sleeping face for a few moments, surprised to see the streaks of grey in the thinning hair of his temples and the laughter lines at the corner of his eyes. Everyone's growing old, she thought and turned to walk away. As she did, he opened one eye and regarded her suspiciously.

'What time is it? Am I early for something or are you late?' He eased himself free of the seat belt and opened the door. 'And which one of us isn't supposed to be where?'

'It's gone three. Where are you supposed to be?'

'Here, but I'm early. What are you doing skulking around admiring men at rest?' As he climbed out of the van, his elbow hit the horn.

Anne's door opened and Bernie Collins stuck her head out.

'You're impatient today, Matt Devine. We're not done with the order yet so keep your hair on will you!'

Matt rubbed his palm over his balding head. 'If I could.' He glared at Lizzie. 'Of course, it'd help if I was getting enough sleep.'

Lizzie laughed. 'Hey, don't blame me, I'm not keeping you awake at night.'

Matt leaned his elbow on the sill and winked at her. 'You could if you wanted, though. You know what they say about bald men...'

'They should wear a hat?'

'Ah, feck off, you.' Matt got back into the van and lay back again grinning to himself.

Bernie laughed. 'He deserves points for trying anyway.' She wagged a finger at him. 'Behave yourself or I'll tell.' Then she ushered Lizzie inside.

Anne's house smelled wonderful. Although it was the house the sisters had grown up in, it never smelt like this when they were children. The kitchen door was shut but the smell of fudge and fruit was everywhere. Lizzie stood in the hallway and inhaled deeply.

'A new recipe. The blackcurrant fudge went really well so we're trying it with raspberries. Do you want to be the taste tester?'

'You bet.'

Bernie opened the kitchen door. 'Anne! Lizzie's here. We can try it on her.'

Anne didn't look up. 'Why not?' She cut a triangle off the slab of cooled fudge on the sideboard and held it out. 'Lizzie always likes to be adventurous.'

If it was meant as a slight, only Lizzie caught it. Anne passed the piece over and cut another. 'Do you want to try it, Bernie? Here – and take some out to prince charming outside.'

Bernie took the fudge and left the sisters alone. Lizzie popped the fudge into her mouth and let it melt. As always, it was perfect – smooth and sweet but with just enough of a fruity tang to make it more-ish. When it had melted she licked her lips till the taste disappeared and waited for Anne to speak.

'Well?' Anne's voice had an edge to it. 'Too innovative for you, is it?'

'Enough now.' Lizzie spoke quietly. 'I was unkind and I shouldn't have been and – ' she bit her lip. Apologies were fine in her head but she hated saying them aloud. She opened her mouth to finish the sentence but no words came.

Anne smiled. She picked up another piece of the fudge and held it out. 'I know, you're sorry for being such a cow. You don't know what came over you but it was probably a menopausal moment which you've regretted ever since.' She turned her attention to the slab, which she started cutting into small squares. 'What's up anyway? I'm sure you didn't come all this way just to add a few inches to your waistline.'

Lizzie pulled out a chair and sat down. 'Actually, I did – ' she saw Anne pause, 'though that was only part of the reason.' She took a deep breath. 'The rest was that you're right about me being a cow. I've been snappy with everyone recently and so I've decided to turn over a new leaf – spring clean my life.'

'Goodness!' Anne put the knife down. 'So you were listening! I never knew I had such influence.'

'You don't – it wasn't all you. I have a new enterprise.'

'Oh dear, what is it? Triangular guest soaps?'

Lizzie bristled. 'Now who's the cow?' She took a disposable glove from the box on the table and started to count out the pieces of fudge into little piles with one for luck, so that Anne could scoop them into the plastic liners. 'Actually, I'm starting a writing project about Rathshannan in conjunction with a very nice man...

Anne frowned. 'Not Matt Devine surely?' She looked from Lizzie to the window where she had a perfect view of the van outside. 'I saw you admiring him.'

'As if! I was just looking. He's aged a bit, hasn't he?'

Anne shrugged, 'Hadn't noticed. Maybe he has things on his mind. Anyway, if not him, who?'

Lizzie took a deep breath. 'I was going to mention it to you last week but I thought I'd wait till I was sure. And now I am... ' and between nibbles of sweet, she told her all about Jim's jigsaw project and her part in it. With their recent falling out in mind, she expected that Anne would be enthusiastic, encourage her to undertake new ventures. Instead, she listened quietly.

'And he's really getting into it. According to Moira he was over at the school looking for old photos as well.' She finished and looked to Anne for reaction.

Anne said nothing. She shook the liner open and began to count squares of fudge into it.

'You don't have to do that,' Lizzie said. 'I've counted them out already.'

'Thanks,' Anne's voice was quiet.

'So what do you think?'

Anne held a piece of fudge mid-air and examined it closely. 'Is he the same fellow Teresa saw over at the church looking at records?' When Lizzie didn't answer, she motioned to Bernie outside talking to Matt. 'She called in here yesterday to give her mother a message and mentioned that there was some artist staying in town who was doing some sort of history of the place, said he was shifty.'

Lizzie laughed. 'Jim's not shifty. Teresa's sulking because she didn't catch his eye, despite her very obvious attempt to squeeze him into the doorframe.'

Anne smiled. 'That good-looking, eh?'

'In a rangy sort of way,' Lizzie could feel the blush starting. 'A bit young and skinny for me. Looks a bit like what's-his-name, that actor, with the monkey? You should come over and meet him, you'd like him.'

'You do anyway.'

Lizzie nodded. 'I do actually. Shame he isn't older.' She pointed a warning finger at her sister. 'And don't say, *or you younger*. I've had enough growing old comments recently to justify an HRT fest.'

Anne winced, 'Sounds painful. Anyway, I need to get these orders filled before your man outside has to fly off on another job so if you're not busy, do you mind giving us a hand?' She lifted some boxes off the shelf on the back wall and passed one over to Lizzie and one to Bernie as she arrived back. 'Thirty in each, rows of six of each flavour, then a box of thirty plain.' The women started counting bags of fudge into neat lines. 'You won't need any extra for the minute, will you, Liz?'

About to shake her head, Lizzie suddenly remembered that she had only a few left. 'Actually, I do. Jim practically cleared me out. Apparently fudge is a weak spot,' she smiled, 'reminds him of his childhood.'

Bernie looked at Anne and winked. 'Ah, sweet! Teresa said you were interested in his weak spot.'

'For goodness sake!' Lizzie sealed the box and handed it to Anne who was now stacking the load in a crate ready for the van. 'Are you lot starved for a bit of gossip or what! I only know that because he happened to mention that he always had a bag of fudge on his birthday when he was a kid and he loves it.' She had to raise her voice to be heard over the crackling of the confectionery bags.

Anne put the last box on the pallet and straightened up. 'Sorry, I missed that. What did you say?'

'Doesn't matter.'

'Right so. Let's get this lot loaded and we can relax.' They each picked up a crate and headed for the door. When they were finished, Anne gave Matt his delivery order and they waved him off. The women headed back to the kitchen and surveyed the mess. There were bits of wrapping, spills of sugar and crumbs of sweet everywhere. 'Thank God that's done for another day!' Anne said. 'If we keep on at this rate I'm going to have to take on more staff. Cup of tea?'

Lizzie looked at her watch. 'Thanks but I'd better be off.' She looked at Bernie and smiled guiltily. 'I need to pop in on Teresa.'

'Right so. Take a box of plain with you if you want and I'll send some more over later.' Anne wiped her hands on her apron and started filling the kettle.

'And tell that daughter of mine to take it easy, won't you. She should pack the twins off to their father and his floozy for a week.' Bernie scowled at the thought of her errant ex-son-in-law.

Lizzie picked up the box. 'Thanks. I'll put this in the account book and settle for the lot later. Okay?'

'Okay, and Liz?' Anne raised her hand to wave. She looked pensive. 'Be careful with that jigsaw man, won't you? He sounds too good to be true.'

'And a bit snoopy, if you ask me.' Bernie added.

'I didn't.' Too late. Lizzie's sharpness was not lost on her audience as they looked at one another and tried to hide the smirks. Lizzie managed a weak smile.

'I meant... '

Bernie nodded. 'I know, you meant mind your own business, but you are far too polite to say it outright.' She bustled Lizzie out of the kitchen. 'Don't worry. Nice to see someone round here having a bit of excitement in her life,' she winked at Anne, 'even if she isn't really!'

'You're hopeless.' Lizzie left them to it. She was conscious that her cheeks were still red as she turned off onto the main road and knew it wasn't the heat from the kitchen. *You are a silly old woman, Lizzie Flynn. This is definitely a mid-life crisis you're having.* She glanced at the box of photos on the seat beside her. Teresa could wait for another day. The sooner she started on the school recollection the better.

*

*Rathshannan National School*, she wrote on the top of the page. *The year was 1969 and I was eleven years old... Our teacher was Sister Cillian... and this is so bloody boring it's like drawing the proverbial blood out of stone and I haven't a clue where to start!* She threw her pen on the desk and got up to make another cup of coffee. She'd already had three mugs and her nerves and bladder were on edge. It wasn't stimulation she needed – more divine intervention. She prayed for inspiration: none came.

Outside the window a large truck passed by, sending a spray of wet mud over the side of her car. Damn! She should

44

have put it into the garage. She kicked her slippers under the radiator and went into the hall to get her shoes. As she opened the front door, another truck whizzed by and then braked heavily. Something was causing an obstruction in the road further ahead and there was a hold-up both ways. Serves him right. Lizzie pulled her coat across her shoulders and went out to her car. The box of convent photographs was still on the floor on the passenger side. Maybe something in there would give her inspiration.

She backed the car into the garage and was reaching in to get the box when there was a knock on her window.

'What are you doing, skulking in your own garage?'

Lizzie jumped. 'More to the point,' she said crossly, 'what are you doing skulking in my garage?'

'I'm not,' Jim laughed, 'I'm lurking, loitering even.'

Lizzie got out and shut the door. The queue had built up now, and all along the road weary car drivers watched her as she locked the garage with one hand and balanced a grubby box that threatened to fall apart at any minute with the other. Jim held out his hands to help her. As she passed the box to him, she remembered what Moira had said and felt suddenly uneasy.

'Lurking and loitering? That sounds seedy.'

Jim laughed. 'Thanks, Lizzie. Being seedy is not my chosen state really – it's more the one thrust upon me by the massive hold-up.' He leaned towards her and spoke in a low voice. 'Apparently a truck, going too fast, has misjudged the bend and is now jack-knifed on the bridge.' He indicated the queue. 'And unlike the patient, unmotivated people of this

45

worthy village, I was not prepared to sit in my car for the next hour while they clear it. I parked on the kerb, walked to the front, found out what was going on, and I was en route back to collect a few things before abandoning it there for the next few hours while they decongest. Hence the loitering. It's my unique way of getting on with my life as best I can – carless.' He made a face at her, 'And instead of sympathy, I am accused of being seedy!'

Lizzie smiled. 'Well it's better than being frustrated anyway!'

Jim furrowed his brow in mock concern. 'Lizzie Flynn, are you sure you want to share that with me?'

The flush to her cheeks caught her by surprise. 'I didn't mean... !' She grabbed the box and pushed past him through the door. 'You'd better come in.'

Jim was laughing openly now. 'I don't know if I should.'

Lizzie dropped the box onto the table. She pulled off her coat and glared at the slippers she had kicked at the radiator earlier. They looked old – like granny slippers. Jim was following her into the kitchen but she gestured towards the study door. 'No,' she said. 'In there. I'll bring in the coffee and show you what I mean.'

When she came into the study, Jim was standing by the fireplace looking at her books. 'You're quite a reader, then?'

'More a collector of books I would like to read. There's never time. Have a seat. Milk and sugar?'

Jim turned and sat. 'What has you so busy then? Do you have family?'

'Don't you know? I thought you'd done your research.'

Jim looked at her in surprise. Lizzie flushed. What on earth had she said that for? What was wrong with her?

'I meant, when you were looking for someone to help with the jigsaws.' She held out a cup and the milk.

'I like it black, thanks.' Jim took the cup but he was still looking puzzled. 'I didn't do research. I drove through, spotted some places which were pretty, evocative or both and checked in to the nearest B&B. After a couple of days of wandering around, I went to the library and asked the lady there to recommend an authority on Rathshannan who was also sufficiently literate,' he glanced again at the shelves of books, 'to help me research the village. She said you.' He sipped the scalding coffee and looked at her.

Lizzie spooned two sugars into her cup and stirred noisily. She would be up all night. 'Oh, right.' That sounded perfectly reasonable. She hoped he would say more, tide her over the awkward silence which was growing, but he said nothing. She took a mouthful of coffee and made a face. She didn't even like sugar. 'I have a sister,' she said. 'Just the one. She's nearly five years older than I am but she doesn't look it. She's divorced and lives on the other side of the village in the house where we were brought up. It was a farm then but now she runs it as a cottage industry with a few of the local woman.'

'Making homemade fudge?'

'That's right.'

Jim sipped his coffee again. 'And the women she employs... ?'

'All old friends.' Lizzie smiled. 'Anne likes to keep things close. She was away from Rathshannan for years, studying then working. When she'd saved enough to start her own business, she came back. She's done well.'

'I know, I tasted it. And you, did you ever marry?'

Lizzie shook her head. 'No. I was the one who stayed at home.' She paused. 'Our father died young and our mother couldn't carry on alone. I looked after her. She died just before Anne came back.'

'I'm sorry.'

'Don't be. The timing was perfect. I didn't want to stay in the house so Anne bought me out and I moved here. The farmland is let so that looks after itself and I run a small curio shop for the local in need of a birthday present and the tourist in need of a souvenir.' She put her cup down. 'Speaking of which – ' she reached over to the table and pulling the sheaf of papers towards her, handed him the top one, 'read this.'

Jim skimmed the few lines. 'Oh dear, it's not going so well then?'

'No, I haven't a clue where to start.'

'*Rathshannan National School...* ?'

'Ha bloody ha.' She took the page from him. 'I mean, what do you want me to say? What exactly do you want to know?'

Jim shrugged. 'What it was like, to be there, you know.'

Lizzie remembered the box she had just carried in.

'Is that why you were looking for pictures at the school?'

Jim smiled and held out his hands. 'Caught red-handed. I thought I could do the groundwork myself. But they couldn't find them so – I need you.'

'And fat lot of good I am. I've drawn a blank.' She got up and left the room. When she returned, she was carrying the box. 'But I got what you wanted. Here,' she pulled a brown envelope out and passed it to him. 'There are only a couple of '69. They're at the top – I had a look earlier.'

Jim eased the photos out as if they were fragile. 'These ones?'

'Yep.' She took one from him and pointed to a skinny girl sitting on a bench at the front of a class group. 'This was taken at the beginning of the year. That's me.' Then she placed another photo on top. 'And this was the end of that school year.' She laughed. 'One of the fathers had just bought himself a brand new Yashica camera and he offered to take photos of all the classes for free. Of course the nuns didn't say no. There's me again.'

Jim held the two photos side by side. He studied them for what seemed a long time until his wrists must have become tired because his hands started to shake. Lizzie put hers out to steady them.

'Coffee,' Jim said softly. 'It kicks in eventually.'

Lizzie sighed. 'I've had it by the bucket today.' She wiped a speck of dust from the photo. 'So what do you think?'

Jim shrugged. 'It must have been a good camera for its day. These are very clear.' As if to belie his statement, he leaned closer and peered into the faces. 'You look a lot older in the second one.'

Lizzie straightened up. 'It was a strange year.'

'Some of the other girls look different too.' He pointed to a couple in turn, tracing one from the first to the second picture and commenting on hair cut, heights achieved. Then he stopped, pointing to a large girl at the back of the first photograph. 'She looks old for the year.' His voice was shaky too. He wasn't joking about the coffee. He ran his finger along the line in the second. 'And she's missing from this one. Where'd she go?'

Lizzie peered over his shoulder. 'That's Bernie – Bernie Healey that was.'

Jim sat very still. 'So why's she missing here?'

Lizzie put her finger to her lips. 'Scandal, I'm afraid.' She took the photos. 'Like I said, '69 was the year it all happened.' And as she slipped them back into the envelope, she sighed. 'Poor Bernie, she had to leave school after that.'

'And when did she die?'

Lizzie frowned. 'Who said she died?'

'You did – Bernie that was.'

'Eejit, I said *Healey* that was. She married since. She's not *Healey* any more.'

Jim opened his mouth then shut it again.

Lizzie sat down again. 'Anyway, all this talk of people past doesn't solve the problem of my writer's block. I need to get back to the point.'

Jim nodded. 'They are the point, Lizzie. Our jigsaws aren't about places, they're about the people who belonged to them in the past and the people who want to belong to them now. And that's what you have to do. Evoke the feel of the place by reawakening the people who made it real.' He noticed his photo on the table and pointed to it. 'At the moment, your memory is in black and white. Get right into it and look around at who's there with you. Once you can see them, you can see the colours, hear the sounds, smell the smells. Actually,' he put his cup down and leaned towards her. 'That's a good place to start. Shut your eyes and go back to, when did we say, '69. What can you smell?'

Lizzie grimaced. 'Chalk dust, sweaty bodies, the sharp oniony smell of prepubescent girls... ' She opened one eye, 'Do you need to hear any more?'

Jim wrinkled his nose. 'No thanks.' He put his cup down and stood. 'Can I leave you to it then?'

'Yep. What you say makes sense but I still don't know how to do it.' She made a face. 'That's what I meant when I said frustration, young man.'

'I know.' He smiled. He reached into his satchel and pulled out a small Walkman. 'Here, d'you want to use this? It has a mike so you could shut your eyes and just recall everything. Afterwards, play it back and pick the bits you want to keep.'

Lizzie took it. 'Thanks, that's a good idea. I have some blank tapes somewhere. You sure you won't need it?'

'No.' He took a tape out and put it into his pocket. 'I use it to remind myself of routes to good places to shoot but I think I've got notes on all I need for the minute.' He slung his bag over his shoulder. 'Bye then. Good luck!'

'Bye!'

As she opened the door to let him out, the queue started to move and a slow procession of cars crawled past the house. In the middle of it was a small green Polo with Anne and Bernie inside. Anne was concentrating on the traffic ahead so she didn't turn but Bernie did. She raised her hands to wave and Lizzie was about to point her out to Jim as the girl in the photo but he had noticed the traffic too and was already hurrying to get his car into the flow before it all stopped again.

So Lizzie stood there, one hand mid-air, waving into space. Bernie was smiling at her, eyebrows raised in enquiry. Lizzie dropped her hand and hurried back into the house, where Jim's cup was still warm where he had left it.

Beneath the radiator in the kitchen her slippers were warm too.

## Rathshannan National School
## 1969

**B** Y TWO O'CLOCK IN THE AFTERNOON it was quiet in the sixth class classroom. All the pent up energy of the morning boosted by the lunchtime sandwiches was wearing off and the air was stuffy and warm. It smelt of thirty bodies and one nun – though she didn't count, as nuns don't smell. It was customary for this to be quiet reading time, or doing corrections in your copybook time, or just gazing at the specks of dust in the air in a way that made you look as if you were figuring something out time. Lizzie loved this. For her it was the time when she thought about all the things she had seen and all the things she had heard and put them all together. By the time the bell went and Sister Cillian called the girls to stand for the final prayer, Lizzie had the world figured out to her satisfaction, usually.

\*

'Now girls,' Sister Cillian sang, resting the tips of her fingers together and staring at them intently, 'what is it that a Good Catholic Girl should hold most dear?' She raised one eyebrow and glared meaningfully at her index fingers.

Nobody moved.

'Well?' The other eyebrow rose.

Beside Lizzie on the bench, Kathleen O'Donnell shuffled uneasily.

'Miss O'Donnell?'

'God?' Kathleen sounded neither convinced nor convincing.

Sister Cillian sighed, a weary, long-suffering sound.

'Is it Jesus, Sister?'

Cillian lowered her hands and spread them out in a gesture of defeat. 'Stupid girl.'

Lizzie tried to stop her eyes from wandering to the picture above the teacher's desk where a blue-eyed, white-skinned Jesus stood barefoot on a path, holding his arms out to a motley crew of sick and sinners. Above his head two angels flew a banner between them, on which was embroidered the words, 'Jesus is the answer.' Lizzie's hand shot up. 'But, Sister... ?'

Sister Cillian glared. 'Are you being impudent, Elizabeth?'

Lizzie shook her head.

'Then kindly attend to matters in hand.' She held her fingertips up again. 'As I was saying,' she nodded towards an empty desk at the back of the classroom, 'You will have noticed that we have an empty desk in the classroom today.' The children nodded assent. 'That desk was most recently occupied by Bernie Healey, isn't that right?'

More nodding.

'But Miss Healey will not be occupying it for the time being.'

Some of the older girls, those who lived in farms further outside the town, sniggered quietly; the others looked at one another, puzzled.

Sister Cillian waited till she had their full attention again. 'That's right.' She lowered her voice and it took on a different tone, heavy with foreboding. 'Bernie Healey has left us, girls. She's had to go to...'

Jail? Bernie Healey had to go to jail? Lizzie clutched the sides of her bench in anticipation. Oh, please God let it be that Bernie Healey had to go to jail. While most of the class was eleven, or ten going on eleven, Bernie Healey was fourteen. She had seven brothers, a bra and a funny smell off her. If she caught you on your own she pushed you against the wall and took your money or your pens. Lizzie's mother called her 'a bad lot' and warned her daughters to stay well away from her. And now she's been caught and gone to...

'England.'

There was a strangled sound from the back row and Lizzie turned to see who it was. Bernie's two cronies were staring at the nun as if she had just said something really dreadful. One of them put her hand up.

'My Mam says she had to go to Dublin to get her appendix out.'

'Yea,' the other agreed, 'or her tonsils or something.'

'Indeed.' Sister Cillian's voice was scorn-weighted. 'And doesn't your mother have a lot to say on the topic, Miss Farrelly? I don't doubt but that your brother might have a word or two to say as well.'

May Farrelly stood up, her face bright with fury. 'My brother had nothing to do with it!'

Sister Cillian was calm. 'As you're standing anyway, Miss Farrelly, may I suggest you take yourself to the other side of the door and position yourself there till the end of the lesson when I will come and speak to you.'

May pulled her jumper defiantly over her backside and stomped to the door. As she pulled it behind her, she raised two fingers at the nun's back and stuck her tongue out at the girls in the front row. Lizzie tried to avoid her eye.

When the vibrations of the door banging died away. Sister Cillian spoke again. This time her voice was quiet as if she was sharing an intimacy. 'Girls,' she said, 'this is a sad situation. We must pray for Bernie and for us all, that we will not go down the same path.'

Like the others, Lizzie lowered her head and clasped her hands. She couldn't think what the fuss was about. You can't give yourself rotten tonsils or a sore appendix. And anyway, people were always having stuff out though it seemed a bit extreme to go to England for it.

'Let us pray, that God in His wisdom and mercy will provide guidance and solace in her hour of need to our sister, Bernadine. That He will help her see the error of her ways and that He will protect these children here present from that most insidious of temptations – temptations to which we all fall prey. Help us to treasure that which our Blessed Mother calls on all decent Catholic girls to hold most dear – '

Lizzie held her breath. Tonsils? Appendix?

'Her virginity.' She paused to let the impact of her words strike home. 'And where does the loss of a girl's precious virginity start?' She looked around the room, carefully avoiding the eyes of the back row experts, then turned and wrote on the blackboard – Impure Thoughts. 'We must guard, girls, at all times, against impure thoughts. Please take out your Examination of Conscience lists and add this to them. And remember, any girl who fails to guard against such a weakness could end up then same way as Bernie Healey. In England. And now we pray, Hail Mary... '

*

By the following morning Lizzie was feeling sick with anxiety. Despite all her efforts to stay on the right side of the good girl rulebook, Hell looked like a certainty. Whatever impure thoughts actually were, she was pretty sure she hadn't had any. So if she confessed to them in a confessional when she hadn't, then she'd be telling a lie to a priest, and that would be a sin. If she left them out, having been told to add them, she'd be guilty of disobedience to a nun, and that would be a sin too.

*

'Lizzie, will you please stop dawdling and get off to confession!' Mam's voice was more tired than cross. There was no sign of Da and Anne was up and away already. Lizzie didn't hear her come in from babysitting the night before but it must have been late. She scraped the last few cornflakes out of the bowl and stood up.

'Leave it – I'll do that – you get yourself off before your father sees you still here.'

Lizzie glanced at the clock. It was only five past nine. Confessions didn't start till half past, even later if it was Father Doran, and it took only ten minutes to get there. Mam was making it sound as if she was doing something wrong and if Da came in now and was cross, it'd be Lizzie's fault.

But it wasn't. It was Saturday and nobody had to get up and do things early on a Saturday. Mam was just trying to pretend that whatever the row was about it was someone else's fault. That's why she was standing at the sink doing everyone's dishes so she could be the good one. Huh! Lizzie scraped her chair under the table as loudly as she could and stuck her tongue out at her mother's back. Mam was so unfair.

'Hurry now, pet, and don't worry about the paper. I think your father is picking that up.' Her mother turned. Her face was pink and her eyes shiny as if she might sneeze in a moment. She was smiling. She held her arms out. 'Give me a hug and then off you go. I don't want you rushing crossing that main road.'

Awkwardly, Lizzie came forward into the hug, glad to hide her burning cheeks in her mother's embrace. She felt aggrieved. Her mum had a way of doing that, making you cross with her and wanting to please her at the same time. And she had a funny smell off her too. It was a morning after the row in the evening smell. Lizzie recoiled.

'I'll go so. Maybe I'll catch up with Anne. What time did she leave?'

Her mother stiffened. 'I have no idea. She's very quick off the mark this morning.'

'I'll lock my bike to hers and then we can come home together.'

'Do that. Hurry now – go.' Her mother let her go and turned to the sink again. Lizzie waited to see if she would say more but she didn't. In her mouth, Lizzie's tongue curled and she rubbed her arms crossly to get all the warm of the hug off them. One minute hug, next minute go. She pulled her cardigan off the banister and left the house without another word.

By the time she got to the church there were quite a few bikes stacked in the stands at the side. Lizzie scanned them but Anne's wasn't there. The side gate to the schoolyard was open and from inside you could hear the sounds of people laughing. Damn! That meant the older kids were there. Even though the bicycle shed belonged to the primary school, the older kids always took it over at the weekend when the nuns couldn't see them. They stacked their bikes at the front and then clambered in behind to tell jokes and smoke cigarettes and even sometimes kiss each other. If someone was in love, which someone usually was, they got the shed to themselves and the others did lookout for nuns, priests or parents who might be on the prowl. And when the prowlers arrived, the ones outside gave a signal and everyone ran like hell, sometimes having to leave their bicycle behind. The nuns took the bicycle then and chained it to the front of the convent railing so that the person who owned it had to knock on the front door to ask for it back. A while ago, May Farrelly's brother's bicycle was chained to the railing for a week. Sister Cillian kept looking out the window during the day, waiting for him to come and collect it but he didn't. One of the gardai came, with a message to say that somebody had stolen the bicycle and could the nuns please explain how they came to have it attached to their railing? They had to give it back then and Sister Cillian had it in for May Farrelly ever since.

Lizzie wheeled her bike around towards the yard, through the swing gate and sighed as she saw the stack there. One of the older boys was leaning against the side of the shed, one leg resting on the other as if he thought he was a cowboy. He held his cigarette between his thumb and forefinger so that as soon as he took the last pull he could aim it into the hedge and whatever it hit, he would say, 'bull's-eye!' as if that's what he was aiming at all along and then he'd swagger away, thinking he was a great fellow. Lizzie's cheeks burned. Those big fellows were horrible. If they said anything it was rude and if they said nothing but just looked at you slowly, it felt even ruder. She swung her handlebars round to leave before he spotted her but it was too late. As soon as he caught sight of her, he threw the cigarette away – exactly as she knew he would – and turned to say something to the people in the shed. Everyone stopped talking. Then he uncrossed his legs and started to move towards her. No way. Lizzie hurried through and pulled the gate shut behind her. Her bike would be fine with the others – outside.

When she got into the church confessions had already started. There was a line of repentant sinners waiting to go in to the confessionals on either side and at the top and bottom of the church; those who had already been forgiven were mumbling their penances. Mostly the ones with quick penances went up the front so everyone would know how good they'd been and the bad ones went to the back so they could scuttle out when they were done and not be too ashamed of how long it took to get out of there. Lizzie took her place at the end of the shorter queue and shut her eyes. There wouldn't be time now for a proper examination of conscience or to decide which of her impending sins – lying to priests or disobeying nuns – was preferable. She sat in the pew watching the candle flicker outside the confessional and prayed for guidance.

When she opened her eyes again to shuffle along the bench, she noticed her sister, Anne, waiting her turn on the other side. Lizzie coughed loudly to try and catch her attention but Anne was deep in thought. She was sitting staring at the statue of the Holy Family. Lizzie tried one more cough then resigned herself to watching Anne's profile. She was so pretty. Unlike Lizzie's straggly crop, Anne's hair was long and wavy. Since her fifteenth birthday last month when Mammy had given her a ream of coloured ribbons she had taken to wearing it in a plait down her back, the ribbons threaded through it. At the sides of her head, small curls escaped and framed her face. Her pale skin accentuated the pink of her cheeks and she was sighing gently. Lizzie watched and wished she could look like that – romantic. A wave of love swept over her. Anne looked so gentle, not a bit like Bernie Healey. Then she had a terrible thought. If misfortune could befall a big tough girl like Bernie Healey, how is a good girl like Anne to avoid having an hour of need? She shut her eyes and prayed.

*

When she opened her eyes again, the other people in the pew ahead of her were gone and it was her turn to go into the confessional. The curtain of the central cubicle was pulled shut so she couldn't see which priest was on duty this morning. She hoped it was Father Doran. He was always asleep after the first few confessions anyway, and lay slumped in his chair, snoring. If it was him you could say everything and emerge in credit, ready to sin all week if you chose to.

*

It was Father Doran. And he wasn't asleep. Though his eyes were shut and he was breathing deeply, as soon as Lizzie mentioned the words, 'impure thoughts' his eyebrows shot up and he peered, bleary-eyed through the grill.

'Impure thoughts? Is that what you said?'

'Yes, Father,' Lizzie whispered.

'And you say you've been enjoying them, is that right?

Lizzie wasn't sure. She'd been told to add them to her list but nobody had said how she was supposed to feel about them. 'I don't know, Father,' she said eventually. 'I'm not really sure. I was just told to say about them.'

'Who told you?'

'Sister Cillian.'

'Ah-ha.' In the gloom she could see him nodding to himself. 'And why did she tell you in particular?'

'She didn't.' Lizzie wasn't used to cross-examination like this. Usually she just listed off her sins, sang the Act of Contrition, collected her Hail Marys and got out. Usually, the priests didn't listen. Father Doran was all ears now. She took a deep breath. 'It's because of Bernie Healey. She has to go to England to get her appendix or her tonsils or something out and Sister Cillian said it wouldn't have happened if she hadn't had impure thoughts.'

Through the grille Father Doran smiled. 'Indeed. And so she made you add impure thoughts to your list, did she? As a precaution?'

'I think so.'

'Very wise.' Father Doran was smiling broadly now. 'And how d'you feel about that?'

Lizzie shrugged. 'I don't think I've had any, Father, but I didn't think I should leave them out.'

He laughed. 'Oh, never leave them out, dear.'

He settled back in his chair and looked as if he might be going to sleep now. 'Sins of Omission and all that, you know...' his voice tailed off and when it rose again the words were in Latin. Lizzie recognised her cue and started reciting the Act of Contrition. She tried to sound sincere, 'And I firmly resolve, by Thy Holy Grace, never more to offend Thee and to amend my life. Amen.'

*

Outside the church, the sun was high. She usually felt good after confession but not today. She'd gone in hoping for a bit of guidance but Father Doran treated it as if it was a big joke. And then he'd given her thirty Hail Marys! She'd come out of the confession box, conscious of eyes on her, waiting to see which end of the church she'd go to. Some of the older kids were waiting to go in now so it probably they who were making her feel uncomfortable. She raised her eyebrows slightly, hoping it made her look jaunty and relaxed and headed for the front of the church. Three Hail Marys that end and one on the way down the aisle and another two as she examined the leaflets at the back and loads as she unlocked her bike and she should be able to cover most of them before she left the car park. Any that were left over, she could say on the way home. She glanced around quickly. So many people were muttering their prayers, God was unlikely to notice if a few of Lizzie's were staggered in arriving. Head high, she marched up to the front.

Father Doran must have been on a roll. She was only starting the third prayer when she felt someone slide along the pew and come in beside her. She opened one eye and sneaked a peep. It was Sister Cillian. She had her hands clasped together in gratitude for having all her terrible sins forgiven and she fell to her knees and bowed her head, sighing loudly. Lizzie sighed too. With Sister Cillian there, clicking beads and making smacking noises as she prayed, there was no way God wouldn't notice her – or Lizzie either. Her reputation was ruined! The people behind would think she had done something awful. She folded her arms and squeezed her eyes shut. *Hail Mary...*

So now as she came blinking into the sunshine, many of the bicycles were gone. She looked around the car park – no Anne – great. She'd spent the last hour getting into trouble with nuns, priests, God, and now her sister was nowhere to be seen. She sneaked over to the schoolyard gate but this time she didn't go inside. She peered round the corner but there was nobody there. On the ground, an abandoned Major cigarette box was testament to the recent occupation. Lizzie shook her bicycle loose from the stack and pedalled as quickly as she could across the car park to the huge gates of the churchyard. As she rounded the corner outside, she had to break suddenly to avoid crashing into a crowd. Anne was there, stopped in the middle of the road, surrounded by boys. One was the fellow she'd seen outside the shed. He was smirking at another, a tall fellow with a thin face who was straddling her front wheel and facing her across the handlebars. He had his hands on hers.

'You could have knocked me down,' his voice was soft, 'killed me outright or,' he dropped his eyes to where the wheel was pinned between his legs. 'You wouldn't really want that to happen, would you?'

There was a whoop from the onlookers as if he'd said something really clever and Lizzie's cheeks burned. She couldn't quite understand why they were so amused and it seemed as if they were laughing at Anne. Lizzie waited for her sister to react, to push him off or tell him to get lost or threaten to tell their father. She nudged her bike forward and waited.

Anne said nothing. As the crowd watched in silence, she slowly withdrew her hands from under his and rubbed them, one over the other, as if there was cream on them. Then she tilted her head to one side and narrowed her eyes but her mouth was smiling. The boy held his hands, palms downward in the air above her handlebars for a minute before he spread them in a gesture of defeat and backed away. He was still looking at her but his expression was different now. He didn't look so smart alecky – he looked shy. Lizzie wondered who he was.

As the crowd drifted away, Anne turned and waved to Lizzie. 'Come on you, where've you been? I've been waiting for you for ages.'

Lizzie glared at her. 'No, you weren't. You were talking to a boy.'

'So?' Anne was still smiling.

'You're not supposed to – Sister Cillian said. It gives you impure thoughts and then you have to go to England... '

'Oh for goodness sake, Lizzie. That's rubbish!' Anne was already moving off.

'It's not rubbish!' Lizzie felt her cheeks burn at the unfairness of it. It wasn't rubbish. 'It happened already – you can ask anyone in my class.'

'Like sixth class are the authorities on impure thoughts?'

Now Anne was being the smart Alec. Lizzie bristled. 'Yes, they are actually. One of them has gone to England already.'

Anne braked and turned to look at her sister. 'You're not serious? I never heard anything about that! Who?'

Lizzie was temped not to tell her but you couldn't stay cross with Anne for long.

'Tell me, Lizzie,' she said, her voice gentle.

'Bernie Healey.'

Anne looked puzzled.

'She's going to need an operation. I'm not sure what it's for but Sister Cillian said May Farrelly's brother knows all about it.'

Anne's face flushed livid red. She turned and mounted her bike quickly.

'Anne? Where are you going, Anne?'

But Anne didn't turn around. She had kicked off and was already pedalling fast. By the time Lizzie worked up speed to follow her, Anne was nearly at the humpback bridge. She wanted to call after her to wait but there was something about the way Anne was sitting very stiff on her bike that suggested there'd be no point and anyway the flies were swarming off the canal by the roadside and if you didn't squint your eyes and keep your mouth shut, you'd catch them. Nothing makes sense, Lizzie thought to herself as she pedalled along. A fly landed on her lips and she spat hard at the verge, aiming for a large bunch of nettles. Bull's eye! She'd be better off not bothering even to think about it. Anne could make squinty eyes at whomever she wanted and Bernie Healey could go to America for all she cared. And regardless of what Sister Cillian might have to say on the matter she was never admitting to an impure thought again. They were awful things.

Apart from the fact that there was no way of telling if you'd had one, they kept the priest awake, ruined your reputation – and they earned you serious penance.

\*

'Now girls,' Sister Cillian sang, 'listen carefully then repeat after me, *The long leg of Italy kicked poor Sicily out in to the Mediterranean Sea!*' As she chanted the words, she tapped out the rhythm on her desk with her choir baton.

'*The long leg of Italy...* ' The children sang and Lizzie, confident that the details of Sicily's precise location would be forever remembered, let her mind and her eyes drift out the window beside her desk. There was some commotion at the front door of the school and she had the impression that Sister Cillian was only making them sing loudly so that they wouldn't hear it. She couldn't see who it was because the ivy had grown over the porch lintel but she would be able to in a minute. All she could do for now was listen. It was definitely a man, an angry man because he was shouting and saying something like, 'Well, you'd bloody well better find it because I'll burn the... '

'Mr Healey, *please!* ' Downstairs, Mother Clement's voice was thin and sounded as if it might crack any minute.

Healey! Lizzie's body tingled in excitement. Mr Healey was at the front door shouting the 'f' word at the nuns and his poor daughter Bernie away in England having her tonsils out. He sounded very angry and even with the window shut, his words were clear.

'You tell me where she is or I swear I'll... '

'Girls, girls!' Sister Cillian tapped the side of her desk with her wooden pointer and tried to get their attention but by now most of them were leaning out of their seats and straining to catch what was coming next. Sister Cillian tutted in annoyance and dropped the baton onto her desk. 'Please open your geography books and read page fifteen until I return. Nobody is to leave her desk unless of course, she wishes to spend next Saturday morning helping me to clean out the ink cupboard.' She paused at the door and glared at the girls briefly before shutting it firmly behind her. The girls could hear the tap of her shoes on the staircase.

For a minute there was silence. Lizzie could feel the tension. She didn't know what was going on exactly but as all the other classrooms were at the back of the school, they'd be the only ones to know anything at all about this. Everybody would be crowding around them and asking loads of questions. And she was in the best seat.

She leaned over towards the window a bit and peered out, fizzing with excitement. If the people below didn't move back from the front door a bit she'd have to make bits up about what he was wearing and if he was carrying a weapon. Just as the outline of a plausible description formed in her mind, somebody brushed past and stood in front of her at the window.

'Hey you, May, sit down!' one of the back row girls called out.

'You'll get into trouble if she catches you, so you will!'

Face pressed to the glass, May Farrelly ignored them. Lizzie stretched out her hand and grabbed the edge of May's skirt. 'Go on, sit down, you'll get it if she comes back in.'

Without taking her eye off the front, May yanked her skirt free. Lizzie stood up beside her. If there really was something exciting going to happen out the front there was no way she was going to let May Farrelly be the sole witness.

And if Sister Cillian came back in now, they'd all be in trouble anyway for allowing such sinful disobedience to occur so she might as well be hung for a sheep as a lamb. She wedged herself into the space between May and the window shutter and peered out.

Downstairs, Mr Healey was standing a few steps back from the door on the path. He had his legs apart and his fists clenched on his hips like a cowboy about to pull out a gun. Lizzie shivered in delight. Imagine if he really was a cowboy and he really had a gun and he pulled it out and shot one of the nuns! Wouldn't that be brilliant! There'd have to be a big funeral and they'd all get a day off – or maybe even more because if it was Sister Cillian they'd have to get a new teacher for the sixth class, and as far as she knew, there weren't any spare nuns around at the moment. She pushed her face even closer to the glass to see.

The movement must have caught Mr Healey's attention. Without a word he raised his eyes and stared at the two girls, their faces pressed to the window, then he raised one hand slowly. Lizzie's forehead grew colder as the hand moved towards her. Beside her, May clutched the sleeve of her jumper and she could feel the other girl trembling through the thin wool.

'Is he going to shoot us?' she whispered.

May said nothing. Below them Mr Healey's hand was still and she could see that there was no gun although he had a look on his face that made you think he wished he had. He was pointing at them. As they stood rigid, his lips moved and he made a noise. At first it was an indistinct growl and they couldn't make out the words but the feel of it was hate, pure hate. Then the sound of it became louder until he was shouting at the window.

'Well? What are you fucking staring at, little Missy Innocent? Hiding behind the nuns, are you, like the rest of your fucking cowardly family? Why don't you come down here and talk to me if you're so curious?'

Before they could react, Mother Clement stepped forward from under the porch and when she reached him, turned and looked up at the window. Lizzie waited for her to look cross and motion them to come down this minute and get a fierce punishment but she didn't. Instead she just nodded to them and, holding Mr Healey gently by the arm, turned him away from the window and led him down the path away from the school. When Sister Cillian's head bobbed into view behind her, the girls ducked and landed panting on the floor.

'What's happened? What did you see?' Around them the other girls slid out of their seats and jostled to get close. Lizzie struggled to get her hands under her and stand up. The sweat had dried on her forehead and she felt clammy and there was a smell of fear like fresh-cut onions. She couldn't tell if it was coming from May or from her. She reached out and to pull May up as well.

'Is he gone? What did he want?' All around them, hungry voices swallowed the air and it was hard to breathe. Struggling to get May to move, she wished the older girl would tell them to back off but she didn't. She was slumped beside the radiator and her face was very white. Her lips moved but there were no words coming out. In the clamour of questions none of the onlookers seemed to notice, but before Lizzie had a chance to do anything there was a shuffle at the back and the crowd parted. Lizzie looked up. Sister Cillian was standing there.

'I told you to stay in your places.' Her voice was quiet. The sort of quiet that nuns' voices have when the meaning of what they were saying was loud, very loud indeed. This particular quiet was screaming – you two are in *serious* trouble. 'Well, Miss Elizabeth Flynn,' the quiet voice said. 'Have you an explanation for your disobedience?'

Lizzie looked to May for inspiration. May was staring into space as if she was asleep with her eyes open. Lizzie was inspired. She pointed at May.

'Oh Sister,' she said, hoping she sounded as pleased as she intended. 'I'm so glad you're back! There's something wrong with poor May. I think she's fainted. Look at her! Do you think we could open the window and get her a bit of fresh air? When my sister Anne used to feel faint my mother always used to take her across to the window and – '

'Thank you, Elizabeth.' Sister Cillian didn't sound altogether convinced but it looked like she was going to let it go. She gestured the other girls back to their places and grabbing May under the arm, lifted her onto the nearest seat. With her hand on the back of May's neck, she pushed her head forward and held it down – to let the blood into her brain – muttering soothing words as she did so. For a few minutes, May sat slumped and then the life seemed to come back into her. She shook the nun's hand away and sat up straight.

Sister Cillian leaned down and peered into her face. 'Are you all right, May? Do you feel okay now?'

May looked around the room as if she didn't know where she was. Then she turned back and her face was angry. 'It's not fair,' she hissed, 'it isn't anything to do with us!' She swung around and glared at Lizzie. 'It isn't!'

Lizzie looked at her, shocked. What was all that about? Then she remembered Sister Cillian's rebuke to May on the day that they learned Bernie Healey was going to England and how her brother might know about it. And now Mr Healey was coming around to the school and shouting things about her 'f' word family – in front of two nuns! Wow! This was seriously exciting! This was grown up stuff.

Suddenly Lizzie felt very young. And May, standing at the front of the classroom with her cronies standing around her as if to protect her, looked old. Lizzie sighed and wished the bell would ring soon. Though she didn't want to admit it, Mr Healey's anger frightened her and she wanted to go home.

Where it was safe.

*

There was a creamery lorry blocking the gate when Lizzie arrived home. Da was helping to load the last of the urns and Mam was taking in the cups she had brought out earlier with tea for the creamery men. Lizzie waited till she had washed up and Da had come back inside before she spilled her news.

73

'Mam, Da – wait till I tell you what happened in school today!' She dumped her schoolbag on the chair.

'Was it your spelling test?'

'Nooo! It was even better.' Lizzie gulped the air and waited till they were both looking at her. 'Mr Healey came to the school and shouted the 'f' word at the nuns!'

'Good God! What did he do a thing like that for?'

'Because he wants to know where Bernie's gone and they know and he doesn't and they won't tell him!' Lizzie could feel the excitement bubbling in her throat. It was unusual for her to have all the attention instead of Anne, who was always gallivanting and coming home late and having teenage tantrums.

Lizzie's mother looked at her father. 'Healey? The fellow who was doing the harvest with you?'

Her father nodded but didn't look up.

'And which one is Bernie – the little blonde one?' Her mother was wringing her hands anxiously.

'Uh uh.' Lizzie was keen to get back into the conversation. 'She's the big one, with the curly hair. You know, the one that had that fever and had to stay off school for ages so when she was well again she had to stay back in my year?'

'I know, she helped out with the harvest too, didn't she?'

Da was helping himself to the last of the scones without Mam noticing so he didn't answer.

'Jack?'

He looked up, a bit dreamy.

'That young Healey girl who did a bit of work in the harvest. Apparently she's had to "go away" for a while and her father is looking for her.' She wiped her hands on the sides of her apron and sighed. 'It's dreadful really. A young girl like that and her life in tatters. I suppose it's just too much for the poor man to manage all those children on his own – they're wild.'

Da was looking at the scone very intently as if he wasn't sure whether he should eat it or not. He was squeezing the sides of it slowly so that it began to break up and the crumbs fell onto his plate. Lizzie was about to mention this but he suddenly put the scone down. 'Bullshit! If he wasn't a thug their mother wouldn't have left in the first place!' His voice was quiet but strong. 'That woman took more blows than wheat in a threshing machine, it's little wonder she upped and left him. Bernie, or whatever her name is, has had to be mammy to those kids since she was out of nappies.'

'She'll be up to her elbows in nappies again soon by the sound of things.'

Da pushed the plate away crossly and stood up. 'Stop that! I will not have idle gossip in this house – shame on you – both!' He glared at the two of them. 'You don't know for certain what's going on and I will not put up with any idle speculation in the meantime.'

Lizzie's Mam looked as if she'd had a slap and Lizzie could see her eyes flick towards the larder. That's where Mam went when Da was cross with her and after that she wouldn't talk sensibly for ages – days even. Desperate to smooth things over, she caught her Da's arm.

'But it isn't idle gossip, Da. He really did say the 'f' word and Bernie really is gone to England to have her tonsils – or appendix – out and even the nuns know about it and Sister Cillian said that May Farrelly knows too because it is her brother's fault!'

As she gulped for breath she could feel her father's arm relax beneath her hand. He looked from one to the other and sat again slowly. 'Is that right?'

'Yes!'

Her mother still looked puzzled but she often did. Da was picking at the scone again.

'Definitely.'

Her father smiled. 'Right so, get on with your homework and leave your mother and I in peace.'

Lizzie picked up her bag and turned to her mother. Mam was in a kind of a trance. She was staring at her Da with a dreamy frown and her mouth was opening. Just as she got it wide enough for a word to come out, Da held out his hand as if he was stopping cars on the Main Street.

'Enough! I don't want to hear it!'

But she hadn't said anything. Lizzie wondered if she should mention this but the dreamy look was turning into a cross one. A cross one that might end up in tears. She slung her bag over her shoulder and backed out of the kitchen. She'd been wrong. It wasn't safe here at all. She knew as soon as she shut the door behind her the noise would start. The low rumbling and mumbling that meant her parents were angry and pretending that they were having a quiet chat when they were really having a row that wasn't noisy enough to get all the things said and it would last for ages even after the talking had stopped. It would hum in your head even when you covered it with a pillow.

Lizzie ran up the stairs to her room and shut the door. She turned the dial on Anne's transistor to Radio Luxemburg, then upped it as loudly as she could and sat on her bed. Anne would be livid with her for touching it but already in the kitchen below the low quiet mumbling had started and though the pop songs were loud, the quiet hum was louder still.

Before the battery gave out, her father had slammed out the back door and the house was quiet again.

## Rathshannan
## 2006

*C*LICK! THE TAPE WHIRRED TO THE END and the machine turned itself off. Lizzie exhaled. So that was it – Rathshannan National School 1969. The year when innocence was lost. She looked at the stack of used tapes. And that's where it all started – the day when Sister Cillian told them about Bernie Healey. She picked up the tapes and took them over to the table. Now all she had to do was to listen to it all again and see what she could keep. Most of this was irrelevant. It wasn't to do with the school at all. It didn't tell you what the classes were like or how many children were in each or how strict the rules were. They were the things Jim needed to know. She plugged in her computer and fired it up. What she must do now was listen to the beginning again and make a list of those parts she could use. The rest she would delete. It was memory, revived to no purpose – except to make her cry and in doing so, clean out some of the dusty old memories lurking in the recesses of her brain.

When Jim appeared in the shop the following morning, Lizzie was ready for him.

'You look bright-eyed and bushy-tailed!' He slung his bag on the floor and rubbed the cold from his hands briskly.

'I don't know why.' Lizzie opened the table drawer and took out an envelope. 'I was burning the midnight oil to get this finished. You don't have to read it now.'

He cast a glance over the page and smiled. 'It looks great – lots of detail but... ' he scanned the page again, 'no names.'

'Of course not! Most of the people who were there then are still around today. People born in Rathshannan are notoriously reluctant to leave. It's not an exciting place but it's an easy one to live in. I could be sued for libel if I used the names.'

'Really?' Jim's eyes were smiling. 'That'd be wonderful publicity. Would you be giving away terrible secrets?'

Lizzie thought of the tapes in her study, the memories of those frightening days and nights that followed. She hadn't deleted the tapes yet. She'd wait for the next photo then tape over and those days would be gone forever. In the meantime, Jim had his recollection. When she'd listened through it again she'd shut her eyes and seen it all from the outside. She watched the children file into classrooms in neat lines, pausing as Mother Clement did her weekly measurement of skirt lengths to ensure that no girl was in danger of courting sin by immodesty. She'd heard the rattling of the 'Black Baby' box into which the children had dropped their shiny new decimal coins every Friday – and she recalled the terrible disappointment when the poor little black babies from Africa, for whom they paid pounds by the end of the school year, failed to materialise. She'd already named hers Patrick – but Patrick never arrived. She recounted the dire warnings from the nuns when the summer came round and the girls played rounders on the town field at the far side of the Christian Brothers School. They had to file past the building, eyes forward, muttering prayers to themselves lest they be tempted to peek into one of the classrooms and catch the eyes of a boy. A boy! God help us! Dirty little beasts who tried to do the devil's work and tempt you into sin. If the nuns had only realised the extent to which their Rosary jangling fanned the flames of desire in those prepubescent girls – it was little wonder there was more learned in that bicycle shed than there ever was in the classrooms beyond it.

She watched Jim's face as he read the first page. His lips moved with the words and there was a slow smile dimpling his cheeks. He looked up and caught her watching.

'Are you gloating?' he asked, his voice soft.

'About what?'

He held out the pages. 'This is wonderful and you know it. I can see everything.' He read out one of the lines and grimaced, 'Were they really that awful – the nuns?'

Lizzie shrugged. 'They weren't awful, not really. Some of the things they did were awful but they didn't understand that. Everything they said, everything they did, they did believing it to be right, to be for the best.'

Jim slid the pages back into the envelope. 'So the end justifies the means, is that what you think? Whatever you do must be judged for why you did it and not what you did?' His face was set, angry even.

'That's not what I said.' She sighed and looked around for inspiration. On a side table there was a pile of pretty linens and bedding with pillowcases edged in homemade lace. Lizzie crossed the room and picked one up. 'Do you know what these are for?'

'Beds?'

'Very clever, but not just any beds.' She smoothed the surface affectionately. 'These are for wedding beds. We sell them to young women for their bottom drawers and in the olden days – when I was young and you weren't born – lots of girls had bottom drawers. And they had something else in common as well.' She put the pillowcase back. 'They were often the older or oldest daughter. That's the way it went, you see. In homes where there were lots of children, not every girl could be afforded a dowry large enough to secure her a good match and there was little to be gained from sharing it out and leaving each with a paltry amount – you'd only end up with a load of good-for-nothing sons-in-law – or worse still, a houseful of unmarried daughters to feed. So, one daughter got the dowry and the good husband; one got to stay at home to look after the parents; and the rest were given away – '

Jim raised an eyebrow.

'To God.' She smiled. 'They called it a vocation but for many that's not what it was at all. These girls were forced to devote their lives to God and forsake their sexuality so they became obsessed with their loss. They had to believe everything they did was for the best; otherwise they couldn't justify their existence. God got the blame for everything and it wasn't his fault at all. It was chance – an accident of birth.'

'An accident of birth, I see.' Jim was staring into space. 'And were there many "accidents of birth"?'

Lizzie shrugged. 'I suppose there were. But there were great women as well. I met loads who were there of their own free choice and they were wonderful. It's the few twisted ones you hear about – the ones who drove young girls crazy with their sin and lust and fires of hell.'

Jim was watching her now.

'Not me, if that's what you're thinking.'

He held his hands, palms up, in protest but he was smiling.

'Do you remember the photos I showed you of my class in '69? There was a girl missing in the second one?'

Jim nodded.

'She was a victim of that. Became pregnant when she was very young and was sent away – to England – to have her baby and hide her disgrace. She was never the same afterwards.'

Jim didn't appear to be listening. He was on his hunkers rummaging in his satchel. When he stood up again he had some photos in his hand. 'I remember,' he said, 'Bernie Healey that was.'

'That's it. I was talking to her the other day, actually.'

Jim raised an eyebrow.

'The day you came over. I was just back from Anne's, collecting more of this.' She pointed to the replenished supply of fudge. 'Bernie works for her. She's Anne's chief fudge maker.'

There was a rustle of paper as Jim coughed and the photos fell onto the floor. When he retrieved them and stood up, his face was red.

'Are you okay?'

Jim smiled. 'Too much time spent lurking in bushes looking for the good shots. I catch chills easily. Here, have a look at this and tell me if you like it.' He put a photo on the table. It was of an old Bristol MV tour bus.

Lizzie leaned in close to have a look. 'It's great! Where did you find it?'

'I spotted it,' he said, 'parked in an old barn outside the town. It's rusted and no doubt immobile but it's a wonderful example for its time. Cleaned up I reckon it would be magnificent. You could live in it.'

Lizzie looked at his flushed face and heard the enthusiasm in his voice. 'Jim Nealon,' she said sternly, 'You're not seriously thinking of – '

He nodded. 'I am, it would be perfect. I've always been good with machines and I reckon it'd only take me a few months to get it roadworthy. By that time we should be done with the jigsaw design and then I could use it to travel around in. Save me a fortune in B&Bs.'

'You're crazy.'

'Maybe.' He turned the photo around so she could see it better. 'In the meantime, Miss Flynn, this is your next project. You don't happen to know who used it, do you?'

Lizzie picked up the photo and smiled as a wave of memory washed over her. 'Of course I do.' She grinned at his expression. 'It was in this that I spent some of the most exciting days of my childhood.' She prodded the picture. 'It might look like an old scrap heap to you, but to me it signalled adventure, trips to the big wide world outside Rathshannan.' She put the photo down. 'For one glorious day every year, this was the official Annual Outing Rathshannan National School Bus.'

*

'You've been busy – this looks very nice!' Teresa pushed the shop door open with her backside and eased her way in, heavily laden with bags.

'So have you by the look of things. Have you been shopping?'

Teresa glared. 'That's not bloody likely, is it?' She dumped the bags and stood hands on hips, surveying the scene.

Lizzie put the last of the novelty pens onto a display stand. 'Ease up, Teresa, I'm not the enemy.' She pointed to the chair. 'Leave your stuff there and come round the back. The kettle's just boiled.'

Teresa picked up her bags and moved them over to the table. 'You're right, sorry. Actually, this is stuff I wanted to show you.' She began to undo one of the bags and then stopped. 'I'll have the tea first though, or coffee if you have it, fully leaded – I need the boost.'

'Oh dear.' Lizzie looked at Teresa's face and saw how pale and drawn she was. The pallor and dark lines suggested that whatever she had been up to, it wasn't sleeping. 'Are you going to tell me about it?'

'Two sugars, thanks.' Teresa took the mug and, swinging her hips from side to side, slowly backed comfortably onto the chair. She took a sip and shut her eyes. 'Aah! That's the nicest thing that's happened to me in the last week.' Then she opened one eye and regarded Lizzie seriously. 'Honestly. One by one all the pieces of my world have come apart.' She nodded towards Jim's Balmullen jigsaw, half-completed on a tray on the table. 'It's like one of those. My world is a jigsaw and all of a sudden it's broken up. I was just about coping with it as it was but now all the pieces are in the air and I can see them falling and I don't know how to catch them.' She held her hands out in despair. 'I haven't a clue how to put the pieces back together again.' There was a shake in her voice and she looked near to tears. She took another sip.

'First the twins. They have the Group Cert coming up but as their sixteenth birthday is coming up first, they have informed me that they are done with full-time education. They want to leave school and get a job.'

Lizzie considered this for a moment. With no man in the house, Teresa struggled to look after her twins alone. Maybe if they brought a bit of money home, it wouldn't be such a bad thing. She opened her mouth to suggest this but Teresa pre-empted her.

'Don't say it – I know and you're right. It would be grand to have them bringing money into the house but, Lizzie, let's indulge in a little realism here.' She sighed. 'They're a pair of feckers but I love them.' The sigh turned into a sob. 'And let's face it, in that too I am alone. Who else, who absolutely else in the whole wide world could possibly love my children?'

Lizzie didn't know what to say. Teresa was right. Jason and Kylie Callaghan were probably the least attractive teenagers in the entire world. As little ones they were wild, but with their curly hair and big eyes could charm their way out of any scrape. Now Kylie's hair was pulled back into a tight scalp-restricting ponytail, gelled into immobility, and Jason had shaved so that there was just a faint shadow of hair root to darken his head. Once the swellings from the tattoos subsided, they'd look like a modern day version of Bonnie and Clyde. Neither seemed to have acquired the ability to dress fully either. Kylie walked around in what appeared to be a white track suit that barely covered her pubic bone so that when she walked, her belly stuck out and from the back she appeared to have two pairs of buttocks, stacked one on the other, fighting the band of her trousers for circulation. Jason's ripped jeans hung below his crotch and in the absence of hips were held up only by the distance between his knees as he swaggered along the street looking for trouble. Lizzie looked at Teresa sympathetically.

'Maybe it'll pass?'

'It'll do me in first.' The sob escaped at last and she rubbed her face roughly. 'I am at my wits' end, I really am!'

'Can't their father help?'

Teresa stopped rubbing and her face flushed angrily. 'Are you crazy? He's encouraging them! Said it was a great idea – they leave school and then, when they are no longer in full-time education, he doesn't have to give me another penny for them. His "paternal obligation" as he likes to call it – as they are the only words of more than one syllable that eejit knows, barring marmalade, and he can't spell that either – will be over, finis, kaput!' She banged the mug on the table. 'And while he sits on the lovely new sofa, in his lovely new apartment overlooking the river, holding the lovely soft hand – because she wouldn't know a day's work if it jumped up and bit her little tight backside – of his beloved, awaiting the birth of the child to whom he will be a wonderful father... '

she gulped for breath, 'I am left alone in a bloody mobile home with a pair of lazy delinquents who couldn't find their own backsides even if you gave them a map!' She reached over and pulled one of the bags towards her. 'That's why I came to you. I have a proposition.'

Lizzie winced. Jason and Kylie's hair-brained schemes didn't all come as a genetic inheritance from Gerry. She waited patiently while Teresa rummaged.

'Do you remember the last time I was in here?'

Lizzie blushed. Oh dear, she hadn't managed to see Teresa since. 'Em... ?'

'Well,' Teresa straightened up, a shoebox in her hand and opened it. 'Have a look at these – what do you think?' From the box she took a series of small packets, in a variety of shapes, all beautifully wrapped with exquisite bows. 'D'you remember you said I had a knack for wrapping?' She pushed one of the boxes towards Lizzie. 'And you are going to try some different things in the shop?'

Lizzie nodded.

'Well, that's what I thought I could help you with. If you supplied me with the wrapping paper and the ribbon, I could come in and wrap it all beautifully and you could charge a small fee for the service. I could really do with some extra work at the minute and maybe if there were times when we had a theme to work on – like Valentines – you could commission me to do a load. Maybe I could persuade Kylie to help and that might get her thinking about how she could earn a few euros herself... ' she stopped. Lizzie was staring out the window, apparently in a dream world. 'You've not heard a word I said, have you?'

'Actually, I heard every syllable.' Lizzie picked up one of the little bows. 'And I think it's a grand idea. Nobody likes having to spend money on a full sheet of wrapping and a roll of ribbon when all they need is a scrap so I think it would be a very useful service to offer.' She turned the bow over and examined the underside. 'You are so good with your hands. Do you sew as well?'

'I knit, I sew, I embroider and I even do upholstery,' Teresa sighed. 'But there's no call for it. People don't mend, they replace.'

Lizzie put the bow back into the box. 'Maybe, but I think this will go down well.' She opened the drawer in the table and took out two rolls of decorative ribbon. 'Tell you what. You make a series of bows with this for starters, bring them in and I'll pay you. When we see how well they sell, we can get an idea of how far to take it. In the meantime,' she pointed to the bags still on the floor, 'let me see what else you have in there and I'll show it to the stationery rep when he calls. He'll have an idea where you could go with it.'

There were tears in Teresa's eyes. 'You're a star, Lizzie, you really are.' She sniffed.

Lizzie took the bags from her and put them behind the table. 'Nonsense. If you sell, I sell, so it's good for all of us.'

Teresa passed over the last of the bags and finished up her coffee. 'And thanks for the coffee too.' She put the mug down. 'And Lizzie? If you do hear of anything, legal, that my two could do by way of work, would you let me know?'

Lizzie smiled. 'Of course. I'm sure something will come up for them.'

Teresa shook her head. 'It might but at the rate they're going it could be jail!'

'Teresa Callaghan – have a bit of faith, will you!'

Teresa shrugged. 'Okay, but I don't know what good it'll do me.' She stuffed the rolls of ribbon in her coat pockets and headed for the door. 'In the meantime, I'll tie the two of them to the gatepost with this and at least I'll know where they are! Bye.'

Lizzie waved. Poor Teresa. She took the two mugs through to the back to wash. While she was sorry for Teresa's misfortune, she was glad of the opportunity to help her out. She stepped over the laden bags and sighed. God knows what was in them – might be a great white elephant – but at least it gave Teresa a bit of hope. And she was very good with her hands. She watched the lonely figure disappear down the street. As for finding work for the twins – she couldn't think of anything that pair were good for. Maybe Teresa's suggestion to tie them up was the right one after all.

For goodness sake, where on earth were they going to find someone crazy enough to employ them?

*

Not that there was a shortage of crazy people, Lizzie decided as she locked up that evening and prepared to walk home in the biting wind. It must have been ten degrees warmer this morning and walking to and from the shop had seemed like a great idea. Now, it seemed like lunacy. No sooner had she rounded the first corner than there was a bleeping behind her and Jim's Land Rover trundled to a halt. He leaned over and opened the door.

'Climb in,' he said. 'You'll die of the cold.'

'Fragile old woman that I am,' Lizzie muttered, but she took hold of the handrail nonetheless and pulled herself up. Inside, it was chilly and noisy and smelled of dried mud and freshly cut wood. Jim lifted a rug off the passenger seat and motioned her to put it over her knees. 'You'll freeze otherwise. There's a bit of a draught.'

Lizzie arranged the rug comfortably and then had a good look around. There were boxes and bags thrown into the back and even a sleeping bag. She frowned. 'You don't live in this, do you?'

Jim shrugged. 'If I have to.' He noticed her grimace and laughed. 'It's not so bad. It's not always as cold as this, you know, and when it's too cold I decamp to a B&B.' He revved up and they pulled out onto the road again, Jim shouting over the sound of the engine. 'I've had this for years. It's been everywhere with me – the continent, Africa even. It's the only vehicle I ever owned. Until now.'

In the roar of the engine Lizzie didn't quite hear him.

'It must be near fifty years old,' he shouted. 'I bought if from an old farmer who'd had it for years and it was parked in a shed as a kind of glorified chicken roost. He only sold it to me because he wanted to build a new shed and it was in the way. Took me eight months to get it roadworthy and I've had it ever since.' He patted the steering wheel affectionately. 'I'll be sorry to let it go.'

'What are you letting it go for?' Lizzie leaned over towards him, suddenly conscious of the intimacy of the Land Rover's interior, the rug cosy on her lap and the noise of rattling windows pushing them together.

Jim raised an eyebrow. 'The bus – the old school bus – I told you.'

'You're taking pictures of it.'

He nodded. 'You can't just take a picture and sell it, you know. When I was in Africa, with a camera, I had to be very careful. Some people – ' he pulled the gear stick back and the vehicle crawled up the hill past all the cars that were struggling to cope with the ice. He grinned. 'See, the old bird has her uses. Anyway, as I said, some people believe that when you photograph something, take its image and pin it down, you capture part of its soul. Since then I have never taken a photograph of anything without getting permission. Silly maybe, but I've always been a superstitious sort.'

'Um, that makes sense, I suppose.' Lizzie looked at his lean hands as he steered. 'Is that why you don't sell jigsaws without a history attached?'

'Probably. I never thought of it that way, it just didn't seem right to have an image exposed with no explanation, no background.' He smiled at her. 'So that's what you're doing really, providing the soul.'

'Awakening old ghosts would be more accurate.'

'Yea?'

Lizzie shrugged and pulled the rug closer. 'What I gave you was only a tiny part of what flooded back once I started. I had to listen through the tapes three times to filter out what was to do with the school and what was to do with the rest – the people. In the end I had to be quite ruthless. It took ages.'

'Sorry,' Jim said, 'why didn't you tell me? I could have helped you.'

Lizzie shook her head. 'You couldn't. It wasn't about all the people, it was about what happened to one girl and the effect her story had on the rest of us.'

Jim's grip on the steering wheel tightened as they neared Lizzie's house and he signalled to pull over. With a jangling of brakes the vehicle trundled to the front and stopped. He turned off the engine. Without its roar, it seemed very quiet. Their breath was visible and Lizzie watched as it mingled in the freezing air. She felt very self-conscious.

Jim's face was serious, concerned. 'Was it a sad story?'

'Hers or the rest?'

He shrugged. 'Any of it.'

Lizzie pulled at one of the little balls of wool loose on the rug. Rolling it in her fingers she struggled to keep the emotion out of her voice. 'I don't really know all of her story to be honest with you. There was talk – ' she looked at him and smiled, 'provincial Ireland, as you'd expect, but I don't think any of us really knew the whole truth of it. As for the rest, yes, it was sad, horribly sad, thought I'm not sure if it was actually connected. I think it all just happened at the same time and her story marked the start of it.' Suddenly she remembered what Teresa said earlier about jigsaws in the air. She described the image to him. 'That's what it was like for us then. Bernie's departure unsettled the jigsaw and before any of us knew what was happening, all the pieces were in the air and nobody knew where they would land. And by the time they did, everything was changed. Everything was different.'

Jim pursed his lips and thought for a minute. 'Have I opened Pandora's box?'

'A bit,' Lizzie reached over and, smiling, patted his hand. 'But never mind, dear, I'm sure you didn't mean to.'

Jim pulled his hand away and Lizzie immediately regretted her action. She was only being light-hearted. She hadn't meant to make him uncomfortable. She cleared her throat as she pulled back the rug and prepared to get out. 'Anyway, what were you saying about the old bus?'

Jim's face cleared and he grinned broadly. 'I bought it!'

He laughed outright at her expression. 'I told you it'd be great to do up and so, when I went looking for an owner, I discovered it actually belongs to the bus company in Kilkenny and they have no interest in it at all. I offered them a ridiculously paltry sum to take if off their hands and they said I was welcome. I even rented an old garage where I can work on it. Isn't that great?'

Lizzie shook her head as she lowered herself onto the path. 'To coin Teresa's phrase, Jim Nealon, I think you are a fecking eejit! It looks like a heap and it will take you for ever to sort it out. You'll never manage it on your own.'

'I won't be on my own,' Jim said. As he turned the ignition and the engine roared into life again. 'I've hired a couple of eager youngsters to help me out.'

'That's a good thing then,' Lizzie shouted, her hand on the door handle, ready to push it shut.

'Sure is,' Jim shouted back. 'And they seem like a lively pair.'

It wasn't the temperature outside that froze Lizzie's blood. It was what Jim said next.

'They're twins.'

'Of all the stupid, fool – ' but it was too late.

Before she had time to register the information, Jim pulled out and was now clattering off into the distance. Lizzie glared after him for a minute then shrugged. What's the point – what's the bloody point? She pushed open the front door and dropped her bag in the hallway. After the biting wind, the rumble of traffic and the roar of the Land Rover's engine, the quietness of her house was bliss. She went through to the study and flicked on the table lamp. Its soft amber glow made the room look warm and not for the first time Lizzie sent up a quick thank you for her good sense in moving here – away from the creaks of the farmhouse where she and Anne grew up and away from the drudgery of adult years spent looking after an ailing mother and a flagging farm. She sat in her armchair and shut her eyes. Peace and quiet, that's what she had now.

As she shifted her position, her elbow caught on something on the table and it fell to the floor. Lizzie sighed. It was the new photograph, the school bus. She held it under the lamp and examined it closely. Jim was right in one thing, it made a lovely picture and would be an even better jigsaw. The lines of the bus were simple, roughly rectangular with rounded corners top front and back. It looked so sleek when it arrived and the nuns stood around it, clapping their hands at the realisation that this wonderful vehicle would enable them to broaden the horizons of so many girls who might otherwise never cross the county border. Even now the sight of it caused her heart to quicken at the prospect of adventure. She traced the outline with her finger. Maybe she should suggest to Jim that this one be photographed in colour – the cream and red were so vivid in her mind still. She shifted a little in her armchair. And the seats – not bench-like as on ordinary buses – were high backed and curved at the sides so that nobody had to suffer the indignity of elbows prodding at every corner. Between that and the rolling of the wheels on the long roads to Dublin most people were asleep on the way home. Lizzie smiled. Not her, though.

Too much to miss if you did.

## The School Bus
## 1969

'AND FOR THOSE OF YOU UNINITIATED in the finer things of life... ' Sister Cillian raised an eyebrow and glared at the girls in the back row, 'Mother Clement has agreed to take ownership, on the convent's behalf... ' she paused and joining her hands as if in prayer, lowered her chin onto the tips of her fingers, 'of something that will ensure that you do not leave Rathshannan National School without at least a rudimentary grasp of the wonders of the world outside.'

She paused then and the girls waited to hear that Mother Clement had secured yet another good deal on an entire collection of encyclopaedias that someone else didn't want, or that someone had died and left to the school in his will. Sister Cillian didn't elaborate however, she kept her eyes lowered and appeared to be waiting for something. Unsure whether to risk asking if the encyclopaedias had coloured pictures or not, the girls waited too, trying to stifle giggles as every sound in the room, every sniffle and tummy grumble, was magnified by their silence. After a minute, Sister Cillian glanced towards the window and the girls were aware of a low rumble in the distance. Sister Cillian's hands slid together into a clasp and she smiled broadly. 'Now, girls, what do you think that sound might be?'

The girls strained to hear.

'An engine?'

'Very good, but what sort of engine?'

It wasn't a tractor, it was too smooth and it wasn't a lorry. It was too light for that and too heavy for a van. As the hands went up and the suggestions rejected, Lizzie shot a quick glance out of the window. In the distance she could see stripes of red and cream rumble over the bridge in the distance. She put her hand up.

'Excuse me, Sister? Might it be a bus?'

Sister Cillian smiled indulgently. 'That's correct, Elizabeth, it is a bus.'

'Well, whoop-de-do.' A whisper slithered forward from the back row but Sister Cillian ignored it. She was looking triumphant as if the bus was something she had just won for being inordinately clever.

'It's not any old bus either,' she said, 'it's a Bristol MW, ten years old and in perfect condition.' Her cheeks reddened. 'One of the sisters, who has connections in the motor trade, has managed to secure for the school, the use of this lovely bus...' outside the window the bus rumbled to a halt, 'for outings and excursions of an educational nature.' She stopped, flushed with pride and looked to the girls for a reaction.

Lizzie noticed the pink of her cheeks and the shining eyes and a wave of pity caught her by surprise. Sister Cillian was old, ancient even. Anne said she was thirty something and she had joined the convent when she was only a teenager. Sister Cillian had once said that next to the church, garages were her favourite places. But girls can't work in garages so Sister Cillian went to the convent. Lizzie watched her as she crossed to the window. Looking at her now, you'd never think she liked God better. She never looked that happy in the church.

She turned and ushered the girls into a line by the door. 'Quietly now, we'll go down and have a closer look.'

Outside, the bus was purring, and even the sniggerers had to admit it was impressive. As the door whooshed open, the girls leaned in for a better look. Unlike the rickety old one that barrelled through country lanes every Tuesday and Thursday from Kilkenny, this one did not have slidey plastic benches for seats but separate ones close together so that you could sit beside someone without having her elbows poke into you at the corners when you swerved.

'We will not be swerving in this, will we, Mr Barrett?' Sister Cillian smiled as the driver raised an eyebrow at the suggestion. Then she waxed lyrical about the new bus's other attributes. Mr Barrett sat watching them through his window, with his cap pushed back on his head and a smile on his face. When Sister Cillian pointed out another feature, he'd nod approvingly.

'This Bristol MW,' she said, 'has been imported from England only one month ago. They've been in production only since 1958 so you won't see many of them around for a few years yet.' She patted the side of the bus as if it was a horse and Lizzie wouldn't have been surprised if she had whipped a sugar cube out of her pocket and slipped it under the bonnet. 'We're going to hire it out to earn a bit of money for improvements to the school and use it ourselves when we want to.' She patted the side again. 'Isn't it simply marvellous?' Her eyes were so bright she looked as if there were tears in them and although some of the girls were sniggering at her enthusiasm, Lizzie felt embarrassed. It was as if there was another side to Sister Cillian that she kept hidden most of the time and that was a pity because when her eyes shone she looked so much younger. 'Come along now, girls, back inside and get on with your work.' She waved to the driver. 'Thank you, Mr Barrett, I have no doubt we'll be seeing you again.'

'And soon I hope.' He winked at the girls as she ushered them towards the door.

'If you could take it around to Devine's, they will keep it there.'

'Right y'are!' He tipped his cap forward again and the bus rumbled into life. Some of the girls gave loud, exaggerated coughs at the exhaust and immediately regretted it when Sister Cillian swung around.

'Don't be so stupid. Upstairs now!' As quickly as her good mood had come on it was gone and she was back to her old strict self.

Lizzie shrugged and followed the girls up the stairs. Poor Sister Cillian. Imagine having two things that you love and having to choose only one of them. The noise of the bus grew fainter in the distance and Lizzie looked at the nun's face. She hoped Sister Cillian had chosen the right one.

*

Two weeks later, it looked as if she had. Because their class had done so well in the County Choir Competition, Mother Clement said they were to have an outing to Dublin. The other classes grumbled and said that it was really because Sister Cillian's father had died and left the bus to her in his will. Nuns weren't supposed to own anything and because she belonged to the convent and not her earthly family any more, she couldn't even go to the funeral. Instead, Mother Clement had let her accept a bus for the school's use to make up for it. Lizzie wondered if that made losing your father any easier. Even thinking about it made her sad so she shook the thought away and concentrated on being as good as she could. Most of the other girls did too – Sister Cillian wasn't the worst teacher in the school and if she liked them then maybe they'd have her next year as well and not Sister Mercedes who was known to hate children.

Everybody had to bring in ten shillings to cover the cost of the petrol and the driver's time, as well as a packed lunch, sealed carefully so that it didn't leak out and ruin the seats. They were going to leave Rathshannan at eight-thirty in the morning and drive straight to Dublin where they would first drive around and see all the monuments and important sights. Then they had two hours in the National Museum before lunch. After that it was lunch and a surprise. Everyone wracked her brain to think what the surprise would be.

'I bet it's the Zoo,' May Farrelly said. 'That's in the middle of the Phoenix Park. We'll stop to picnic there and then go to the Zoo.' She looked hopefully at Sister Cillian. 'Am I right, Sister? Did I guess it?'

Sister Cillian pursed her lips. 'You're very knowledgeable about Dublin, Miss Farrelly. I didn't realise you were so well travelled.'

May blushed. 'My brother told me, 'she said. 'He went up to Dublin and took photographs and everything and I saw them.'

'Did he now? I didn't think your brother would have business in Dublin?' The question sounded more like an answer. May flushed scarlet and put her hand down. She offered no more suggestions about the itinerary after that.

\*

As it turned out, she was right. As soon as they got to Dublin, Sister Cillian asked Mr Barrett if he'd drive along O'Connell Street so that she could show the girls where the rebels held out in the GPO at the Easter Rising.

He slid his hands across the huge steering wheel. 'You're the boss,' he said as they fell into line with the other traffic. He seemed to like the bus as much as Sister Cillian did and took every opportunity that he could to overtake. All the way, he pointed out to her how easy it was to change gears compared to this model and that and she nodded and knew what he was talking about. It put her in such a good mood that many of the girls managed to eat their lunches surreptitiously on the way without her noticing and by the time they reached Dublin, many were complaining of feeling queasy.

All that stopped when they reached the city. The girls who had not been to Dublin before gasped at the width of O'Connell Street and the magnificence of its buildings. Mr Barrett, who was a Dubliner, revelled in their enthusiasm. He looked to Sister Cillian for permission and when she smiled and sat back in her seat, he took over as tour guide. He took them past Trinity College, which used to educate only Protestants but now admitted both Catholics and women. Lizzie wondered which was admitted first and how anyone could have considered either unsuitable for admission in the first place. After a quick trip around Stephen's Green, the bus headed for the National Gallery. Mr Barrett helped to offload the girls, and warning them to behave and not give Sister Cillian any trouble, he drove off, promising to be back when they had gleaned all the knowledge they could. Two hours later, minds addled with fact and artefact, the girls were herded onto the bus for the surprise. En route, Sister Cillian made him slow down every few minutes in order that she could point out some important building that formed part of what she liked to call 'our impressive history'. She would tell them the facts and then Mr Barrett would chip in with some story about someone he knew who knew someone who'd been there. Some of the stories were funny and Lizzie wondered if Sister Cillian might think they were unsuitable for the sixth class but she laughed along with the rest of them. May Farrelly said they were only taking their time so that the people of Dublin could get a good look at the bus and know that people from the country had a bit of money as well. Leaving O'Connell Street behind, they travelled past the Mater Hospital, along the North Circular Road through Phibsboro, and then west. As the tour continued, tummies began to rumble.

'How much farther, Sister? We're starving!'

Sister Cillian waved their complaints away. 'Another couple of minutes and we're there. Why don't you just enjoy the views and say grace? It won't be long now.'

May peered out the window for clues. As they passed a sign for the Navan Road, she clapped her hands gleefully. 'I was right! This is the way to the Zoo! I was right, wasn't I?'

Sister Cillian gave a tight smile. 'You were. Now calm down and behave till we get there.'

Lizzie rested her head against the window and looked at the buildings as they passed: neat semi-detached houses, each one bigger than many of the detached houses in Rathshannan and much posher looking; a huge church that looked more like a cathedral from the outside; and as they neared the turn off for the Phoenix Park, large gates with a huge wooden sign attached to them – St Bertrand's Home for Unmarried Mothers. Lizzie bolted upright. Unmarried Mothers! How'd you manage that? She was about to put up her hand and ask when the bus swerved around the corner – so much for Sister Cillian's predictions that it would be a sedate trip – Mr Barrett was as excited as the rest of them. Lizzie liked him. There was a cheer from the girls as the sign for the Phoenix Park came into view. Unable to sit still, everyone rummaged under seats for lunchboxes and bags and coats and Sister Cillian grew hoarse urging them to sit still till the bus was stopped and they could gather their things safely.

*

The afternoon passed in a flash. By the end of it Lizzie was beginning to feel like one of the exhibits herself, herded from one cage to the next, ignored by bored lions, screeched at by exotic birds in small cages and ushered away quickly from the baboon who took the opportunity of having an audience of thirty girls from the country to flash his pink bottom and then rummage between his legs to excite an even better reaction. In the next cage, a gorilla tried to shield her newborn from the prying eyes of visitors but there was nowhere to hide.

Eventually the girls stood in front of the elephant, exhausted and sleepy. He looked exhausted too, shrunken inside his thick grey skin, its folds packed with dust. His pen was a small island with a dry moat. It didn't look as if it would be too difficult to escape from it but the elephant seemed weary and she had the impression that he couldn't be bothered with the effort. While some of the girls 'oohed' and 'aahed' at the sight of the huge creature, Lizzie's heart broke for him. He was pacing backwards and forwards in his tiny corral, stir-crazy with confinement in an environment alien to him. She looked around at the others and wondered why they didn't notice. They were saying things like, 'Isn't he lovely?' and 'Here, Nelly, over here!'

Sister Cillian watched too but she was silent. She was fiddling with the beads that hung from her belt and watching the elephant, with her lips tightly pursed. Lizzie edged closer to her.

'He looks sad, doesn't he, Sister?'

Sister Cillian nodded.

'I don't think he should be kept here like this. I think he should be let go back where he belongs. What do you think, Sister?'

Sister Cillian curved her lips but it didn't quite form a smile. 'I think you're right, Elizabeth. It's cruel.'

'And the silly thing is,' Lizzie warmed to her theme, 'it wouldn't actually be that hard for him to get out, would it?' She pointed to the dry moat. 'It's not that wide. All he'd have to do is come right to the edge and take a bigger step than usual. Then he'd be free.'

Sister Cillian smiled at her. 'Is it that easy, Lizzie?'

Lizzie looked at the nun in amazement. Sister Cillian had just called her Lizzie! That was what her family and ordinary people called her but Sister Cillian always said full names – like Elizabeth. And what was even weirder was that she was waiting for an answer. She had the smile on her face still but her eyes were very bright. Lizzie wasn't sure whether this was one of those questions that nuns liked to ask where you were in trouble for rudeness if you didn't give the answer; and trouble for cheek if you did.

'Well...' she said, playing for time and praying for inspiration, 'em. It might be the way for him to get out but I don't think he will actually.'

Sister Cillian waited.

'Because...' Lizzie swung her arm out and indicated all the spectators, still taunting the elephant to attract his attention, 'what would he do then?'

Sister Cillian nodded slowly.

'I mean, he'd still be an elephant – everyone would know that. He'd have to have someone on the outside helping him to escape so that when he did his jump they could take him to where he was to go next – to where he really belonged.'

'And do you think he will?'

Lizzie looked back at the huge dusty creature and shrugged. 'I don't know. I suppose he'd have to be very brave. It could all go wrong and then he might be sorry he didn't just leave it and stay here, miserable and all.'

'I think maybe you're right,' Sister Cillian whispered. She stopped fiddling with the beads and let her hand fall to her side. It was just about level with Lizzie's shoulder and it looked so lonely hanging there, that Lizzie caught it and squeezed. For a second there was no reaction, then Sister Cillian squeezed back and made a sound like a closed-mouth hiccup. Her hand wasn't hot and sweaty like some people's – it was warm and dry – and it struck Lizzie that it was a strong hand.

'If I was the elephant,' Lizzie whispered, 'I think I'd give it a try anyway.'

Suddenly, there was a gasp from the crowd as the elephant sucked dust from the floor of his pen and blew it onto them. Coughing, they backed away rubbing grit from their eyes. Sister Cillian moved to gather her girls and Lizzie found herself standing alone. As they were herded into line for the short walk to the gate where they were to meet the bus, she felt as if she was in a dream, watching things happening outside her head while other things happened inside. The roll was called and the heads counted and the line moved to the gate. As they neared it, Sister Cillian became more agitated, her real self, and fussed about staying neatly in line and how she hoped he would be there waiting. She couldn't abide people not being where they were supposed to be. Lizzie could feel her shoulders tensing.

Mr Barrett was there. At the gate a line of buses stood purring, and theirs was at the very front – exactly right. Sister Cillian smiled and her shoulders relaxed.

'You're here!' she said.

He tipped his cap. 'Did you think I'd let you down?'

Sister Cillian didn't seem to know what to say. Lizzie wondered if she should put her hand up and say, yes, she was very worried actually, but decided against it. He climbed down to help load the weary passengers and as Lizzie stood back to let him through, he winked at her. Then while Sister Cillian read out the names, he helped the girls up onto the high steps, relaying her instructions about where they were to sit – the bold ones near her in the front, the good ones further away. Lizzie could go in the very back. Most were exhausted and quiet as they boarded and he joked that there would be snores drowning out the sound of the engine all the way home. When all the girls were on, apart from Lizzie and Patricia Whittle who were entrusted with taking the last few pieces of confiscated rubbish to the bin, he helped Sister Cillian up. He must have thought she looked tired because he held her elbow as she stepped up and put his hand on her back – probably to give her a shove if she didn't have the energy for the three steps on her own. Then he waited while she did a final head count before firing up the engine.

As she called out the roll, Lizzie watched her from the back. When she came to Lizzie's name her voice didn't falter nor give any indication that she remembered what had happened. Lizzie frowned and looked at her hand. It was still warm with the feel of a squeeze on it. It had happened. Sister Cillian had definitely squeezed it as if to say, *I think the same as you do; I am sad about the elephant too.* But she wasn't pretending anything. She finished her head count then said something to Mr Barrett as she settled into her seat up the front. Lizzie watched the top of her head shuffle a bit to find a comfortable way to relax against a headrest wearing a veil. Then she was still. Lizzie wondered what she was thinking, wondering if she was watching all the other people outside going home for their tea as if it was an ordinary day and not the day of the Annual Rathshannan Outing in the new school bus. Mr Barrett pointed to something in front of them, then he slid the steering wheel round and they were off, out through the gates of the park and into the traffic.

*

Out on the road it was a different world. The people in cars outside the Zoo didn't look any freer than the animals in cages inside. Men sat waiting for traffic lights to change and some of them tapped their fingers on the steering wheels in time to tunes nobody else could hear. Lorry drivers edged as close as they could to cars in front and van drivers lit cigarettes and stole glances at papers on their dashboards. Some of the girls in the window seats stuck their tongues out as they passed, safe in the knowledge that these strangers were too eager to get home to bother climbing out and rapping on the bus window to tell on them. The traffic was much heavier than it had been earlier and it was already dark when they crawled back onto the Navan Road. In the fading light, the bus was dwarfed by huge green and cream double-deckers blocking off triangles of light from the streetlamps. Farther along the road, people huddled together at a bus stop and as the outside line of traffic was moving faster than the one nearer to the pavement – and Patricia Whittle had fallen asleep beside her and wouldn't be awake to tell – Lizzie decided to take the opportunity to make a few faces at them. She sucked in her cheeks and prepared to stick her tongue as far out as she could when the queue came into view. Already she could see two women holding the hands of struggling toddlers; men with leather cases and black umbrellas; and behind them, some younger girls, their rounded bellies straining against their coats. Lizzie glanced at the gates behind the bus stop. It was the Home. She wiped condensation from the window and pressed her forehead against it for a better look.

Just as their bus moved along the outside lane and reached the stop, a double-decker pulled in on the inside. Through its window, Lizzie could see the people getting on in the yellowing light. The mothers were struggling to keep the toddlers in check while they pulled the pushchairs on board. The businessmen, accustomed to being in front, efficiently stowed their cases and sat. And the young girls, weary with the weight of their growing bellies, hauled themselves up and cast around anxiously for a seat, avoiding the disapproving eyes of the other passengers. As the last girl climbed aboard, Lizzie abandoned her plans to make a face. They already looked as if they'd had too many faces made at them. And anyway, the last girl on wasn't looking. She shouldn't even have been on a bus in Dublin.

She was supposed to be in London – having her tonsils out.

## Rathshannan
## 2006

'THERE SHE IS – what do you think of it?' Jim stood back as the heavy metal door of the garage finally rolled up and inside, his bus was revealed in all its glory. Lizzie folded her arms over her chest and leaned her head to one side.

'That's a difficult one. Implicit in it are so many questions: what do I think of it now; what used I think of it; what do I think it will be like when you're finished with it?'

Jim made a face. 'Have to be difficult, don't you?'

From somewhere up the road came the sound of laughter and shouting. Lizzie recognised the cracked raucous voices of Jason Callaghan and his sister, Kylie. 'I should add, what do I think it will be like when those two are done with it.'

'They're okay, just typical teenagers.'

Lizzie leaned closer. 'They're not, Jim, and I think it's only fair to warn you.' She glanced over her shoulder to where the twins were stopped and taking a last drag from their cigarette before seeing if they could flick the butt accurately over the bridge to the pot on the riverboat beneath. 'They're demons, the two of them, wild and out of control. Honestly, they should be locked away.'

Jim swung around, his face set and angry. 'Is that right, Lizzie? Is that how you handle kids who prove a little more challenging than the rest – lock them away?'

Surprised by the force of his reaction, Lizzie didn't know how to answer. She shrugged, confused. 'I didn't mean literally... I, em...' she watched the twins duck behind the wall. Their butt had missed the pot and hit the river boatman instead. 'No actually, that's not what I'd recommend for all,' she glared back at him, 'challenging, as you call them, children. But in the case of those two, it's exactly what they need. They're horrors, lead their poor mother a merry dance and if you think you'll get any proper work out of them, you need your head examined.'

Jim lifted the bonnet of the bus and stuck his head underneath it. 'I can handle them. Here, Jason, come and have a look at this!'

Jason and Kylie ran up, joshing each other and laughing. By the time they reached the garage, Kylie was holding her tattoo wound and pouting.

'Jason's opened my wound!'

Jim looked concerned. 'Poor you. And poor me – I was hoping you were coming to work for me this morning.'

Kylie dropped her arm. 'I am.'

'Is your arm up to it? There might be some lifting involved.'

Kylie shrugged. 'I can handle it.'

Jim smiled. 'Good girl – knew I could depend on you.' He handed her a clipboard. 'First thing we have to do is work out exactly what we have to do.'

The twins made a face.

'So I'll start at the back and call it out and you write a list of everything I say. Jason, you take note as well and then we'll make a plan of action... ' Kylie appeared to have lost interest already and was pulling on a strand of pink-streaked hair to check for split ends, 'so that I can work out how much I'm going to pay you.'

'In the chipper, they pay twelve euro an hour.' Kylie stuck the strand of hair into her mouth and started to suck it.

Jim raised an eyebrow. 'And you want twelve euro an hour?'

The twins nodded.

He turned his attention to the engine again. 'Okay so. Go work in the chipper.' Then he pulled a spanner from his pocket and started to tap the engine all over as if testing for weak spots.

'But we wanted to work for you!' The plaintiffs were in unison.

'I pay by the job done – so much per job if done in the time specified and to the standard required.' He looked from one to the other. 'You up to it?'

They nodded, sheepishly.

'Good.' He took a pen from his pocket and handed it to Kylie. 'So if you're ready, Miss Callaghan, we'll begin.' He bowed formally and Kylie giggled. She clicked her heels together as best she could with tracksuit bottoms that trailed the ground on either side and saluted.

'Yes, sir, Mr Nealon sir!'

Lizzie watched the show carefully, still bristling from the tone Jim had used with her. She saw the twins wink at each other as they followed Jim to the back of the bus and write studiously as he called out job after job to be done. He explained how he intended to remove the ripped seats and install benches that made a bed and table and screen off the back section to make a small toilet and have a kitchen area. With each new suggestion, the twins cooed and agreed that his ideas were wonderful and how great it would look when they finished. By the time they came to the front of the bus again they were eating out of his hand.

'I can't wait to get started – this is going to be the meanest machine on the roads!' Jason patted the side of the bus as he examined it. 'I can t-cut along here and bring it up as good as new!'

'And I'll clean those engine bits for you.' Kylie pointed to some components Jim had already removed and arranged in jam jars on the ground. 'They'll be perfect.'

Jim smiled at them. 'Yes, I'm sure they will.'

'When can we start?'

'Tomorrow, eight-thirty.'

The twins looked alarmed for a second then they nodded. 'Right, we'll be here.' They nodded their goodbyes to Lizzie and waved at Jim. 'See you then, bye.' And off they went – little angels.

Lizzie glared in their wake.

'They seem fine to me.'

Jim was smirking.

'They would.' Lizzie pulled her bag higher on her shoulder and held it close. 'But time's a great teacher.' She turned on her heel and walked away. Jim didn't call after her. He leaned back under the bonnet and started to sing – softly at first as he swung his hips from side to side – something about having faith. Lizzie's grip on her shoulder strap tightened. What a smart ass. What an insufferable, know-it-all smart ass. She turned around to say so, hoping he'd lift his head to reply and crack it off the bonnet lid – no more than he deserved – but he was already facing her. She opened her mouth but not before he lifted his palm to his lips and blew her a kiss.

'Love you too, Lizzie!' he sang in a high-pitched voice and then turned his back on her again.

Lizzie threw back her head and laughed out loud. He was worse than the twins. She could still see them in the distance as they jostled and pushed each other off the pavement up ahead. Well, he couldn't say he wasn't warned.

*

The arrival of Jim's newly-cut jigsaws aroused curiosity amongst the inhabitants of Rathshannan and Lizzie was both amused and gratified at the reaction. Once word got around that these beautiful pieces were based solely on Rathshannan and its sights, people popped in for a look.

'Teresa told me they were lovely, proper works of art.' Bernie Collins counted the remaining bags of fudge in the basket as she spoke and Lizzie smiled. Of all Anne's employees, Bernie was definitely the most loyal. 'You'll need more of this soon.'

Lizzie nodded. 'I've had a few visitors keen to see how this "photo fella" as he's known, plans to put Rathshannan on the map with his works of art. They have a go at fitting a few pieces and then feel guilty about leaving without buying anything so they look around for something that doesn't break the bank. You know, art for art's sake, fudge for propriety's.'

Bernie fingered the fine wooden pieces. 'They are works of art too, aren't they? He's very good with his hands.'

'Seems to be. He's working on that old bus the school used to have for outings before they sold it off to the Kilkenny Bus Company. Did you hear?'

Bernie turned a piece of the jigsaw one way then the other before slotting it into place. 'I did – he has the twins working for him and do you know what, they love it. Teresa can't believe it, he's so good with them – just the man's influence they needed.'

'I bet.' Lizzie tried to keep the irritation out of her voice. Every time she'd seen Jim recently he waxed lyrical about the twins – how diligent they were and how they were great kids who needed only to be handled the right way.

'Apparently, he's used to working with teenagers.'

'Really?'

'In London. He works in a hostel or something – they do "Artist in Residence" weeks for kids who need a bit of diversion.' Bernie slotted another two pieces into place. 'Do you not know that?'

Lizzie shook her head. No, she didn't know that. She didn't actually know anything about Jim Nealon at all except that he had turned up here with crazy suggestion that she could help him make jigsaws to sell to tourists. And now that two designs of the jigsaws were made, it wasn't the tourists who were interested as much as the locals. Each and every one who had come into the shop had bought one eventually.

*

When she'd told him that, he smiled and said, 'Well, what do you know. Looks like we're stirring up some old memories.'

Lizzie flushed. 'Looks like we are. I've remembered stuff I hadn't thought about for years.'

'Good stuff I hope.'

'Mostly.' She looked at him. 'But not all. It seems as if there's a whole period in the past that I'd buried and rekindling the atmosphere of those days has raked it all up again.'

He said nothing.

'Really – the school, the old bus – it all seems to belong to the same time. You'd think you were doing it deliberately.'

Jim made a face. 'They're your memories, Lizzie. I only wanted to know what it felt like.' He left a pile of boxes on the table. 'Do you want to label these or will I?'

Lizzie took them. 'Leave it to me. As they're proving popular, I'll get Teresa to gift wrap some – she's great.'

He smiled. 'Right little cottage industry, aren't we?'

'Aren't we just.'

Jim put the last of the boxes on the table. 'Right so, I'll leave you to it. Maybe we should get together soon and plan the next ones. I've taken some more shots. I was thinking that maybe I'd get a few more people involved in the recollections – some of the old folk have great stories.'

'Good idea.'

'I'll call. Where's best – here or home?'

Lizzie wrote a phone number on her pad and handed the page to him. 'Ring me at home. After six.'

'Great, it's a date. Now, I must get back to see how my protégés are getting on.'

He picked up his bag and headed for the door just as it opened. He nodded briefly to the woman coming in but his mind was already on the next stop. He didn't wait to be introduced.

*

'It's a pity I didn't get to talk to him just now,' Bernie said. 'He's a nice-looking fellow – reminds me of someone.'

Lizzie raised her eyes to heaven. 'Don't tell me – Clint Eastwood without the monkey – Teresa's already pointed that out.'

Bernie nodded. 'That might be it. She likes him. And not just because she's grateful to him for keeping her devils off the streets. He isn't married or anything like that, is he?'

'I've no idea,' Lizzie said. 'He doesn't talk much about himself though he manages to get everyone else's information out of them.' She fingered the smooth jigsaw piece in her hand before trying to place it. She tried it one position then another but it didn't slot in. 'I'm no good at this,' she said. 'I can't seem to get them in the right place.'

Bernie took it from her and turned it upside down. 'It's not the way you look at it – it's the way you see it. If it doesn't fit as you expect, try turning it on its head.' She slotted the piece into place. 'It's like life.'

Lizzie sniffed. 'Aren't you very philosophical in your old age?'

Bernie took a bag of fudge and left a euro on the table. 'And fat – I'll have to cut down on this stuff – I love it though.' She tore the bag open and popped a piece into her mouth. 'Uum, delicious, mother's milk! I'm off.'

Lizzie waved and then started to sort the boxes on the table into piles. Jim had cut some of them into larger pieces with whimsies for children and others into pieces so fine and smooth to the touch they were works of art in themselves. The unfinished one on the table was in the middle range – small enough to be challenging but robust enough to withstand the variety of customers who tried their hand at completing part of it. Absentmindedly, Lizzie sat and looked what they had assembled already. The school outline was there with the heavy ivy overhang along one side. Two of the windows on the ground floor were there and the front door. All the rest was still in pieces on the tray. Lizzie picked one up. It was a piece of wall with the pattern of brick showing. Hopeless. There must be nearly a hundred of those. How were you supposed to know where to start? She was about to drop it when she thought about what Bernie said. It's the way you see it. She looked at the piece again. Bernie was right. It wasn't like all the others. It was darker, like the bricks nearer the ivy. She turned the piece sideways and looked at the half-completed puzzle and suddenly she could see where it went. The piece slotted into place and something about teaching old dogs new tricks flashed into her mind. She smiled. Maybe Bernie was right about the other as well. Jim was the right age for Teresa and he'd be good for her. Maybe they would get together and settle down and Lizzie would stop all the foolish notions that were catching her unawares recently. Silly menopausal old woman that she was. It was a bit late in the day for her to casting about for a man, especially one who was too young for her, who had come into her life all of a sudden and was likely to leave it just as abruptly when his business was done. She picked up another dark brick piece and tried it. It didn't fit.

*

It was a week before Lizzie saw Jim again. She had finished her tea and was settling down to read her book when there was a knock on the door. Jim was standing there in oily overalls, looking even more dishevelled than ever.

'So you got dressed up to come and see me then?'

He held his hands out in gesture of defeat. 'Guilty as charged. But my hands are clean.'

Lizzie stepped back. 'You'd better come in. I think. Are you wet?'

'No. It's all dried in – days of lying on my back trying to figure out how three decades of self-taught mechanics have managed to mangle the engine of my bus. I'll tell you what, they couldn't have made a bigger mess of it if they'd got knitting needles and tried to knit the repairs.'

'Jim Nealon, I hope you're not casting aspersions on the mechanical skills of our local craftsmen, are you?'

Jim shook his head. 'Not really. I'm more frustrated with myself. Over the years some of the bits that should be there have gone awol and I've had to order them. Until they arrive the engine is out of bounds. The interior is great though. Those kids – '

'Don't tell me, they're God's gift to the renovator and you don't know what you'd have done without them.'

Jim grinned. 'I mentioned them then?'

Lizzie made a face. 'Come in to the kitchen and tell me why I've been graced with a visit at this unlikely hour.' She pointed to the casserole dish on the sideboard. 'Have you eaten?'

Jim shook his head. 'No but I'm not dressed for it. I'll grab a bite later in the pub. Actually, I was going to ask if you'd join me but it looks like I'm too late.'

Lizzie nodded.

'What about a drink then – do you fancy keeping me company while I eat? My treat?'

'In Reardons?' Lizzie wondered what her face must look like. She couldn't remember the last time she had crossed that threshold. She must have been nine years old, getting out of her father's Anglia to follow him into Reardons for a bottle of Fanta with a straw and a packet of salt and vinegar Tayto crisps to celebrate Anne's great Inter Cert results. Anne Flynn, the big brain box who would get even better Leaving Cert results and go off to university in Dublin. Even at nine Lizzie understood that people weren't all the same. Anne was the one with the beauty and the brains and Lizzie was the one who sat in the wings with her Fanta and her crisps and watched.

'Do you know,' she lifted the teapot to check if there was still a cup in it she could offer Jim, 'I haven't been in that place for decades. Tea? It's not long made.'

'Thanks.'

'My father was a regular but I wouldn't have considered going there in an million years.'

'Why not? The food's great.'

'I'm sure it is.'

'So come with me then. You can order a sweet and I can show you some more photos that I've taken.' He must have noticed her hesitate. 'Unless you can think of a good reason why not.'

'I can't. You're right – live dangerously and all that.' She poured him a cup of tea and handed it over. 'Was that it then, why you called?'

Jim took a sip and shook his head. 'No, actually. I need to ask you a favour.'

Lizzie felt a shiver of suspicion and berated herself silently. In the few weeks since she had met Jim he had never been anything but straight with her. They got on well, his jigsaws were selling and she was gleaning a healthy profit from them, yet she did not feel entirely at ease with this man. Many locals interviewed him in their own unsubtle ways and each declared him a fine fellow. The twins thought the world of him and thanks to their efforts the bus was becoming increasingly habitable. Even Teresa who had called ostensibly to 'check they were behaving', had been roped in to help with the renovations. Seeing Jim struggle with the interior design, Lizzie suggested he ask Teresa to help make the padded benches he planned would double as sofa and bed. With her needlework skills Teresa was the ideal candidate for the job and when he offered it, she readily accepted. Lizzie hadn't had a chance to ask him how it was all working out with her yet, but if she knew Teresa as well as she suspected, more than padded benches would be well and truly sewn up before the bus was complete. So what did he want from Lizzie? She raised an eyebrow.

'That tea's just what I needed, thanks.' He put the cup down. 'To business – I mentioned I had ordered some engine parts?'

She nodded.

'Well, I haven't anywhere to store them and I wondered if you would let me have them delivered here into your garage till I need them?'

'I thought you were renting from Devine's?'

'I am, but only for the month. Matt reckons he needs to use it himself after next week and I am on the lookout for a new place. In the meantime, I need an address to have the parts delivered. It should only be for a few days.'

Lizzie considered the request – straightforward enough.

'What do you think? I'll pay, of course.'

'How much "stuff" are you anticipating?'

'A crate, a couple of boxes – it wouldn't take up much space.' He watched her hesitation and held up hand. 'Don't worry – if it bothers you having it here, forget it – it doesn't matter. I'll find somewhere else.'

'No, no, it's fine. Of course you can. There's plenty of room at the back where the old freezer was – leave what you like there.'

Jim caught her by the shoulders and kissed her on the forehead. 'Lizzie Flynn, you are a lifesaver. Thanks. These parts took me an age to track down and I'm keen to have them as quickly as I can.'

With the touch of his lips still on her forehead, Lizzie could feel the heat rushing into her cheeks. She hoped it was a blush – which would be bad enough – and not a hot flush, which would be disastrous. She turned towards the sink and started to wash his cup. 'If we are going for that drink,' she tried to keep her voice steady, 'you had better get changed, hadn't you?'

Jim looked down at his stained overalls. 'I will. Should take me half an hour and then I'll pick you up.'

Lizzie's face was still burning. She didn't think she could bear to get into the car with him. 'It's okay. It's a fine evening and I could do with the walk. I'll meet you there.'

'Okay. It's coming up seven-thirty now so, say eight?'

'Grand.'

'And thanks again. I'll bring the photos with me and you can choose the next scene.' He turned and headed for the front door. 'I'll let myself out. See you at eight.'

'Don't be late – don't want to be sitting in a pub on my own,' Lizzie called out to him.

'And there I was for a minute thinking you were desperate to see me!'

Jim laughed as he pulled her door behind him.

With the sound of the door still ringing in her ears, Lizzie put her hands to her burning cheeks, soapy suds and all. What was the matter with her? One affectionate peck in gratitude for space in her garage and she was blushing like an adolescent – if adolescents nowadays ever had such modesty. She was too old to blush over a man and certainly too old for a man like Jim Nealon. Anyway, what would she need a man for? She didn't. She dried her hands and conscious of the traitorous heat of her body, headed upstairs for a shower. Teresa was the one she should be encouraging Jim to have his eye on. Jim and Teresa – perfect.

*

Thirty-five minutes later, Lizzie walked down the street trying to ignore the lightness of her step and the fluttering in her heart. For all she had persuaded herself that her intention was to play matchmaker, she was still looking forward to the prospect of the evening ahead. She pushed open the door of Reardons Lounge Bar and stopped in amazement on the threshold. In the forty years since she had been here the place hadn't changed a bit – or if it had, all that was achieved was to make it look as much the same as was possible. The floor was still flagstone, and on the far wall a huge fire blazed out from the stone fireplace. Above it, a collection of mirrors advertising Jameson, Paddy and Bush-mills Whiskeys made the room look bigger than it was but Lizzie was surprised to find that it was still not as spacious as the Reardons of her memory. At nine she'd had to stand on tippy-toe to try and catch her reflection, now it stared back at her – a middle-aged woman, all made up to look younger and wrapped up to be warm. She looked around the tables – mostly old Singer sewing machines with mahogany tops polished to a gleam in the dimmed lights. Lizzie caught her breath when she spotted Jim, sitting at a table in the corner, checking the contents of a number of large brown envelopes. It was only half an hour since she'd seen him but she was struck by how – she didn't know how to describe it – how familiar he looked. And how young. Stop it, Lizzie!

Jim looked up and smiled. He didn't stand but gestured to the seat beside him. 'Hello! Come and have a look at these.' He held out his hand for her coat and laid it on the seat on the far side of him. 'What do you want to drink?'

'Hot port – thanks.' Lizzie pulled off her gloves and took the envelope from him. As he went to the bar she examined the contents. They weren't what she'd expected at all. As she slid one behind the other, close up shots of engine parts, wheel hubs, half-dismantled dashboards presented themselves and when she had seen them all, she turned to see Jim coming back from the bar, grinning broadly. She held out the pack to him and shook her head. 'Tell me you didn't drag me out in the cold and dark to look at a series of pictures of your bus restoration project?'

Jim put the drinks down and slid in beside her. 'What's that? Oh sorry, wrong ones.' He reached over and took another envelope. 'This is what I meant to show you. I spotted it a couple of weeks ago and I'm trying to find the owner. It looks derelict but it must have been magnificent in its day. It's definitely going to be your next project.'

'Not another bus?'

'Ha ha – very funny. For snide remarks like that you don't deserve to see it yet.' He put the envelope into his pocket and sank his lips into the creamy head of Guinness, shutting his eyes. 'Uuum, wonderful. How's the port?'

'Lovely, thank you, have you ordered?' Lizzie tapped the pile of pictures on the table. 'I can't believe you taking a roll like this. I'd never have figured you for a secret anorak.'

Jim laughed. 'I'm not an anorak! I just happen to love old vehicles, and this bus is a particularly fine old vehicle.' He took a deep slug and Lizzie had the impression that he was about to go into detail.

She held her palm up to stop him. 'Don't – spare me, please. You're worse than Sister Cillian and my father put together.'

Jim leaned closer. 'Scandal, is it? What did your father have to do with Sister Cillian?'

Lizzie laughed. 'Nothing, it's just that they were both vehicle enthusiasts as well. She was the reason the school had the use of the bus in the first place – ' she saw his raised eyebrow and waved his interest away. 'Long story, I'll tell you about it another time. And my father, who was in no way connected with this bus, was a tractor enthusiast. Whatever was the latest model, he had to have it. And even though they were all working tractors, they were always kept in sheds and barns overnight, pristine. It was his little eccentricity. And when he took delivery of a new one, he would be out with it for ages and we all knew what was coming next.' She paused and sipped her port. 'This,' she indicated the pictures, 'reels of boring photographs of wheels and engine parts to be admired. You'd have been his best friend.' She made a face. 'I was never impressed.'

Jim picked up the pictures. 'Poor man, a solitary passion. Didn't you have brothers?'

'No, just Anne and my mother and me. My father would have loved a son to follow him around but,' she took another sip, 'my mother had what was politely called "a delicate disposition".' She tapped the side of her glass. 'Or a liquid one, if you want to be more precise.'

Jim said nothing.

'What about you?'

Jim lifted his glass. 'I have a very solid disposition, thank you, though I can't get enough of this stuff. It tastes so much better this side of the water.'

Lizzie tutted. 'That's not what I meant. Family – have you brothers?'

Jim shook his head. 'Just me, and my father liked philately. We didn't get on.'

'Shame – you'd have been fine round our place – would have fitted in perfectly.'

Jim smiled. 'Maybe. I've never been the fitting in type.' He took another slug. 'As you say, long story. And speaking about stories,' he raised an eyebrow, 'my bus?'

'I haven't had a chance.' Lizzie picked up one of the menus wedged between the salt and pepper pots and scanned it. 'Once I've had a nice plate of something I don't need, I will go straight home and write up my memories. I presume that's what you were asking about.' She pointed to the third item down the sweet list. 'I'll have that when you're having yours.'

Jim took the menu from her and stood up. 'I've already ordered. I'm not bothering with afters. I'll ask Teresa to bring them over together.'

Teresa? Lizzie turned to the bar to see Teresa there, taking orders between rolling cutlery into serviettes and arranging them neatly in a flat basket on the bar counter. She looked up and waved.

'I didn't know you worked here!'

Teresa shrugged. 'I work everywhere. Especially for your man there.' She inclined her head towards Jim. 'He's a slave driver.' As Jim pointed out Lizzie's choice she nodded and called through a hatch to the kitchen to order it. 'Won't be long, I'll bring it over.'

'You're a good girl, so efficient.' Jim pursed his lips at her.

'Feck off, you.' Teresa laughed.

Lizzie watched his grin as he sat down. From the brief exchange it was obvious that Jim and Teresa's relationship was coming along just fine without any prompting from her – and she was shocked at how peeved she felt about that. She fished the slice of lemon from her glass and bit into it, glad that its bitterness afforded her the opportunity to wince. Stupid, stupid old woman. What did she expect? Teresa was young and capable and could help Jim prepare for the future; Lizzie was coming up to fifty and could only help him recall the past. She sneaked a glance at Teresa up at the bar. All the worry about the twins had taken weight off her and, with a close-fitting top and a bit of make-up, she was looking radiant. Young and desirable, like Jim. Oh shit – stop it! Lizzie sucked the last of the juice from the lemon and threw the peel into her empty glass.

'Why do you do it if it makes you so miserable?'

She looked at him in horror. Was he a mind reader too?

He pointed to the peel. 'Lemons. Why do you suck them if you don't like them?'

Relief made her laugh. 'I do.'

'It didn't look like it.'

'Don't look then.'

Jim raised his eyes to heaven. 'There's no pleasing women, is there? I had Teresa earlier telling me to hurry up and let her know how I wanted the benches done and now she's complaining that I'm slave driving her and you – ' he noticed her glare and held his hands up. 'You're just fine, don't mind me. Do you want another one?'

'No, thanks. I'll have a coffee in a minute.'

Teresa came over to the table with a tray. As she unloaded the plates Lizzie watched her closely. She definitely had an air about her that was different.

'Bon appetit!' She flicked a crumb off the table and went back to the bar, swinging her hips.'

'Teresa looks well.' Lizzie tried to make it sound like a compliment though her inclination was to add, *damn her*.

Jim was concentrating on sawing through his steak. 'She's a honey,' he said, without looking up. 'Bloody hell – forget what I said about the food in here being good. I'd love to know what this particular bull died from.'

130

Lizzie knew she should laugh but suddenly the fizz had gone out of her evening. She'd arrived here with every intention of alerting Jim to Teresa's many attractions only to discover that he'd noticed them already and they were getting on fine without her. And she felt peeved. She picked up her spoon and eased a sliver of sponge out of her dish. It looked lovely but when she tasted it, found that it too had lost its appeal. It was too much, too nice – too cloying. She put her spoon down and pushed the plate away.

Jim didn't even notice. He was busy piling chips and mushrooms onto a fork and was the picture of contentment. And why wouldn't he be? Lovely Teresa and her well-behaved twins helping him to create the perfect home in which they would all travel around the world – together. Angry with herself for her bitchiness, she slid the dish back and heaping custard onto her sponge, stuffed it into her mouth. If she was going to be left behind in Rathshannan, as always, she might as well make sure she had plenty of warm cellulite to keep her company. She swallowed the mouthful quickly and was about to stuff another one after it when the door of the bar was thrown open and Kylie Callaghan burst in. She ran towards her mother at the bar.

Teresa dropped the tea towel with which she had been polishing glasses.

'Kylie? What's the matter?' Teresa lost her radiance in an instant. Kylie looked as if she was about to start crying when she noticed Jim and stopped, staring at him in horror.

Lizzie looked from his face to hers and realised he was slowly getting to his feet. 'Kylie,' she said calmly, 'why are you here?'

Kylie turned to her mother again and now the guilt was plain for all to see. 'Oh Mam, we didn't mean it – it was an accident, honestly.'

Teresa was coming around the side of the bar.

Kylie wrung her hands and started to back towards the door but not quickly enough. 'Honestly, we didn't mean it.'

Behind Jim, Lizzie was pulling on her coat.

'Where's Jason?' Teresa had reached her daughter.

'He's fine, Mam, they got him out but – ' she turned to Jim, 'we're sorry, we really are.'

And then she pushed open the door again and they all heard it.

The siren of a fire engine.

*

For a while there was complete panic in the village. Matt Devine had a small store behind the garage where he kept his emergency supplies and behind that again the huge warehouse where his minibus and coach was kept. While some fire-fighters kept the flames at bay, others organised to clear the sheds further back. The front garage was a dead loss. Jim's bus was like a giant lantern and all the hard work they had done gone up in a blaze. Flanked by her children Teresa stood watching in horror as the walls of the garage crumbled and the torched bus inside was revealed. She looked from one to the other but neither Jason nor Kylie would meet her eye. She was so dispirited that Lizzie felt sharp pangs of guilt for her jealousy earlier. Didn't the poor woman deserve some happiness? Shivering with cold, she was wringing her hands and muttering something. Lizzie went over and put her arms around her.

'Hey, Teresa. It'll be all right. Nobody was hurt.'

Teresa scowled. 'You don't understand! Everything was going so well. For the first time in years things were actually looking up. Now,' she glared at the twins, 'thanks to these two, he won't want anything to do with me. That'll be the end of it.' Her voice broke and tears poured down her cheeks from puddles of mascara.

Lizzie felt impotent. Teresa was shaking from a mixture of cold and rage but when Lizzie's arms went round her she melted into them. The twins took the opportunity to close ranks and held one another loosely by the hand. They scuffed the ground with filthy trainers and were at least two steps back before Lizzie realised what they were planning.

'Don't you dare!' she hissed at them. 'Don't you bloody dare slink out of here after this and leave your mother to cope on her own!'

Jason stuck his chin out. 'What can we do? It was an accident.'

'Yea – we didn't mean for this to happen.'

There was a thin line of anger tracing its way up Lizzie's spine, and she could feel the roots of her hair tingle. She wanted to reach out and slap Kylie as hard as she could. Instead she clenched her fists and hugged Teresa even tighter. Through gritted teeth, she spat the words out slowly.

'Nobody ever means for accidents to happen, you unbearably stupid child. But they do happen and someone is always to blame.' She glared at Jason.

His eyes were wide and he looked shocked at the venom in her tone. His lips were working and she knew he wanted to tell her to butt out and what right had she to talk to his sister like that, but she knew as she held his gaze that he wouldn't. In her arms feisty Teresa, who wouldn't normally allow anyone to disparage her offspring, was holding her breath. Lizzie nodded. 'That's the way it is. Regardless of how deliberate it wasn't, you can't back out now and wash your hands of it. You did it and now you stay and help clean up the mess.'

The twins looked at one another, then Jason rolled up his sleeves. 'Com'on,' he said and headed for the human chain that was passing buckets of water down to try and quell the fire. When he reached the start of the line, Matt Devine was there, covered in soot and looking desperate. This property was his pride and joy and now it was in flames. He glared at Jason as he approached and looked as if he was about to tell him to clear off. He paused a second, bucket in hand and as he did, caught Lizzie's eye. He must have noticed Teresa slumped in her arms because there was a flash of understanding. Nodding to the next man who moved away slightly, leaving a space for the twins to join the chain, he passed Jason the bucket. Like a Mexican wave, the chain flowed smoothly again.

'The twins are helping to put the fire out,' Lizzie whispered in Teresa's ear.

'The least they could bloody do.' Teresa sniffed. 'I could kill them!' She lifted her face and looked Lizzie in the eye. 'I probably will once I get them safely home out of this. Oh God! Listen to me! What am I saying? Jason could have been killed!' Torn between laughing and crying she turned to look at the fire. Even with half the village out, it was still blazing lustily and they could see Matt and Jim moving people back.

'Move away!' Matt shouted. 'There's no point in trying to save any more here at the front and no point in risking lives over it. Move back and let it burn itself out!'

Reluctantly the crowd did as they were told. Still holding buckets, they edged away to a safer distance where the sparks could not reach them and stood there, silent, watching. Without the sound of voices the noise of the blaze like a huge waterfall was deafening. Lizzie shook her head at the irony of it.

'It's a nightmare, isn't it?' Teresa said.

Lizzie shrugged. 'No, it's terrible but nobody was killed. Nobody was even hurt as far as we know.'

Haloed by the orange flame, Jim walked towards them. He looked weary and Lizzie fought the urge to move forward and wrap him in her arms.

'He is,' Teresa said, 'he was really enjoying that bus and now it doesn't exist.'

'There'll be other buses to renovate.'

'Not in Rathshannan, there aren't.' Teresa took a step towards him but as she did, Matt called out and he changed direction and walked away again. The two women watched. 'I wonder if he'll stay,' Teresa said.

The suggestion was a cold slap and Lizzie looked at her, horrified. 'Why wouldn't he? He's got work to do here. He's the jigsaw maker.'

'Yea, but do you really think he's going to want to hang around making jigsaws in Rathshannan after this? There are plenty of prettier villages he could go to, ones where he doesn't hire a pair of little shits and treat them like family and then have them burn his dreams down.' She started to cry again.

Lizzie put her arm around Teresa's shoulder. 'Maybe you're right.' She could hear her own voice, flat and monotone against the roaring fire. On the far side of the street, Jim and the other men were loading some of Matt's stores from the sheds onto a trailer to be taken to safety. Matt was wiping the sweat from his forehead as he urged people to stay back, not to risk getting hurt.

'Damn it,' Teresa said, 'I've gotten used to having him round.'

'Me too.'

'And it'd be a shame to go back to the way we were. I don't think I could bear it.'

'Me neither,' Lizzie whispered.

The two women looked at each other. Lizzie saw how, even with the blaze reflected in Teresa's eyes, the light she'd seen in them earlier had gone out. She smiled ruefully. Poor Teresa, always hoping that there was a better future up ahead. Not like Lizzie. She didn't worry about the future, expected nothing from it but to be left alone and usually wasn't disappointed. She noticed the twins, still huddled together shamefaced as they caught the eyes and remarks of the other onlookers. It looked as if they had taken what she'd said on board. They couldn't run away and pretend accidents just happen. Somebody had to take the responsibility. She shivered suddenly, wished she had taken her coat with her as she left Reardons but it wasn't really the cold.

Someone was always to blame. She was just glad that this time it wasn't her.

*

By three in the morning the fire was finally under control. Only a few smouldering ashes remained glowing in the darkness and the air was full of the acrid smell of charred wood and scorched paint and metal. Lizzie found herself back in Reardons. The fire engine had left but the last few stragglers were tidying up as best they could for fear a gust of wind would carry a stray spark to a nearby building and the whole thing would start up again. Another human chain, sparse but smooth flowing, carried buckets of water to wherever embers dared to glow. Lizzie and a couple of other women offered to help but Matt, still wired with nervous energy, asked if they could get a bite to eat prepared instead.

In the kitchen, Kate Reardon had already organised the food. She was boiling kettles and buttering bread for toasted sandwiches. Lizzie's half-eaten pudding was still on the table where she had left it and she realised that she was starving.

'Lizzie! Come in and warm yourself up. We'll all have hypothermia after that. Here, you butter those and don't make a mess!' Bernie Collins held a knife out to Kylie. 'And I don't want to hear another word about how tired you are and how you need your beauty sleep. You'll need to have a lot more than beauty going for you in the morning when the Gardai come asking questions, I can tell you.'

Sullenly, Kylie took the knife from her. She looked as if she might retort but the door opened and the men arrived. Jason was with them, flanked by Matt and Jim and, judging by his face, he'd had the same idea but had wisely abandoned it. Lizzie stood up and held Jim's jacket out to him.

'You're perished, Jim. Put this on.'

He took it from her.

'Are you okay?'

He shrugged. 'Tired, sweaty – nothing a hot bath and a good night's sleep won't cure.'

'And the bus?'

He smiled. 'That's more than a night's sleep worth, I think. We may draw a line under that one.' He took the mug of tea that Bernie had come over to offer him and wrapped his hands around it. 'Thanks.' He made a face at Lizzie. 'I'm afraid that chapter is well and truly closed.'

Lizzie remembered Teresa's prediction that he might leave Rathshannan now. She watched him drink the tea and fought the temptation to cover his hand with hers and say, don't leave, I want you to stay. She didn't realise how close the tears were till one escaped and she felt it slide down her cheek.

Jim jumped to attention. He put the mug on the table and wrapped his arms around her. 'Hey, none of that! It's only an old bus! I didn't realise you were so fond of it. And I thought *I* was the anorak!' He was making fun of her.

She pushed him away, crossly. 'I'm not upset about the bus.'

He raised an eyebrow.

'I'm not – and you're right. You do need a bath.'

Jim laughed. 'Thanks – and there I was thinking you were going to offer me tea and sympathy.'

Lizzie indicated the mug. 'You got your tea.'

'I did, don't think I even thanked her for it.' He looked around to where Bernie was berating Kylie for making a mess. 'Oh dear – '

'Looks like Kylie's fallen foul of her grandmother as well.'

'Grandmother? Teresa's mother?'

'Yep, do you want me to introduce you?'

Jim watched Kylie cower under the onslaught. He turned back to Lizzie, grinning. 'No, thanks, I think I'll just drink my tea and be off to my bed. There'll be enough trouble to face in the morning without looking for more tonight.'

Lizzie smiled. 'You're probably right.' She watched as he finished the tea and stuffed a sandwich into his mouth. 'You're taking it very well, I must say.'

Jim shrugged. 'Can't say I'm not upset but it's nothing I won't get over. Accidents happen.'

Lizzie felt the old flash of anger. 'No, they don't. Someone's always to blame. You can't just brush it off like that. Someone has to pay.'

Jim looked over to where the twins were now sitting at a table with Bernie on one side and Matt Devine on the other. They looked close to tears.

'Aren't you going to say anything to them?'

Jim shook his head. 'No, I'm not, Lizzie, not tonight. What happened happened, and all the whys and the retributions can wait. We've all been through enough – them included.'

'But – '

He held a hand up. 'Enough. No more.'

'You're – '

He put both hands on the table and leaned towards her. '*I'm* nothing. Whatever is going on in your head is not about me – it's you. I'm not into this Irish Catholic need for guilt and retribution.'

She flashed angrily at him – patronising bastard.

'Normally I'd love to stay and talk to you about it but now it's – ' he wiped the soot from his watch and groaned, 'three-thirty, and I am completely whacked so I'm going to bed. Do you need me to walk you home?'

'No, thank you,' Lizzie said stiffly. 'I know my way.' She buttoned her coat and made her way to the door.

Jim followed her. 'Suit yourself.'

When they came level with the table where the twins were, Jason stood up and caught Jim's arm.

'I'm sorry, Jim,' he said. 'I really am.'

'Me too.' Kylie's voice was a whisper behind him.

Jim nodded. 'I know you are – you ought to be – but I guess you've been told that already.' He acknowledged

Bernie and Matt then he smiled at the twins wearily. 'You can tell me all about it in the morning. Just go home now and try to get some sleep.' Teresa was watching from behind the bar and he went across and kissed her on the cheek. 'You too. You look done in.'

She motioned the twins to stand. There was an awkward moment when they all stood looking at one another. Somebody was definitely due to make a remark but nobody seemed to know what to say. Matt broke the silence. He nodded to where Lizzie's half-eaten pudding sat cold and congealed in the dish where she had abandoned it hours earlier.

'So, Lizzie,' he said. 'You don't like syrup sponge then. You didn't need to go to such lengths – you could have just said!'

There was a burst of laughter and a sudden flurry as coats were collected and everyone spilled out into the freezing air. Where the garage had been there was complete darkness and people disappeared into the night. Lizzie watched Jim's silhouette as he headed up the street towards the B&B where he was going to stay.

'Goodnight Jim,' she called softly after him but he didn't turn around. She walked quickly up the street, conscious how loud her steps sounded on the cold pavement. The tears were flowing freely before she reached her front door and she could hardly get her key into the lock.

'Damn you, Jim Nealon,' she sobbed crossly. 'Damn you and your damned jigsaws.' She threw the keys on the hall table and opening the cupboard, took out a bottle of gin and poured herself a large glass. She downed it in one and winced at the taste. How did her mother ever get through so much of this stuff – it was disgusting. At the thought of her mother the tears started again and she poured another glass. 'And he's wrong about the retribution thing, so he is,' she blubbed aloud. 'Somebody *does* have to pay when they make an accident happen.' She took another mouthful. 'And I don't know why I'm feeling so horrible about this one – it isn't my fault. *I* didn't burn down the bloody bus and now he's going to leave and all I have left is a bloody photograph – ' she took another gulp, 'which I've probably lost.'

Staggering, she felt her way to the study where she had a bus jigsaw completed on the table. Poor bus. Poor dead burned-out bus. Careful not to let her tears fall on it, she traced the line of the bus and realised she was smiling fondly through her hiccups. She took another sip. And why wouldn't I smile? It was a fine bus in its day – we had some good times. She sank into her chair and sniffed. Good times, great times. She shut her eyes and felt the exhaustion wash over her.

*

It was not the sandman who eventually brought sleep to Lizzie the night of the fire. It was a grit lorry, heavily laden with energetic gritters each carrying a shovel which he used to fling great heaps of hot itchy grit into every recess of her brain. And when she tried to open her eyes the following morning, they were full of it.

She opened one, just a fraction, and shut it again as a wave of nausea rushed up her throat. She groaned. The grit was forming into golf balls in her head and they rolled from side to side when she tried to move. Shit! She slid her hands along the sides of the chair and leaned forward. *I can't have drunk that much.* Even in her head, her own voice sounded accusing. Another wave of nausea then the phone rang. With the harsh light from the window and the humming in her ears, it sounded more strident than usual – urgent. She took a deep breath and lurched to the table.

'Hello?' Her voice was deep, gravelly.

'Lizzie? Is that you?' Anne's was anxious. 'Are you okay? I heard about the fire. Bernie's just told me. Why didn't you ring?'

Lizzie rested the receiver on her shoulder and, slumping into the chair, held her head with both hands. 'There wasn't time. It just happened. Nobody was hurt.'

'Lizzie? I can't hear you – your voice is muffled. Do you want me to come round?'

'No. I'm fine – it's...' as she shifted her position on the chair, her foot hit something on the floor which rolled into view. It was the gin bottle; it was empty. *It's nothing more serious than a hangover*, she ought to say now. *We should be used to that.* 'I dropped off in the chair – '

'You poor thing, you must be exhausted. Will I pop round and make you something to eat? You can go back to bed for the day.'

Lizzie shook her head before remembering Anne couldn't see her. 'I'm fine, really. I'll grab a coffee to wake

143

myself up and then I'll be fine.' She could sense Anne's intake of breath at the other end in preparation for the next question and realised that she didn't have the energy for it. 'Let me get myself sorted and then I'll call you, okay?'

'Grand, let me know if there's anything I can do.'

'Sure, bye.' Lizzie dropped the phone. She leaned over and picked the bottle off the floor. 'Oh bloody hell!' She turned it over but nothing fell out – it was completely dry. Supporting herself with one hand she knelt down and felt along the edges of the rug – that was dry too. Nothing had been spilled. She had managed to empty a half bottle of gin, neat, on her own. All the gritters in her pulsing brain paused their shovelling and shook their heads in disapproval. *Tut, tut, Lizzie – you know what downing the gin on your own leads to – there's no excuse – not for you.* Still holding the side of the chair for balance, she hauled herself upright and padded to the kitchen. Under her stockinged feet the floor tiles were cold and she welcomed the shock of it. Everything else was too hot, too sharp. She filled the kettle and pulled back the kitchen curtain.

\*

As she had predicted, the high street was busy. Already, someone had delivered two huge skips and teams of men were filling them with lengths of charred wood. In the place where the garage had been the remains of the bus stood, forlorn, a blackened skeleton of its former self. Lizzie tried not to look as she passed but it was impossible.

'Hey, Lizzie! I didn't expect to see you up this morning! How are you feeling?'

'I'm feeling fine – why shouldn't I be?' Did she look that bad? Were the dark glasses too obvious? She didn't think she could function without them.

Matt Devine pulled off the heavy gloves he was wearing and came across the road to her smiling. 'You can't have had much sleep, it must have been near four by the time you got home.'

Oh, that's what he meant. 'I had a few hours – what about you?'

Matt turned and looked back at the damage. 'Not till this lot is cleared. I kept thinking I heard crackling and of course it was nothing, just the wind.' He sighed deeply. 'Bloody shame all the same. He was doing a great job of it and the work Teresa did on the inside was like nothing you've ever seen, pure professional.'

I bet. Lizzie managed a tight smile. 'How did they manage it anyway?'

'Who?'

'The twins. How did they manage to start the fire – it was hardly deliberate.'

Matt pushed his cap back and scratched the top of his head. 'God no, they wouldn't do a thing like that. They're not bad kids.' He must have noticed Lizzie's eyebrow shoot up above her sunglasses. 'They're not, really. They're devils but they're not malicious, and they think the world of Jim. They all do.'

Lizzie folded her arms so that her clenched fists were buried deep in the folds of her elbows. She motioned to where the men were beginning to dismantle the bonnet of the bus and pile it into the huge skip. 'It doesn't exactly look like it, does it?'

Matt smiled. 'No, I suppose it doesn't but – '

Lizzie held her hand up. 'Don't tell me – it was an accident.'

'More stupid than accidental to be honest. Will I tell you what the eejit did?' He leaned closer to her. 'The two of them were in the bus – Jim had left them with the key to lock up because Jason was finishing a paint job and Jim was keen to get off early... '

Lizzie blushed. He had come around to see her.

'So they decided to have a crafty smoke before going home. Teresa had warned them there'd be hell to pay if she caught them smoking at home now that she's taken up clean living and given it up.'

Lizzie looked at him in surprise. 'Teresa doesn't smoke any more!'

Matt laughed at her surprise. 'Amazing, isn't it? She's a reformed woman.'

'Wonder what brought that on?'

Matt pulled his cap forward again and cleared his throat. 'Do you want me to tell you the story or not?'

'Sorry, carry on.'

'Right. There's the two of them in the bus, pulling on the fag, when Kylie notices a piece of thread hanging out of the seat of the bench her mother was sewing. Now, as you know,

Teresa is very particular and Kylie was joking that she'd left a loose bit, and should she cut it off? *Not at all,* says Jason, the clever boyo, *let me fix it,* and he reaches over and puts the tip of the fag to the end of it. The two of them watch as the thread burns – all the way up, till you wouldn't see it. And when it gets to the place where it should stop, it doesn't. It keeps burning, till there's a little orange ringed hole where the seams meet and when he puts his nose to it – a bit of a smell. *Put it out,* says she. *How,* says he? *Spit on it* – so he does.'

'Oh dear.'

'Oh dear, exactly. By all accounts he did a grand job and nobody would ever have known if they'd had the sense to leave it at that but of course, they didn't. He presses the spit into the hole and rubs it hard so his mother won't notice. Kylie decides to go off to the shop for another packet of fags and leaves Jason finishing the last one. Left on his own, he decides to check that there aren't any other loose ends needing his attention. Fuelled with success, his expertise knows no bounds now and by the time Kylie returns, he's found three more and the smell is stronger. He can't smell it but she can. And no sooner does she manage to convince him that all's not well, than they notice a thin line of smoke oozing out from the seam nearest the original thread.'

'The stuffing was on fire?'

Matt nodded. 'He'd put out the bit on the outside but when he pressed the spit into it, he must have managed to push a lighted bit into the back of it as well. Of course it travelled all down through the wadding and by the time the eejit realised what he'd done, it was too late. There was smoke filling up the bus and they had to get out of there. Kylie came over to the pub to call her mother to see if she could come and sort it out and someone saw the smoke through the open garage door and called the fire brigade.' He shrugged. 'And the rest, as they say, is history.'

'And now there's no bus and no garage.'

Matt nodded. 'Right.'

'Were you insured?'

He grimaced. 'I was – up to recently.'

'Oh Matt – not like you to let something like that slip.'

'I didn't.' His expression hardened. 'I was going to pull down the old garage anyway – planning to extend the house out the front and keep the business in a separate yard out the back. The work wasn't due to start till the summer so it suited me fine to let Jim have the use of it for the time being. I don't even know what his insurance details are. He's probably lost the lot.'

'He didn't keep any of his photographic equipment in there, did he?'

Matt shook his head. 'That's over in the B&B. Most of it anyway – the rest is in his car, or in the sack on his back!'

Lizzie smiled. 'Thank God for that.' She looked across to where the work was continuing at a great pace. Most of the men she recognised. Jim wasn't there. 'Where is he anyway? I thought he'd be here.'

'Nah – he was here earlier but he's gone over to Teresa's.'

Lizzie stiffened. Of course.

'For the inquisition – and a bit of tea and sympathy – he'll need it.'

Lizzie smiled. Matt was a good man. 'You too, I suppose.'

Matt shrugged. 'Oh, I'm okay. Anything out the back that's damaged is insured and I've lost nothing out front that I can't replace.' Then he smiled and there was a twinkle in his eye. 'Might even help my cause.'

Lizzie was puzzled. His cause? Then she remembered. 'You mean the extension?'

He nodded. 'Something like that.' Across the road the last of the bus was being pulled onto a huge trailer. Soon the site would be razed to the ground. Empty.

'Seems a bit drastic if all you want is an extension, Matt.'

He was grinning. 'Ah well – every cloud and all that.'

Strange man. Lizzie nodded but she wasn't sure she was following him at all. She watched as the chassis of the bus was roped to the sides of the trailer and with a puff of exhaust, the whole thing started to move slowly away. They were silent as it passed and when it reached the bridge at the end of the street, held their breath while the driver negotiated the narrow turning and the trailer disappeared from view. Matt raised his hand in salute.

'Well, there she goes, the end of an era.'

'She's not the only one – the nuns won't be sorry to see the back of her. They didn't want her back in Rathshannan at all.'

Matt laughed. 'I bet they didn't.' In the distance the sound of the heavy trailer faded. 'Does Jim know the story?'

'No.'

'You should tell him.' Matt pulled his heavy gloves on. 'Right, much as I'd love to dally and waste the day chatting up women in dark glasses, I must get back and help these fellows finish.' He raised a hand in farewell. 'Mind yourself – be good.'

'Chance would be a fine thing.' Lizzie smiled and turned towards the shop. As she opened the door, she noticed ash and flakes of soot on the front windowsill. She reached out and rubbed it with her finger. Then she went into the shop and, careful not to knock off the soot, took a picture from the shelf above her table. It was in a small frame, cream and mulberry striped and inside it, a postcard. Very carefully, she prised open the back of the frame and slid the postcard out. On the back of it there was her name, written in ink in a beautiful flowing hand and beside it, a short note: *Sometimes one is brave enough.* She pressed her finger on the clean space in between and smiled at the blackened print. Then she slid the frame back into place again and put it onto the shelf. An appropriate farewell.

As she took her coat off, she realised that her hangover had eased in the morning air and her recollections from the night before seemed less urgent now. It had bothered her what she could tell Jim about his bus – school outings weren't that exciting if you weren't on them – but that wasn't what she would tell him about his bus at all. She smiled. She'd tell him what she'd never explained to anyone else before – why she kept that funny postcard on the shelf wherever she was. It wasn't even a pretty scene. It was just a single image.

An elephant – with wings.

\*

150

It was past four when Anne arrived, dishevelled and carrying a large basket. She backed in the door and dropped her load. 'That weighs a ton – I'm knackered!'

Lizzie got up to help her. 'What have you in there – the week's washing?'

Anne smiled. 'No. I thought I'd make some treats for the victims of the Callaghan twins' latest escapade – give you all the energy you used up battling the blaze in the dead of night.'

Lizzie peeped into the basket. There were trays of fudge, plates of fancies covered in cling film and a couple of fruit loaves. 'That looks lovely, Anne. You must have been busy all day.'

'Bernie helped me. She's mortified at what happened and doing her best to put a brave face on it. No matter what awful thing anyone said about the twins today, Bernie either said something worse or got in early and said it first! What she hasn't called them isn't worth noting.'

'They deserve it.'

'They do. Try this.' Anne pulled some cling film off one of the plates and handed her a piece of sticky cake. 'It's another new one.'

Lizzie bit into it. The outside was crunchy but inside was moist and full of fruit. 'This is gorgeous!' She took another bite. 'And I'm starving. This is the first thing I've eaten all day.'

'That's not good for you. What's up? Did last night frighten you that much?'

Lizzie realised she was blushing. It wasn't last night's excitement but this morning's hangover that whipped her appetite but she didn't want to go explaining that to Anne just now. She would have trouble explaining it to herself. Instead, she popped the last of the slice into her mouth and rummaged in the basket for something else.

'Here, let me put it on a plate and I'll stick the kettle on.' Anne lifted the basket onto the table. 'You should really have let me come round this morning and look after you. Sometimes it takes a while for the shock to register and you think you're fine but you're not.'

'Anne! For goodness sake! You're fussing – leave it. I was across in Reardons eating ham sandwiches at three in the morning; it's little wonder I don't feel up to eating much today.'

Anne turned and looked at her puzzled. 'Yea – what about that?'

'What?'

'You, in Reardons in the first place? You never go in there.'

Lizzie nodded. 'I don't. Jim had come round and said he was going there for his tea and suggested I join him for a drink.'

Anne's eyebrows twitched. There were questions lining up in her brain, waiting to be asked. Lizzie tried to deflect them.

'Teresa works there part-time, did you know?'

Anne nodded.

'She looks well – or at least she did before last night's fiasco.'

'She'll be fine. Teresa has weathered worse storms than this one.' The questions were lying down but they weren't asleep.

Lizzie decided to go for it. 'I was glad to see her there because I'd been hoping to catch up with her and ask how she was getting on with the upholstery work on the bus. Jim says she was doing a great job.' Actually, it was Matt said that. 'Said it was pure professional.'

'Matt Devine waxed lyrical when he called for the deliveries last week.'

'Shame that job's ended. She's worried he won't want to have anything to do with her now.'

Anne smiled. 'I don't think she needs to worry. I may be an old romantic but I think he'd forgive her anything – even her offspring.'

'Really?' Lizzie hoped she didn't sound as surprised outside her head as she did in it.

'He's had a soft spot for her since the first time he saw her – I don't think she even notices.'

'She does. She said so.'

Anne rubbed her hands together. 'Oh goodie! I love a bit of romance. Wouldn't it be lovely.'

Lizzie shrugged. 'I suppose,' then pulled herself together quickly, 'I mean, of course it would, lovely.'

For a minute Anne said nothing. Then she leaned over and looked at Lizzie closely.

Lizzie held her breath, glad that she'd eaten the sweet cake but conscious that it wouldn't quite mask the hangover smell that had been on her breath all day. She knew her eyes were still red but she could blame that on the tiredness.

'Lizzie.' The word was a statement. 'Are you going to tell me what's wrong or shall we spend ten minutes insisting that nothing is and then you tell me?' Anne had her hands on her hips and looked very solid for a slight figure.

Lizzie smiled. 'You're so astute.' She pushed the sheaf of papers she had been writing on across the table towards her sister. 'To tell you the truth, I'm worried about being sued for libel. Read this.'

Anne picked the papers up. She skimmed the first couple of lines then smiled broadly. 'You are a worrier – this is fine – it's good. What's it for, the local newspaper?'

'No. You've seen Jim's latest jigsaw is a beautiful photograph of the now defunct bus. I've been battling to find an angle to write about for it – school outings, local historical trips, mystery tours – but I wasn't getting any-where. Then Matt mentioned about when the nuns got rid of it and he suggested I tell Jim the story. So I wrote this. What do you think?'

Anne perched on the edge of the table as she read. Lizzie watched her eyes move back and forth across the page, occasionally pausing and smiling. When she eventually finished she turned and smiled. 'I hadn't realised the nuns sold the bus afterwards.'

'They regarded it as a threat to the moral integrity of the convent – a vessel of wanton passions and all that.' Lizzie took the sheets from her. 'I wonder what happened to her afterwards, if she's still alive.'

'She got married,' Anne paused and for a second, Lizzie had the impression that she had not intended to mention it. She took a deep breath. 'I met them in Dublin, you know.'

'What! You never told me!'

Anne shrugged. 'Didn't think it was important.'

Didn't think at all more like it. 'You met Sister Cillian in Dublin and you didn't think I'd be interested?'

'She wasn't Sister then – she was Mrs Barrett by then.'

'And? The rest?'

'That's it – they were married, his people lived in Dublin and I think they planned to stay there a while and set up a business of their own – Barrett's Buses. I lost track of them after a while. Anyway, I'd better be off.' She lifted her basket off the table, dislodging the pages which fluttered to the floor. She bent to pick them up and as she handed them back to Lizzie, seemed to be avoiding her eye. 'This is good.' She held them out. 'It's a great story and would complement the photograph if he decides to go ahead with it now.'

Her words echoed Teresa's and Lizzie felt afraid. 'Why wouldn't he?'

'Would *you*? I'd be out of here in a flash.'

'I'm sure he's not superstitious like that.'

Anne smiled. 'Well, you know him. Anyway, this is good stuff and you shouldn't worry about libel – there's nothing offensive here, just the truth. I like it anyway – the Runaway Nun – it's catchy. She pushed a bag of fudge and a plate of cakes across the table. 'Give these to your jigsaw man when you see him. Might cheer him up a bit.'

Lizzie was about to say she mightn't see him either but it struck her that she should take them anyway. She could use them as an excuse to call – a peace offering. 'Thanks. I'll tell him they're from you.'

But Anne was already at the door, waving over her shoulder as she left. Lizzie watched her pass the window, fighting the frustration she often felt after a conversation with her sister. Anne had a way of leading into a topic then turning tail and abandoning you there while she moved on to the next thing. That's what she had done today – mentioned Cillian and Mr Barrett and then nothing. Ah well, *plus ça change* and all that. She gathered the pages up carefully with sticky fingers, smiling. At least she had a title for it now.

\*

'Afternoon!'

Lizzie looked up to see a very weary Jim in the doorway.

'I've just been accosted by a bohemian lady carrying a large basket who informed me that as I must be the jigsaw man, she had left something for me here! Can you shed light on the subject?'

Lizzie smiled. No need for peace offerings then. 'That'll be Anne, my sister. She heard about the fire and decided to make a batch of goodies to give us all our strength back. Here – these are yours.' She held out the plate of sweets.

Jim took them. 'What a kind woman. I should thank her but she had gone before I got a chance to lift my safety visor.'

'I'll introduce you some time, though you won't be news. She'll have heard all about you from Bernie.' It seemed to Lizzie that Jim held the plate tightly. 'Are you okay?'

He was still for a moment. 'What would Bernie what's-her-name know about me?'

'Jim Nealon, this is Rathshannan. Everyone knows everything about everyone around here. You talk to Teresa who tells Bernie who mentions it to Anne... you get the picture.'

'Oh right – ' Jim looked thoughtful. He opened his mouth as if to say more but changed his mind. Instead he pulled open the wrapping on one of the cakes and gently easing it out, took a large bite. 'Um – your sister is an angel! Did she make all of this?'

'Between them they make it, I don't know who is responsible for what.' Then he noticed the sheets of paper. 'Hey, is that for me?'

'If you still want it.' Lizzie picked up the sheets and tapped them into order on the table. 'If you don't use it you might like to read the story anyway.'

Jim held his hand out for the sheets. 'Why wouldn't I want it?'

'After last night – we weren't sure you'd want to, you know, go ahead with the jigsaw scheme.'

Jim looked puzzled. 'Why would that change anything? I didn't come here to renovate a bus, Lizzie. I came here – ' he turned the pages over as if he was reading off the back of them. She had the distinct impression he was playing for time.

'To make jigsaws?'

He was still hesitating. 'That's right but – '

Lizzie felt that shiver of anxiety start the long climb up her spine again. So there was something else. Teresa hadn't bought the story – she'd said right at the beginning that there was more to Jim Nealon than met the eye. Anne was suspicious of him too. And Lizzie had defended him, said he was all above board. She leaned forward, waiting for him to tell her everything.

And just as Anne had earlier, Jim seemed to switch off. He stuffed the last of the slice into his mouth and apologised as some crumbs dropped to the floor. He bent to pick them up and then, holding them tentatively with the tips of his fingers, he put them in the bin. Then he pulled a grubby handkerchief from his pocket and began to wipe his hands. 'Gets everywhere, doesn't it?'

He ignored the glare she knew she was giving him. 'So, tell me your bus story.'

'I thought *you* had a story for me?'

Shoving the handkerchief back in his pocket, he leaned against the table and scanned the pages. As he read, his eyes lit up. 'An escapee! Great! What a romantic tale – you should have told me this before.'

'There wasn't much opportunity. You've been so taken up with your bus and the renovations I didn't get around to it.' That was meant as a statement of fact but spoken aloud, it sounded more like a peeve. She blushed. 'I mean, I probably would have gotten round to it but I wasn't actually thinking about that till Matt mentioned it this morning. My memories started earlier – almost a year earlier.'

Jim was watching her closely. 'Not happy memories?'

Lizzie shrugged. 'Neither happy nor unhappy.'

'Go on then.'

Lizzie stood up and put her hands on her hips. 'Jim Nealon, tempting as it is to recount my fascinating memories to a captive audience, there's a little voice in my head which says, *hold on there Lizzie. This fellow stands in your shop and tells you there's more to his presence than meets the eye – and then he clams up and changes the subject. Are you really going to satisfy his curiosity when he leaves you burning with your own?*'

Jim pursed his lips and winced as if the decision was not a comfortable one.

'Of course, if you don't trust me... ' There was more than a hint of truth in her jest.

'It's not that, Lizzie. Trust doesn't come into it.' He held out his arms and indicated the shop. 'Look at this. What do you see all around you?'

Lizzie looked. 'My shop?'

He shook his head. 'In the shop.'

Lizzie looked again. All around her, on shelves and display stands there was an array of lovely things – scented candles, cards, pictures, pottery, ornaments, household linens, handmade toys, jewellery. She tried to think of a word to sum it all up. 'Lovely things to have or give as presents? Luxuries.'

He nodded. 'Possessions. Things that tie you down.'

Lizzie bristled. 'There's nothing wrong with that. They're treats, they make you feel nice.'

He nodded. 'Yes, but they also identify you, bracket you.' He picked up a vase. 'If I want to give you a gift and I choose this for you, it will be because it belongs in my picture of you, what you're like. For you it will be part of the picture of our relationship. For ever afterwards it takes on an identity greater than the reality of it – ' he turned it over, 'a simple pottery vase with a flower painted on the front.' He handed it to her. 'It binds us.'

It felt warm in her hand.

Without warning, Jim took the vase back and threw it in the air. Lizzie reached out for it but he reached higher and caught it as it fell. She glared at him. 'What was that for? You could have broken it!'

He shrugged. 'And? I would have given you the twenty euro and so you wouldn't have lost out.'

'Yes, I would.' She was angry now. 'You're playing games.'

He smiled. 'I'm just trying to explain. Once you surround yourself with things, you think you possess them but in fact they possess you. What happens to them affects you even though they are supposedly inanimate. Because of our sentimentality, we imbue our possessions with meaning and that takes on a life of its own – it ties us down.'

Lizzie considered his words. She looked around her shop and felt defensive. When she bought this shop it had been an ironmongers. Everyone came here for the brushes and buckets and soaps they needed for their daily toil.

Lizzie's first action was to hold a huge stock sale – practically give it away and then she painted and restocked. Where it had once sold the necessities, the shop now sold the luxuries, the little treats and extras that cheered people up, made them feel special. It was a deliberate choice after years of looking after her mother who in her depression shunned luxuries as being only for the deserving, not for her. And the shop flourished. It wasn't ever going to make a fortune but it ticked over, every purchase brightening someone's day.

'What I sell makes people happy,' she said.

Jim smiled. 'I know it does. And I'm not saying it's a bad thing to tie people down either – it's just not for me.'

Crossly, Lizzie took the vase out of his hands and put it back on the shelf. 'Don't throw it around then.' She turned. 'Is this by way of explaining why you're not making too much fuss about the fire; or by way of failing to explain exactly what you're up to?'

Now he laughed. 'Both. I am annoyed about what happened. I was really enjoying that and it would have been a lovely way to travel round – '

'And you were enjoying the workforce.'

He nodded. 'I was thoroughly enjoying the workforce but – I would have left them behind in the end.'

'Would you?'

'Of course. I always travel alone.'

That sounded very ruthless.

'What are you thinking?' he asked gently.

It came into focus. She looked at him. 'I think you're a hypocrite.'

He raised an eyebrow.

'You are,' she said, seeing it all more clearly now. 'You arrive here with a idea – what was it you said – *to capture one person's memories so that other people could feel part of them.* For weeks now you have been combing my memories and capturing them on paper and on wood and yet you preach about travelling light and not being possessed. You are a hypocrite.'

His face was angry. 'I am not. Memories don't weigh. Regrets weigh heavy so I don't carry those but memories are light. They carry us – make being alone something entirely different from being lonely. Without them, you're empty.' Lizzie had the impression that he was about to leave. She reached out and touched the sleeve of his jacket. She nodded.

'You're right – there is a difference.'

Jim relaxed. 'I'm always right.'

'Don't push it. There's still a flaw in your argument.' She picked up one of the jigsaw boxes. 'These beautiful and justifiably expensive works of art are possessions too. You are here creating possessions which, by your own admission, you disdain.'

He ran a hand through his hair and shrugged. 'I know, but the jigsaws aren't the point, they're a way of earning money. It's the memories I'm after.'

Lizzie held her breath. So he had come here looking for something.

'If I remember rightly, you walked into this shop looking for me?'

He nodded.

'I don't understand. Why are you after my memories?'

'I'm not,' he said simply. 'The memories I'm looking for aren't yours, they're mine.'

*

'Aha! How did I know I'd find you here?' The door burst open and Teresa bustled in, flushed and looking none the worst for her late night. She smiled broadly at the two of them. 'Just the people I was looking for. Lizzie – are you closing soon?'

Lizzie nodded, dazed. She smiled weakly at Teresa. 'Jim was just telling me the real reason he came to Rathshannan.' Maybe two pairs of ears would hear more clearly what was being said. She looked back at Jim. 'Weren't you?'

But Teresa was on a roll. She practically skipped across the shop and linked her arm through Jim's. 'You don't have to tell me – I know exactly what he's up to.' She winked at him. 'You came here looking for the love of a good woman, didn't you?'

Jim's face cleared and he smiled at Teresa – gratefully, it seemed. He patted the back of her hand. 'Actually, my dear, you are completely right.'

Teresa swept a stray lock off her forehead flirtatiously. 'I knew that.' Then she let his arm go. 'Come on, Lizzie. Close up here and come over to Reardons with me.' She pulled Lizzie's coat off the back of the chair and held it open for her. 'After all the activity last night, you won't have the energy to cook and so I have arranged your tea, complete with a fresh syrup sponge for afters, so that you can get a bite to eat and then be off home to your bed for a good night's sleep.' She shrugged. 'It's by way of a thank you and – ' she looked at Jim, 'a heartfelt sorry, for what happened.'

Jim smiled. 'It wasn't your fault but it's a nice thought.' He indicated the plate of cakes on the table. 'Fortunately, I haven't eaten too much of that so there's plenty of space for more. Are you coming, Lizzie?'

Lizzie was standing still, watching the pair of them. She was so furious that if she opened her mouth to speak she was sure a scream would come out. Teresa was holding out her coat, her eyes shining as she joked and flirted with Jim and he responded. Two-faced bastard! It was obvious to Lizzie that, whatever his professed reasons for coming here, he was simply playing a game. Teresa was in love. Her shining eyes and the blush in her cheeks were evident and he had allowed that to happen. No doubt Teresa thought, as she had, that he intended to return her affections but by his own admission, he didn't. He was having a bit of fun, creating for himself some happy memories then he was off, light with the experience, leaving a trail of broken hearts behind. Hypocritical bastard too. He didn't make jigsaws – he broke them.

'Lizzie?' Teresa eased the coat gently over her shoulders and took her hand. 'Lizzie, you look pale. Are you okay?' She ushered her towards the door. 'I'll lock up for you if you like. You go over and get something to eat.'

They were by the door now. Lizzie felt as if she was moving in a daze. Should she turn and spit it out or should she talk to Jim alone first? She looked at his face but his expression was inscrutable. The curtains were down again.

She snapped. Shaking off Teresa's guiding hand she pulled her coat from her shoulders. 'Actually, I'm not hungry, thank you. I – ' she looked around the shop, at all her lovely possessions that tied people down and made them commit to a specific identity. Made it possible for others to see what they were dealing with. 'I have a couple of things I need to see to here.' She went over to the table and picking up the plate of cakes, held them out to Jim. 'These belong to you, I think,' she said, biting each word off. She shoved the plate towards him.

Jim looked bemused. He took the plate and pulled the foil over the top to seal it again. 'Thank you. I'll enjoy these.' He turned to Teresa who was watching the scene, baffled. 'But not before I accept your wonderful offer of a warm meal.'

Lizzie couldn't leave it at that. As they reached the door she called after him. 'What do you want anyway?'

He looked bemused.

'Today, I mean. What did you call in for? To get something?'

'Lizzie,' he said, as if he were speaking to a child. 'I'm not quite sure what's going on here.' He rummaged in his bag and took out a large manila envelope. 'There were a few things I wanted to talk to you about. This is one of them.'

She raised an enquiring eyebrow. 'More pictures?'

He nodded. 'I had left a box with some photographs in the bus. They're gone now and I haven't had a chance to sort out what I have left. I wanted to leave this lot with you so you could have a look and tell me if there are any you reckon we could use.' He passed it over. 'Also, the delivery I mentioned last night is en route and I'll have to send it back when it comes. I wanted to sort that out with you too.' He paused and held his hands out, palms upwards. 'That's what I called in for really – and to see that you were okay after last night. It was a bit dramatic.'

Lizzie's eyes welled up and before she could stop them, huge tears spilled down her face. She felt like crumbling to the ground and sobbing her heart out but she couldn't for the life of her explain what she was crying about. She tried to speak but before a sound came out, Jim moved forward and wrapped his arms around her. 'Ah, Lizzie, what's wrong?'

Teresa came round behind her and stroked her hair gently. 'She's probably exhausted. Matt said she was in here early this morning claiming she felt fine. It's all probably hitting her now.'

With her head pressed against his shoulder, Lizzie could feel him nodding. 'Can the tea hold a while?' he asked.

'As long as you like. Are you going to drop her home?'

He nodded again.

Lizzie pushed away. 'I am perfectly capable of getting myself home, thank you.' She pulled her coat on properly and avoided their eyes. Then she stuffed the envelope into her bag and slung it over her shoulder.

'You shouldn't be alone,' Teresa said.

Lizzie wiped the tears off her face and smiled weakly. 'As you said, Teresa, I'm knackered, exhausted. That's all. A breath of fresh air on the way home will do me the world of good and I'd prefer to be alone anyway.' She looked from one anxious face to the other. 'Really, I'm fine. You go ahead and have your tea and I'll call you tomorrow.'

Teresa looked doubtful. 'Well, give me a call when you get in so I know you're okay?'

Lizzie nodded.

Jim leaned over and kissed her on her cheek. 'Go safely, okay.'

Lizzie wanted to wipe his touch off but she didn't have the energy. She looked at him to see if there was any guilt on his face but he looked guileless. He raised an eyebrow at her scrutiny and for a moment she wondered if she could have got him wrong. But she hadn't. He'd clearly stated that he came to Rathshannan to find memories so that he could travel lightly. Teresa was linking his arm again and even with the concern on her face she was glowing. Couldn't he see how he would break her heart if her left now? Didn't he understand how you can't just matter to people and then brush them off, leave them behind? A picture of Jim's face when she first mentioned the twins flashed into her mind and she realised why it had made her uncomfortable. He'd winced, as if he knew exactly how difficult teenagers could be – as if he's had experience of them before. And maybe he had. Maybe Rathshannan wasn't the first place he's stolen memories from. Maybe he had kids of his own, abandoned somewhere.

'Did you want to ask me anything?'

She must have been staring. 'No,' she said.

'Right so, if you're sure you're okay we'll leave you to it.' He motioned Teresa towards the door. 'Call as soon as you get in, okay?'

She nodded and turned her back on them. She could sense the puzzled glances but she didn't care. They probably thought she was mad – or menopausal – or both. And they were probably right. She was mad to have allowed herself to become fond of a travelling fly-by-night; mad to have allowed herself to think that her life could ever be any different from the one she had safely cocooned herself into. She picked up the little pottery vase and smiled. Mad to think there was anything wrong with surrounding yourself with an identity that is recognisable and permanent and safe. She paused a minute before letting the vase fall to the ground where it broke into pieces. Only one part remained intact – the central piece with the painted flower.

She leaned down and picked it up. Brushing the clay dust off the flower she placed the fragment on the shelf beside her elephant picture. *Nothing wrong with being safe either, Sister,* she whispered, *sometimes the ones who stay have to be brave too.*

*

Lizzie didn't call either Teresa or Jim when she got home. She threw her bag onto the table in the study and rang Reardons to leave a message. As she put the receiver down, she tried to block out the picture in her head of the two of them laughing and joking as they ate their tea: Teresa thinking that this was just the start of how it would be in the future; Jim thinking, what a nice memory this will make. One gullible; the other ruthless – she didn't know who she despised more. Abandoning the notion that she could stomach a tea, she made herself a mug of cocoa and went to bed.

She must have fallen asleep straight away. When she woke up the cocoa was still on the bedside table, its surface congealed with cold milk, but her body was on fire. Her nightdress was stuck to her skin and though her forehead felt cold, there was sweat dripping from under her hairline, down her face. At first she thought she must have left the electric blanket on but she hadn't. She threw the duvet back and rolled off the bed. The floor beneath her feet was cool and so was the air in the room. It was just her body that was burning. She padded uncomfortably downstairs to get some water, pulling the damp cloth away from her skin as she went.

In the kitchen, she rummaged around for a thermometer. Her first thought was that she might have caught a chill, shivering in the cold air as she watched the men battle the fire. But she didn't feel sick. Her glands weren't up and her bones weren't shivery as they usually were when she was brewing a bug. It was just her blood – it was boiling. She poured a large glass of water and took it into the study where the carpeted floor would be more comfortable under her feet than the hard kitchen tiles. As she passed the mirror in the hallway, something caught her eye. She stopped and looked in shock at the woman who was standing there.

All their childhood days, people remarked on how different the Flynn sisters were. Anne was the spit of her mother, petite, fine featured, with long pre-Raphaelite hair; Lizzie was tall, gangly and dark like their father. Standing in the hallway now, Lizzie leaned closer to the glass. She wasn't there. The woman looking back at her was not an older version of the girl she once was but a taller version of the woman her mother had been. Time greyed her temples and she had not bothered to dye her hair. The brushstrokes of grey against the black gave her an air of composure and made her look distinguished. Tonight the grey seemed to have spread and she looked more extinguished than distinguished. Her eyes were hooded from lack of sleep and what had been the suggestion of crows' feet were now very definite statements. And her cheeks were suffused – bright pink. How often had she seen her mother's face like that?

'Oh bloody hell!' she said as she realised what was happening. 'You're not ill, Lizzie Flynn, you're bloody hormonal. This is the first flush of old age – the last flush of youth.' She threw her head back and shouted into the silent night. 'And I'm not ready!'

Almost in reply, the heat started to drain from body and she began to shiver. She went into the study, flicked on the gas fire and sat staring into the flames. So, that's it – the menopause. Last chance saloon for a different life just shutting up shop forever. In front of her the flames gave theatrical little bows on their artificial stage and she raised her hands in farewell. 'Show's over.' She didn't know whether to laugh or to cry – what difference did it make anyway? She was nearly fifty, safe, secure and independent. She hadn't ever wanted it to be any other way.

Leaning back in the chair she shut her eyes and tried to relax but the sweat on her nightdress had cooled and was uncomfortable to lie against. She ought to go upstairs and change. Instead she reached for her bag and pulled out Jim's envelope of photographs.

The first few were fairly predictable – an old farmhouse with ivy trailing over the windows, suggesting that someone was in there, looking out; a water pump at a roadside with flowers jostling for position at its base; the dry-stone wall of a field with the hill in the distance; the same wall close up as you looked at it through a gate, with an abandoned ploughshare in the foreground and in the background, an old barn. Lizzie smiled. He had done well – the photographs were beautiful. Especially the last one. He had a good eye for evocative scenes, places where anyone might have stood. She turned on the table lamp to have a better look and flicked through the pictures again. As she turned over the last one, her hand suddenly stopped.

'You heartless bastard!' She turned over the photograph and held it close to her face. No wonder she found it evocative. She knew exactly where he went to get this picture.

He must have started under the chestnut tree at the bottom of the lane and wondered what was up there. And with his uncanny skill in sniffing out the place that would prise open your hidden memories, followed his nose. He must have gone all the way up the lane to where the hedges grew so wild you had to guess your way in the dark if you left it too long before going home. Then he'd have found the gate with its heavy wooden bars, the sides now secured with rope. He'd have looked at the barn and thought, what a fine building, what wonderful memories someone must have of that. And then he'd have lifted the camera to his eye, and squatting down, found himself looking through those bars, as a child might, to the field beyond. Not for one second would he have considered that if someone had abandoned a barn it might be because they never wanted to see it again. Maybe they might want to do as he does – pack their memories up and walk away unscathed. But then, one click of the shutters and the barn door creaks open and all the memories stir and rise and glide slowly towards the light outside. And there they'd spot Jim, on his hunkers behind the gate, capturing them in his lens. And when the shutters close and they are packed safely inside he'd stuff them in his satchel and walk slowly down the lane again, oblivious to how much his passion for capturing memories was going to cost.

And who'd have to pay the price.

Lizzie held the photograph in shaking hands and felt as if she was going crazy. Maybe he was doing her a favour, tonight of all nights when she realised that she would never be an elephant with wings, by reminding her of when it all started. When Lizzie Flynn first learned that your future is not your own. Your past is all you get to take with you.

A trickle of sweat slid down her neck from under her hair and she held her breath as it flowed slowly to the top of her spine. Now it should flow down her back but she knew it wouldn't. As if being guided by an invisible finger it crept along the top of her shoulder and stayed there. It was cold and she sat perfectly still, not wanting to turn her head and look as the stain came through her clothing, dark and menacing in the half-light.

She held the photograph in front of her face. She should have guessed. If this jigsaw man was here to take apart the pieces of her life, this one had to be there. He'd already brought her the school, then the bus. This had to be the next one.

In her head the memories stirred and began to sit up. Lizzie knew there'd be no more sleep for her tonight. Tonight she'd have to revisit the barn.

# The Barn
## 1969

J ACK FLYNN'S BARN WAS HUGE – the biggest one not only in Rathshannan but probably in the whole county. With its window set in a high, pitched roof, it commanded a view of the countryside for miles around. Sometimes, when their Da was working nearby, Anne and Lizzie were allowed to climb one of the ladders, set on either side of the central beams, which led to a large loft space over the front door. That was the best place of all.

Lizzie loved it. If there were no one listening, she would stand on the edge of the loft, facing her imaginary audience, and with a piece of rejected fence picket for a guitar, give the performance of her life. Da had put the loft in especially and the window too. Because it was over the door, you could see who was coming but they wouldn't see you because they'd have their back to you as they came into the barn. Da said that was a great idea. If there was rain due and they were in a rush to get the harvest in, he and the lads who helped could work till sunset, grab a few hours sleep in the sweet-smelling loft, be up at dawn to steal a march on the day and get finished before the rain fell. Lizzie wished she could sleep up there sometime – but not on her own.

At the front of the barn were two huge doors. On hot days they were either wide open so that inside would be dry and airy for winter storing, or bolted and secured against the tinkers who sometimes broke in, looking for tools they could sell. Da kept a lot of tools there: huge pitchforks needed for the harvest hung from the beams that crossed the barn from one side to the other; along with great bales of rope suspended high off the ground. Da was very safety conscious. It wouldn't take much to step on the end of a fork half-hidden in the hay and land yourself with a split head, or worse, trip over loose rope and end up pronged like a sausage. And with the thick walls of the barn to dull the sound, you could yell all you liked and nobody'd hear you. Even with all his precautions, the girls were not allowed to go to the barn on their own. Da gave strict instructions that unless he was there, it was out of bounds. Which was a shame. The barn would have been heaven on earth – if it wasn't so spooky.

*

Like today. Seemingly deserted but with the door slightly ajar as if someone had just come in – or was just about to go out. Lizzie crept as quietly as she could across the spikes of cut wheat towards the barn.

'Da!' she called. 'Are you there? Mam says your tea is ready.'

There was no response.

She moved closer. 'Are you in there, Da?' She stuck her head around the door and peered in.

The barn looked even bigger that usual. It was like a cathedral. Light from the door and the window threw long wands of dust-speckled daylight into the cool darkness inside. All the bales were neatly stacked at the back and along the sides, sacks of feed lay slumped, facing each other. In the shadows, they looked like rows of fat-bellied men sitting quietly, waiting for her to speak. She pulled the door further open and felt the hairs on the back of her neck stand on end as the breeze sent the pitchforks swinging. Their movement set up a slow rhythmic creaking. She thought she heard a shuffling noise. She took a deep breath, cleared her throat and tried to sound confident.

'Da, Mam says the tea is on the table in five minutes but that was ages ago and so I think you'd better come or the two of us will be in trouble and now I have to go to get Anne as well.'

There was a shuffling and it was coming from above her head in the loft. Lizzie froze. If it was Da she wished he'd say so that she wouldn't be terrified and if it wasn't Da, but a thief or murderer, she wished he'd say too before he legged it down the ladder after her – intending to murder her and leave her broken body rotting in a deserted barn not to be found for days. She was too young to rot. She ran. Whoever it was, he knew the tea was ready and that was all she'd been asked to do. As she raced across the field to the gate, the sharp stalks of straw grazed her ankles; she made a mental note to wear Wellingtons in future – if she survived.

Somewhere amongst the crisp snapping underfoot and her own heavy breathing, she could hear someone behind her. They seemed to be running away. Then she thought she heard someone calling but she didn't stop. 'Lizzie! Wait!' If she could reach the gate, she'd at least get a head start down the lane. The other person sounded far behind.

'Lizzie! Will you hold up? I need to lock the door!'
Lizzie turned around.

Anne was at the barn door. She was standing there, not running at all. There hadn't been anyone chasing her. She waved to let Anne know she'd heard and then waited while Anne pulled the heavy bolt into place, fitted the padlock and turned. 'What's your hurry?' she called out. 'Why didn't you wait for me?'

'I didn't know you were there. I was looking for Da. You're not supposed to be there on your own anyway.'

'He's not there. There's no one there.' Anne picked her way carefully between the rows, and when she reached the gate, pulled herself up beside her sister. She looked dishevelled.

'What were you doing in there anyway?'

Anne jumped off the gate and started to walk crossly down the lane. 'I'm fifteen for God's sake – don't you start nagging. I just wanted some space.'

Lizzie looked at her and sighed. Anne had broken one of Da's cardinal rules, as he called them, and if he found out there'd be fierce trouble. He'd rant and shout and then Ma would get involved and shout at him and eventually nobody would remember how it started because it would grow so horrible and take days to sort out. Silent days. Days when Da would be gone before you got up and Ma would mope around the kitchen red-faced, sipping clear liquid from the glass she liked to carry everywhere with her; not talking, because if she did, her words wouldn't come out properly. They'd all suffer and Anne would be to blame.

'There'll be trouble... '

Anne turned and smiled. 'There won't. Only you and I know and we won't tell.' She kicked at the loose stones as she walked. 'Anyway, I was only enjoying a bit of peace and quiet, there's no harm in that. Da makes those fussy rules about using the barn to keep us safe and I really think at fifteen I can be trusted not to stand on a pitchfork, can't I?' She smiled and Lizzie melted. She was right. Da was a fusspot – even Mam said so. It was because he'd have liked boys to work alongside him but he only had girls and then after Lizzie, Ma wasn't strong enough to have any more – she said. And so Da was very protective.

They were now at the bottom of the lane near their house and they could see their mother on the step waiting for them.

'Damn! Com'on Lizzie – she's on the look out – hurry.'

They ran the last few steps. As they got to the gate and slowed, Anne caught Lizzie's arm. 'Not a word, mind.'

Their mother spotted them and turning, went back into the house.

Lizzie nodded. Of course not. Anne was right. She was old enough to be trusted to look after herself. As they headed for the door she reached out and pulled something from her sister's tangled curls. It was a length of straw.

*

Da was already back when they got home. He was sitting in the kitchen holding the paper out on the table in front of him. Their mother stood in the doorway glaring at them.

'Where were you?' she demanded.

'Up the lane.'

'I sent you to call your father for his tea.' Mam slammed a platter of sausages onto the middle of the table. 'Can nobody in this house do what I ask them to do? Can't they?' She raised two pink-edged eyes and looked from one to the other. 'Is it too mush to ask?'

As if she had heard the word come out wrong, she paused and blushed, casting a quick worried glance at the back of the paper. Their father didn't react. Usually he would lower the paper slowly and look at their mother over the top of it and she would be quiet for the rest of the meal.

'Sorry, Mam,' Lizzie said.

'Where were you anyway?'

'We were – ' Lizzie looked to Anne for guidance but she was watching her plate.

'At the barn,' she said, without looking up.

There was a rustle of paper and their father's face appeared. 'What were you doing there?'

'Looking for you, Da.' She looked at Lizzie to continue.

'Mam said to call you for your tea and when you weren't in the yard, I thought I'd try up the lane.'

He nodded and lifted the paper up again.

'You didn't go inside, did you?'

Under the table, Anne touched Lizzie's foot. Mam was watching the two of them and if she told a lie, Mam would know. Even when she was tired and her words were slushy, she knew if people were lying. She was looking from the girls to their father as if she was trying to figure something out.

'I didn't go inside. There was no need. Anne checked and Da wasn't there.'

A moment's silence and then their mother started to prong the sausages, flicking them crossly onto the plates. Their father folded his paper and picked up his knife and fork. It seemed the matter was closed.

As she ate, Lizzie stole glances at her family. Da was dipping his head appreciatively as he ate his food. Mam and Anne kept their head bowed. It seemed to her that they were all thinking and she wondered what might be going on in their heads. After tea, Anne excused herself saying that she had to go down and pick up some homework from a girl in her class. Mam started to question her about it but Da picked up his paper again and stuffed it under his arm as he headed for the sitting room to watch the telly. 'Leave her alone – the girl can go and see her friend if she wants to. Do you want a lift, Annie?'

Anne smiled at her father. She was his pet. She reached up and kissed him on the cheek. 'Thanks, Da – I'll be fine.' She looked back at her mother. 'It's just some biology I need help with.' Then she giggled. 'I won't be late. Bye!' And she was gone.

Mam glared in her wake and then at her husband. 'And I will stay behind and clear up, is that right?'

'I'll help you.' Lizzie picked up a tea towel but her mother took it from her.

'Don't bother. You should have some homework to do as well. Didn't you have to write a composition or something?'

Lizzie nodded.

'Then get on with it. Not in here. Do it in the dining room, I need peace and quite.'

Humph. Her father made a noise he sometimes made that sounded like a laugh stuck in your throat. He raised an eyebrow at Mam and left the room. She flushed and flicked the tea towel at Lizzie. 'Go on then, do your work and let me get on with mine.'

'Yes, Mam.' Lizzie went out to get her schoolbag from the hall and took it into the dining room. Anne's books were already spread on the table there and as she pushed them aside to make space Lizzie was surprised at how forgetful her normally fastidious sister had become. She wouldn't be getting much biology done.

She'd left her book behind.

The composition took ages and by the time she was finished, it was late and Anne wasn't home yet. Mam was still in the kitchen, sipping her water and humming along to tunes on the radio. Da was snoozing in the armchair in front of the telly where Charles Mitchell, the newsman, was talking to himself. Nobody seemed too interested in checking her handwriting – which was just as well because she'd grown tired after the first page and it all slanted to one side and eventually fell over. Sister Cillian would kill her about it tomorrow anyway, so there was no point in showing it to either of her parents just so that they could start giving out to her too. She decided that the best thing to do would be to go to bed and attract as little attention as possible. She packed her bag ready for school and went upstairs and was asleep as soon as she hit the pillow.

*

The kitchen was quiet the following morning when she came down for breakfast. Usually the radio was on and her father would pass a running commentary on world events. Today there was only the clink of cutlery on china. She stuck her head around the door.

'Oh, you're there! Where's everyone? Was it really late when you came in last night – it was already the news when I went to bed.' The questions were fired out as she scanned the cereal boxes.

Anne said nothing; she just sat there, staring. Lizzie sat opposite her and even when she reached out to take a plate, Anne didn't move.

'Anne?'

No answer.

'What's wrong?'

Before Anne could say anything there was a noise from the hallway. The side door opened and their mother coughed and stamped her feet on the mat. As she came into the kitchen, Lizzie could see her face was flushed and on her cheeks thin purple veins showed like spider's web below the surface. She looked at the girls as if she expected them to speak. Anne was looking at her plate again.

Lizzie spoke. 'You're out early today, Mam.'

Their mother peeled the cardigan off her shoulders and let it fall onto the chair. 'We don't all sleep so soundly in our beds at night, Lizzie. You need to have a very clear conscience for that.' She glared at Anne. 'I imagine you're tired still?'

Anne shrugged.

Lizzie looked from one to the other. If crossness were a piece of twine, there'd be a thick rope of it stretching all the way across the kitchen from Mam's face to Anne's, pulling the two of them towards each other, getting tighter and tighter. One of them was going to have to say something soon or it would snap and knock them over. Anne was the one to let go.

With her hands still flat on the table, she stood and scraped the chair back. She didn't lift her head properly till she was standing and when she did; she looked every bit as angry as her mother.

'Yes, I'm tired and no, I didn't sleep – okay? What else do you want me to say?'

Their mother shrugged. 'I think everything's been said, don't you?' Her voice was quiet now, her words distinct. The crossness in her face was blurring and she was beginning to look sad instead. She sniffed, 'Oh Anne...' and began to raise her arms in a hug but Anne didn't go to her. Instead she stepped behind the chair and pushed it roughly under the table. Then she ran out of the room and Lizzie heard her feet thump on the stairs. Their mother didn't call her back as she usually did. Lizzie wasn't sure what was coming next. Anne was silent, then shouting; Mam was angry, then soppy. Lizzie was out of there.

She stood and picked up her plate. If she could get it to the sink before Mam noticed it hadn't been used, she'd be fine. She needn't have worried. The plate was rinsed, dried and back in the cupboard and still her mother was in the middle of the floor, staring sadly into the distance. Outside in the hallway, her composition with the sideways writing was hidden in her bag, ready to be picked up and taken safely away from inspection. Lizzie rushed out and grabbed it. 'I have to get to school early today, Mam. I'll go straight away.'

Her mother ignored her. She had come out of the kitchen too and was standing at the foot of the stairs looking after Anne as if she expected her to reappear any minute.

'Bye, Mam, bye Anne,' she whispered and when she got no response, left the house as quickly as she could and headed off to school.

*

Outside in the yard everything looked normal – except that Da wasn't there either. Lizzie had a quick look in the shed but it was empty. His car was gone. Then she remembered him saying something about having to go into Kilkenny sometime in the week for winter feed. She'd meant to ask him about that. The barn was full of the stuff; she couldn't think why he'd need to buy more. They stocked up enough to see them through to *next* Christmas never mind *this* one.

Christmas! That was it! Lizzie grinned to herself as she rounded the side of the house. Even though the girls knew about Santa Claus, Da was a softie for tradition and loved surprises. Maybe he'd gone into Kilkenny on Christmas business.

Through the open kitchen window came the sound of plates banging and pots being stacked roughly. Mam was on the move again. Lizzie sighed. If it was Christmas business she wished Da had taken her mother too – she could do with being cheered up. Once she got into a rage like this everyone suffered. Lizzie decided not to stay around and be one of them. She pulled her cardigan closed, hugged her schoolbag close and headed into a barrage from Sister Cillian.

It didn't happen. The day started with a sewing lesson, then choir, then reading. After lunch – which Lizzie forgot to pack in her hurry to leave home – they got out the paints and Sister Cillian allowed them to paint one another while she read through the compositions. Two people forgot theirs and she didn't even get cross with them. 'Bring it tomorrow, dear,' she said. When she got to Lizzie's she frowned with her forehead but her mouth wasn't cross. She beckoned Lizzie forward and pointed to the second page.

'This is so interesting, Elizabeth, but I find myself distracted about here by having to turn the page sideways to read. Try to keep the writing neat, won't you?'

Lizzie nodded.

'Good girl – now get on with your picture.'

And that was it. The bell for the end of the school day went and the girls filed out feeling so relaxed it was as if they hadn't been to school at all. There was no homework either. Lizzie strolled home, kicking pebbles along the road in front of her, daydreaming.

As she turned in the gate at home, reality struck. The kitchen window was open and her parents were inside. They were rowing. First her mother spat angry words at her father, and then he growled back – low furious noises. If she walked in now, one of them would turn that anger on her. They liked to pretend they weren't fighting when you caught them and instead pretended that it was something you had done that made them be in bad humour. She stopped and considered the likelihood that she could get inside and make it up the stairs without being caught. Not very. The lane up to the barn looked like a much better proposition.

She got no further than the first bend. About a hundred yards from their front gate, a large sweet chestnut tree overhung the path, its branches laden. Lizzie had to run underneath to avoid being hit by the prickly capsules as they fell. She took a deep breath, pulled her sleeves down and ran. It didn't work. A gust of wind shook the branches as she passed underneath and a cluster of nuts fell on her head. Rubbing the sore spot she kicked the capsules crossly at the wall and smiled as they burst apart, shiny chestnuts spilling onto the path. They were perfect – brown and smooth. She picked one up and tried to peel the shell. Her finger slid over the waxy surface and she couldn't prise her bitten nails underneath. She tried to bite it open but it was no use. The shell was bitter in her mouth. Bloody bloody! She threw it crossly over the wall and turned to walk off.

Another cluster of nuts fell onto the lane in front of her and this time Lizzie didn't kick out. Now the thought of a fresh chestnut was enough to make her regret skipping breakfast and walking out without lunch. Even a quick slice of bread would have been worth listening to Mam's giving out for five minutes. She realised she was starving. Pulling the cuffs of her cardigan over her hands for protection, she tapped the capsules and gathered as many nuts as she could into her pockets. When they were full, she headed further up the lane to where there was a rock she could sit on to eat her feast.

Settled comfortably there a few minutes later, she looked around for something to open the shell with. There was nothing obvious. She tried her teeth but they slid over the nuts' shiny surface and her nails were no good – she'd have to get something from the house. She packed the nuts back in her pockets and crept back to the gate. The kitchen window was shut now and it was quiet. From the side you could see that Mam's reading light was on in the sitting room. Da was nowhere to be seen. On tiptoe, she crept around to the door and opened it as quietly as she could. If Mam was out of the kitchen she could sneak in there and get a knife. She eased the door shut behind her and padded quietly towards the kitchen.

She was nearly inside when a noise alerted her. It was a clink and Lizzie knew her mother was in the pantry, easing her bottle back into place behind the jams where, she said, the light wouldn't get to it and ruin the flavour. As if you could ruin the flavour of bottled water. Lizzie held her breath and waited.

There was a crash. One of the jars must have fallen. Now Mam would really be blazing. Even a pocketful of fresh chestnuts when you're hungry wasn't worth staying for that. Lizzie turned to sneak out again and as she pulled the door open, her father's coat, hung on the peg at the back of the door, swung out and wrapped itself around her. She nearly giggled aloud. It felt lovely. Like Da, it was big and although the surface was rough to the touch, it was warm, comforting.

Untangling herself she was smoothing the sleeve back into place when her hand felt something small and hard in the pocket. It was Da's penknife. She slid her hand in and pulled it out. Wow! She'd only ever held it for a few seconds before, as it had been Granddad Flynn's and was very precious so nobody was allowed to touch it. The handle wasn't like an ordinary knife – it was mother-of-pearl – and the blade was so sharp that Da said it could slice through leather. Lizzie stroked the handle, loving the hard smoothness of it. Wedging what little nail she had on her thumb under the blade's edge, she eased it open. As if oiled, it unfolded and she was surprised at how delicate and shiny it was. And pointy too.

'Anne! Lizzie! Is that you?'

Her mother's voice, slurred and upset, broke the spell. Lizzie panicked. She snapped the knife shut, barely missing her fingers and tried to put it back in Da's coat but one of the huge sleeves got in the way and she couldn't find the opening.

There was a shuffle across the kitchen floor and Lizzie knew she'd be caught if she stayed there any longer. Then she'd be in trouble. Either she'd have to clear up the mess in the pantry and get in trouble for not doing it properly or her Mam would be weepy and want to talk to her about how lonely she was and nothing you said was the right thing when she was like that. The only other option was to run for it. She might be seen but if she stayed out long enough, it might be forgotten by the time she came back. Worth the risk. She pulled open the door and ran.

This time the tree was no obstacle. With the knife clutched in her hand, she held the top of her pockets shut as she ran. Behind her she could hear her mother shouting but she wasn't stopping now. Mam might come after her as far as the gate but she'd never try coming up the hill. Head down, Lizzie ran, and ran. When she eventually stopped, exhausted, she was at the gate at the top, looking through the bars into the field with the barn commanding its view of the countryside. Lizzie waited a couple of minutes while she got her breath back and worked out what to do next. In her palm the knife was sweaty, and the pockets of her cardigan bulging and pulled. She rubbed her hand dry on her top and smiled. You'd think she'd planned it. The barn was a hiding place; the nuts were food and the knife? She slid the blade open again – perfect. Checking that no one was watching, she tried to slide the latch of the gate and finding it too stiff, climbed over and picked her way between the rills to the big doors.

Inside, it was quiet like it always was – quiet and creaky. Opening the doors, even slowly, set the pitchforks swinging back and forth but not enough to wake the sleeping sacks on the side. Almost apologetically, Lizzie raised her fingers to her lips. *Shuush! Don't get up* and started to climb the ladder to the loft above. She'd never been up here on her own before without people in the field outside. In the half darkness with the great doors shut it was seriously spooky. The pitchforks were creaking a steady rhythm on the beams like a row of clocks ticking and specks of dust whispered in the air of the loft. It wasn't as tidy as down below with tools propped along the sides and a couple of bales of straw pushed over by the window. The string had come undone and the straw was strewn across the floor like a big cushion, high on the sides and flattened in the middle. Just right for a girl to climb into and eat her feast. Kicking her shoes off, Lizzie slid onto the bales and propped herself on the window side so that she could eat and watch the lane at the same time. Then she emptied her pockets on to her lap and holding the knife carefully so that she wouldn't cut herself she slid the blade along the edge of the nuts. It worked beautifully. She wriggled into a nest and settled into a slow, peeling rhythm – peel, scrape, chew – perfect!

*

It was growing dark when she woke up. She must have slept all afternoon! Sharp stalks of straw were poking the sides of her face and scraps of chestnut shell were scattered all over her lap. Despite a faint itchiness it was very comfortable and she wondered what had woken her. She sat up and peered out the window.

From here it was possible to see their house way down at the bottom of the hill. All the lights were blazing. In the village beyond lights were blazing too and Lizzie's forehead went cold in panic. She didn't have a watch but if it was this dark it must be late and they were probably all out looking for her. Mam was always on about turning off the lights and usually they were on only in the room where everyone was sitting. She looked again – every light in the house!

Without bothering to brush the mess off her lap, she felt around on the floor for her shoes and stuffed her feet into them. Laces dangling, she stumbled down the ladder, across the field and scrambling over the gate, ran for her life. All the way down the lane she prayed out loud for help. Even in the darkest places, where the hedges overhung the sides and she had to run through pitch, it wasn't the darkness that frightened her. All she could think of was the trouble she would get into when she emerged into the light.

When she reached the gate at the end she stopped to catch her breath. She ran her fingers through her hair, catching and discarding the stalks of straw caught in it. Her mind flashed back to when she stood in the same place and tidied Anne's hair. She wished she could turn the clocks back to then – or even to after school – and change everything. She would stay this time and put up with Mam's ramblings. Then she wouldn't have been so hungry and picked up the chestnuts and gone to the barn to eat them and fallen asleep and had to rush home in the dark and – oh no! A fresh wave of panic hit her as she realised what was missing. In desperation she patted her pockets though she knew they were empty. There were no chestnuts left in them. And no knife. Da's precious penknife was gone! Holding her hands over her ears, she tried to replay the sounds of the lane. Had there been a clink as she ran and dropped the knife? She couldn't remember. All she could recall was the frantic scuffle of her steps as she ran and the odd rustle of the bushes as she brushed past them in the darkness. She glanced back up the lane wondering if it was worth trying to retrace her steps and find it but there was no point. The grey of the sky had given way to inky black and even if she did come upon it, she wouldn't be able to see it in the dark. It was hopeless. She was going to be murdered. Pure murdered.

She took a deep breath and headed for the house.

*

Everyone was in the kitchen. There was the deep rumble of her father's voice and the high quaver of her mother's. Anne was there too. She sounded as if she was crying. Every so often she'd try to speak but her voice came out like a tiny squeak that would break into a sob. Lizzie stood in the hallway flushed with shame. Her sins were piling up by the minute. First, she'd run off and not stayed to help her mother; she'd stolen and then lost her father's precious knife; she'd fallen asleep and now her whole family was sick with worry about her. Oh bloody bloody! When they found out that she was alive and well, they'd kill her!

'Oh Annie, why? How could you let this happen?' her mother's voice, high pitched, slid out from the edge of the kitchen door and pricked her forehead sharply. It sounded as if poor Anne was getting the blame for her going missing. That wasn't fair, it wasn't Anne's fault. And the longer she stayed out here, the longer they'd worry. She took a deep breath and stepped forward ready for the attack.

Inside, the kitchen table was set for tea. It looked as if they had all been sitting there drinking tea for hours. She dismissed the notion that they would have been better off searching for their missing child. At one end her father was sitting facing the door, and at the opposite end Mam had her back to her. Anne was in the middle, side on, staring across the table, her face set pale in shock. Lizzie's heart lurched at the sight of them.

'Mam?' Lizzie's voice was low but her mother heard her and turned slowly. Lizzie was shocked at her expression. Where she had been pink and flushed earlier, now she looked as if there was no blood in her at all. Her eyes were far back in her head and from the inside edges of them, dark lines fanned to either side of her mouth.

'I'm home, Mam.' She waited for the outburst.

There wasn't one. Her father looked up and Anne turned but neither of them seemed to see her. They didn't jump up and wrap her in their arms and say *Oh Darling, you're safe!* like they did on telly nor did they leap out and bang the table and say, *Where the Hell have you been!'* Nothing. They just sat there.

'I wasn't lost. I fell asleep. I was asleep for hours!' Still nothing. 'And I'm home now and you don't have to worry any more.'

Her mother smiled weakly. 'That's nice, pet. I'm glad you had a nice day. Go on up to bed now.'

'But...' This wasn't right. Here she was after nearly worrying the life out of them and all they could say was *that's nice?*

'Bed, Lizzie – now!' Her father pointed his finger at the door.

Well, so much for celebrations when the prodigal returns! It obviously only works for sons in the Bible. They get fatted calves. Eleven-year-old daughters get *that's nice*. And no tea. Lizzie turned fuming to the door, which she banged behind her. Her father's coat, still on its hook, swept out in the draught and caught her as she passed. For a second the memory of his missing knife shamed her but she didn't hold the thought for long. If he was that unconcerned about her arriving home safely, he didn't deserve to find it. *Hope you never do!* She turned and glared at the closed kitchen door. From behind it, muffled sounds showed they were talking again but now it sounded a bit calmer. Maybe they really were glad she was back. Pity they couldn't think to tell her. She stifled a sob and went upstairs to bed.

Having spent hours asleep in straw, Lizzie was wide awake when Anne came up. Her legs were itchy and she was sure she must have picked up ticks that were even now gorging themselves on her fresh blood. By morning they'd be huge – pot bellied with feasting and it'd be impossible to pull them out without breaking them. The tiny heads would be embedded in her skin and she'd have to put up with Mam pulling them out with hot tweezers, fussing about diseases and wondering how she got them. She was about to turn on the light and search for them when she heard voices come out of the kitchen. Then Anne was on the stairs.

Instead of coming straight into the room Anne went to the bathroom and Lizzie heard her in there, splashing water on her face and gulping great mouthfuls of air. She washed her teeth and as she spit the toothpaste out, started gulping again. Lizzie wondered if she was all right but decided against going to check. Nobody had bothered to check on her and if Anne was in trouble for letting her get lost in the first place, she deserved it. Imagine having one sister and not even searching for her. She turned over in the bed, pulled the blankets above her head and waited. When Anne came into the room, she deliberately slowed her breathing so that even to her own ears it sounded loud and forced.

'Lizzie? Are you awake?'

She didn't answer. Through the covers she heard Anne taking off her clothes and the creaks as she climbed into bed. For a while there was shuffling and twisting then Anne fell into a deep sleep. Lizzie lay awake listening to her, waiting for her parents to come up. Her mother did but her father stayed in the kitchen, probably having a last cigarette before bed. With the growing stillness of the house, Lizzie started to doze.

Sometime in the early hours she was woken by the sound of rain on the window. She lifted her head and listened. Fairy footsteps – that's what it sounded like. But it wasn't just the sound of fairies. There was someone running across the yard downstairs. They seemed unsteady. She heard a car door opening and then it drove away. 'Lizzie? What are you doing?' Anne's voice was groggy.

'Someone's outside.'

'Who?' Now Anne was sitting up.

Lizzie remembered that she was cross with Annie and decided not to answer. Instead she craned her neck and tried to see down the lane toward the road.

'Tell me, Lizzie, please.' Anne swung her legs onto the floor but she was still half asleep because instead of standing up, she groaned and fell back on to the bed.

'It's okay, I think it's only Da, he's coming back.' Lizzie watched headlights catch the drops on the window pane and send long streaks of light into the room as a car swung around the gate and lurched to a halt at the front. Someone got out and as he stood there looking at the house, Lizzie realised it wasn't her father. He was bigger than Da and had his hands on his hips like a cowboy. She pressed her face closer to the window. It was Mr Healey! He was standing in their front yard looking at the house the way he had stood in front of the school.

'Anne! Come here quick!'

Anne leaped out of bed, swaying as she tried to stand then picked her way across the floor to the window. No sooner had she reached it than there was the sound of a siren in the distance. It didn't sound like it was coming in their direction but it was enough to make Mr Healey get back into his car and drive off. When his tail-light disappeared at the bottom of the lane the two girls looked at each other in the darkness. Anne put her arm around Lizzie's shoulder and kissed the top of her head. Her breath was stale and through her nightdress she was shaking. There was a funny smell off her.

'What's happening Anne? What did he want?'

Anne shook her head. 'Mr Healey's a weirdo – everybody knows that.'

Lizzie shook her away crossly. 'So why's he in our yard? People don't come into your yard in the middle of the night for nothing!'

Anne let her hand drop and leaned forward, pressing her face close to Lizzie's. In the darkness her face was pale, almost luminous.

Lizzie gasped. 'I've got it! He's looking for Art Farrelly, I bet he is! And he thinks he might be hiding in one of our sheds – like an outlaw!'

Anne shook her head. 'I have no idea.' She turned and peered out into the darkness. 'Maybe he's drunk or something. It's nothing to do with us anyway. Go to sleep and I'm sure we'll find out about it in the morning.'

Lizzie got back into bed and lay in the darkness listening to the sounds outside. Anne stayed by the window, peering through the side of the curtain. After a while, they heard their father's car turn into the yard and his heavy step as he came into the house. Lizzie was tempted to sneak downstairs and ask him what was going on but she was warm now and the excitement from earlier made her sleepy. Maybe she'd wait till he came up: maybe he'd even come in and sit down and tell her all about it because that was the thing with her Da – he was a great one for sitting down and having a chat with you when you were nice and cosy in your bed and feeling sleepy, really really sleepy...

*

The following morning both girls slept late. Anne was still out cold when Lizzie woke to the sound of the phone ringing downstairs. Mam was talking to someone, asking questions excitedly and sucking her breath in sharply, shocked as she listened to the answers. Lizzie pulled on her jumper and skirt from the pile at the end of the bed and opened the door. As she got to the bottom of the stairs her mother put the phone down and turned to her.

'Lizzie, have your breakfast then go and get your father for me.' She was fussing.

'Where is he?'

Mam pointed at the back of the door. The coat was gone. 'Out somewhere. Just get him, will you? Something's after happening...' she paused and glanced up the stairs, 'and you'd better tell your sister to come down.' She rubbed her hands on the sides of her apron, frowning. 'No, I'll do that. You go have your breakfast.'

Lizzie shrugged and went into the kitchen. If Da was out in his coat then he was bound to put his hands into the pockets of it and discover that they were empty and then she'd have to admit what she did. Who knows when she'd be given anything to eat after that! She cut two thick slices of bread and stuffed them into the toaster. Best to stock up now – just in case. As the kitchen filled with the smell of toast, she practised excuses in her head that she could use when the storm came. By the time she'd eaten the fourth slice, she had almost completely absolved herself and jumped when Anne and their mother came back into the kitchen.

'Lizzie,' Mam's voice was the sort of calm you get just before someone shouts at you. 'Are you sure it was Mr Healey in the yard last night?'

Lizzie nodded.

'Did he say anything?'

'He just drove off. There was a sound of a Garda car and he went off.'

Mam sat down, thinking hard.

'What's happening, Mam? Is he in trouble?'

'Big trouble. Seems he beat someone up last night and was arrested in the early hours of the morning. The Farrellys are up in arms.' Behind her Anne sniffed and her mother glanced around at her quickly. It seemed to Lizzie there was a warning in her look. 'Has either of you girls seen your father this morning?'

They shook their heads.

'Then I need you to go and get him for me, tell him it's important that he comes – now.'

Lizzie licked the traces of marmalade off her fingers and jumped up. Nothing like a bit of excitement to distract a father from his daughter's boldness – this was great. She caught a glance of Anne's pale face and felt guilty. Someone was beaten up – that wasn't good really. Suddenly she remembered how frightened May was when Mr Healey came to school. She turned.

'It wasn't May, was it?'

'Who wasn't May?'

'That he beat up.'

Mam shook her head. 'No, it was her brother.'

Two high spots of colour flashed in Anne's cheeks. 'And he has a name. His name is Art.' Then she grabbed Lizzie's elbow and pulled her towards the door. 'And now we'd better find Da – come on.'

*

Their father wasn't in the yard anywhere.

Lizzie kicked at the loose stones. 'He isn't far away because his car is here and the tractor is still in the shed and it's cold. That means, by my calculation, that he's gone for a walk.' She tapped the side of her nose. 'And since it was raining last night and he is a heavy man, there may be clues nearby as to where he's gone – footprints maybe. Follow me, Holmes.' She smiled at Anne, expecting the usual indulgent smile.

Anne didn't even look at her. She was glancing around, distracted. Lizzie grabbed her elbow.

'I said, follow me, Holmes, look for clues.'

Anne yanked her arm free. 'Oh shut up, Lizzie and leave me alone!' Her voice broke and she ran towards the gate. Lizzie started after her, hurt. What was wrong with everyone in her family at the moment? She kicked her way around the yard, looking into sheds but her father was nowhere to be seen. Eventually, she decided to find Anne and headed out the gate after her.

The lane was empty. Even with the thick wet mud after last night's rain, you couldn't tell which way the footsteps were going. Anne might have headed down towards the village – that was most likely – or turned right, up the lane to the barn. Da wouldn't have gone up there without taking the tractor because it wasn't the sort of place you went to with just yourself and nothing to bring back that required a tractor and trailer even. What would Sherlock Holmes do now? The logical thing, of course. If Da was unlikely to be in the barn, and Anne unlikely to have gone to look for him there, then this was the perfect opportunity for her to go and find Da's penknife – hopefully before he realised that it was missing. When she got back, she could say she'd gone that way because Anne had gone the other and so it was the most efficient way to conduct a search – brilliant! With a last glance back at the house to see if Mam was watching, she set off.

*

Lizzie got to the top of the lane expecting to have the usual struggle with the gate, which she didn't relish climbing over as it was wet and freezing and then she'd have to spend the whole day in cold damp knickers. To her surprise, someone had slid the latch across already and the gate was pushed wide open. Bloody, bloody. Now she wouldn't have a chance to find the penknife. She'd kept her eyes peeled in the lane to no avail so either Anne found it on her way up here or it fell off her lap when she jumped up to go home from the loft yesterday. It might still be there.

Too late. Just as she reached the door, Anne came out, pulling it closed behind her.

'No Da?'

Anne shook her head. 'No, nobody here. I thought I was in luck when the door was open but it's empty.'

Lizzie felt her face burn. Of course the door was open – she hadn't bothered to close it behind her last night. Anne would be bound to mention that and then she'd be found out. She felt the panic bubble up inside her again. Everything was going wrong. Now she'd have to confess to Anne about yesterday and beg her to keep the secret, maybe even help her find the knife. And sooner rather than later. She took a deep breath.

'Anne?'

'What?'

'Can you keep a secret – a big one, about something really terrible?'

Anne's cheeks reddened and she nodded slowly, turning her face to Lizzie and staring hard into it. 'If I have to,' she whispered.

'You do. Please, Anne, it's a matter of life and death.'

Anne's lips curled but it wasn't much like a smile. 'Go on then.'

Lizzie looked around. It had started to drizzle again but even so, they seemed very exposed on the hilltop. Lizzie could imagine her confession caught on a gust of wind and blown straight down into the kitchen at home – where Da had probably arrived back in his big coat with the empty pocket and was even now trying to figure out where his knife had gone. 'Come into the barn,' she said. 'I'll tell you in there.'

Together they pushed the door open again and shivered as the air from inside pulled a gust of damp behind them. All the pitchforks started to swing in protest and even as she stepped further inside, Lizzie felt some drops fall on her shoulder through the floor from the loft above. She brushed them off and noticed when she let her hand fall that it had a dark stain on it as well. She wiped her hands together.

'Well, get on with it – it's freezing in here. The door must have been left open all night. Da will go mad if his stuff gets damp.'

'That'll be my fault too... ' Lizzie began and told Anne the whole story. As she spoke the stupidity of her actions became all the more apparent and when she finished she expected a tirade of abuse. Instead, Anne smiled and this time it looked real. She reached out and put her arms around Lizzie.

'You silly girl,' she said affectionately. 'Is that your awful crime?'

Lizzie nodded, sniffing back the tears of relief that were threatening. 'Da will kill me, won't he?'

Anne laughed though it sounded sad. 'I don't think so, Lizzie. I think he might have heard of worse things than that. Anyway, maybe we can fix it before he ever finds out,' she patted Lizzie's back. 'Hey, what's that on your cardigan?'

Lizzie pulled the shoulder across. The stains were dotted on the top of it. 'I don't know,' she muttered. 'Some oil from the gate probably. I must have knocked against something.' As she spoke, she could feel another drop from above her head. 'Hey, it's raining in here. If the roof has a leak Da'll be furious.' She giggled. 'Something else to distract him! Come on, will we go look for the penknife.' She turned towards the ladder.

Anne grabbed her arm, her eyes still on Lizzie's shoulder. Her face was set, stern. 'Lizzie, don't.'

Lizzie had her foot on the bottom rung. 'It's okay, I always hold on to ladders safely. I climbed down this one in the dark yesterday, remember?'

'Stop! Come down!' With both hands heavy round her waist, Anne pulled Lizzie off the ladder causing both girls to stumble backwards onto the floor.

'What was that for?' Lizzie got up first and brushed herself off angrily. 'Why are you being so rough? I'm only going to see if I dropped the penknife in the loft.'

Anne stayed where she was. 'And if you dare put another foot on that ladder, I'm going straight home to tell on you.'

Lizzie was furious. How unfair was that? One minute nicey-nicey older sister, I'll look after you and the next – bossy. She stomped to the door. 'Fine then, do what you like.'

'Thank you.' Anne's voice was a whisper as she got up slowly and brushed herself off. She went to the foot of the ladder and held on to the sides, looking up. As if she could see from there.

'Well, go on then, seeing as you want to be the one to do everything.'

Anne took a deep breath and started to climb. Slowly.

Lizzie watched her, sucking in the sides of her cheeks, so resentful she could choke on it. Anne was being *such* a cow. She knew Lizzie was worried about the knife and wanted to find it as soon as she could and here she was, taking one step at a time as if each of her legs weighed a ton and it was all such a terrible effort. 'Hurry, will you?'

Anne continued to climb. When her face came level with the loft floor she moved even slower. She lifted herself up the next two rungs and then stopped, letting her breath out in a sharp puff. Then she was still.

Lizzie tapped her foot impatiently. 'Well, is it there?'

Anne said nothing.

'Is it?' Now her knees were tapping and Lizzie wanted to pull Anne's skinny feet off the ladder onto the floor below and give her a good punch. 'Come on, stop being so mean...' There was still no reply. Lizzie flipped. All the worry from last evening, and the comings and goings in the night, and then the weird atmosphere and funny looks this morning came together in her head, and she'd had enough. She leaped at the ladder, straight to the second rung and scrambled for the top. 'That's it! If you won't tell me, I'll come and look for it myself! Is the knife there or not?'

Anne's voice, high and panicked, stopped her where she was. 'Lizzie, don't look!' She jumped the top rung onto the loft floor and disappeared. There was a scrabble in the loft and suddenly she reappeared above her, holding something in her hands. 'You don't need to come up here, Lizzie,' she whispered. 'Go back down. Look, I found the penknife. I'll pass it to you. Stay there.' With the light from the small window behind her, it was hard to see exactly what she was doing but Lizzie could make out her outline as she bent down and rubbed the blade on her skirt, very slowly, as if she was cleaning it. Then holding it carefully as Da had taught them, she eased it back safely into the handle and passed it down to Lizzie. As their hands touched and Anne stood upright again, Lizzie felt a prickling down her back. Something was wrong. They'd found the knife so they should be happy but there was a kind of humming in the air as if someone was going to scream. Very loudly. Anne was standing like a statue on the platform of the loft facing the window. She didn't look like she was coming down. She was supposed to be coming down. She had done what she wanted to do in the barn and now they had to go and do the next important thing. They had to go and find their father. In her mind, Anne's movements a minute ago replayed in Lizzie's mind. The way she bent over. The way she wiped the knife. The way she said, 'Don't look.'

And suddenly Lizzie knew what it was Anne didn't want her to see. She slipped the knife into her pocket and stepped up until she could see over the floor above. Anne didn't try to stop her, didn't even turn to face her. She was still standing stiffly with her hands by her sides but now her shoulders had started to jerk – up and down – as small, tight gulps escaped from between her clenched teeth. Lizzie kept her eyes on her sister and then slowly turned to see what she was seeing.

At first it looked like nothing. Just the usual jumble of straw and mess. Just like yesterday. Only yesterday, the straw smelt like summer and it was dry and comfortable. Today it smelt different – familiar. And there was a dark stain on the edges of it and Lizzie knew as she squinted into the darkness what the drops were that had fallen onto her shoulder from between the floorboards of the loft above. And as she made out the outline of her father's great boots, the soles facing her, she knew too why the smell was familiar.

She'd done messages for her mother often enough.

In the butcher's.

*

The scream was in her head. It grew out of a cold place on her forehead then burst from her mouth, off the loft floor, through the gates and down the lane to their house where Mam was sitting at the kitchen table waiting for them to come back with their father. When it wrapped itself around her she got up and came slowly to the door, looking out into the darkness for the news to arrive that would change their lives forever.

By the time Anne and Lizzie came down the lane she had moved to the gate. She didn't say, 'Where have you been?' or 'Where's your father?' She just leaned close and looked into her daughters' faces. In her expression were a hundred questions and as the girls looked at her, they opened their mouths to answer but Lizzie couldn't remember if any sounds came out. Mam's red cheeks grew paler as she searched their faces until hers was as white and bloodless as the hand Lizzie had seen in the straw of the loft, lying palm up to the roof, stiff with the cold.

In the end, Anne gave Lizzie's hand one last squeeze and then let it go. 'Mam,' she said. 'Da's dead.' She turned her head and looked back up the lane towards the barn. Then she walked past their mother and into the house.

Mam began to shake, slowly at first. 'How?' Her voice was high-pitched and she looked past Lizzie's head to where the stains, purple and angry, had dried on her shoulder. She reached out and touched them. It seemed to Lizzie that she wasn't as much touching as pointing. Lizzie shuddered and let the cardigan slide off. Her mother was holding it, her eyes never leaving the stains. When it slid as far as her wrist, she tugged a little and eased the cuff over Lizzie's clenched fist. The one with the penknife in it. Then she held the cardigan to her face and started to cry. Lizzie didn't know what to do. Even though they were standing close together, her mother felt miles away. Lizzie knew that if she tried to put her arms around her, it would make no difference. Her mother's body was trembling and shaking and huge gulps were coming out of her mouth as if she was drowning. Any second now the scream that preceded them down the lane would come out of her and even though there were miles of countryside all around to swallow it up, Lizzie knew the noise would still be able to fill all the space and she would drown in it too. She turned and ran into the house.

Anne was in the hallway with the phone pressed to her ear. 'I'm still here,' she was saying, her voice calm, 'Yes, I'll hold.' She caught sight of Lizzie and her eyes filled with tears. She was drowning too. 'Please come – quickly.' She dropped the receiver and held her arms out. Lizzie fell into them. Anne held her little sister tight, stroking her head. 'Don't cry, Lizzie, don't be frightened. It'll be okay.'

Lizzie lifted her eyes and looked at her, surprised. 'Will it?' she said, for one crazy moment hoping that maybe she had got it wrong. Maybe 'Lizzie's wild imagination' as their parents like to call it, had gotten in the way of what she was looking at and she hadn't really seen what she thought she had. 'Is Da not really dead then? '

Anne pushed her away and holding her arms by the sides, bent close to her face. 'Da's gone, Lizzie, do you understand that?'

Lizzie stared back. That didn't make any sense. Anne said it would be okay but that was only true if the rest of it wasn't. If their father was asleep or resting or pretending or something. Not if he was lying flat on his back with his arms out by his side and his great boots facing you as you came up the loft ladder – blocking out the picture of the rest of him; his check shirt not moving up and down the way it was supposed to when he was resting, but still and spattered in dark stains that were everywhere – on his coat, on the straw, on the wall behind him. She'd wanted to move closer to him, to see if he realised the disorder and was upset about his tidy barn being messed up like that. She'd wanted to see his face.

But as she'd moved forward, Anne put her hand out to block the way.

'Let me, Anne – I want to see Da's face. '

'You can't.' Anne's arm was strong and Lizzie couldn't budge it. 'Leggo, Anne! I want to see his face!'

Anne swung around and her eyes were blazing. 'YOU CAN'T! DO YOU UNDERSTAND ME – YOU CAN'T!'

Lizzie pushed and while she didn't get past, she did manage to peer into the dimness beyond where the light from the window shone into the corner of the loft to the top of their father's body, where his head was. Where his face should have been.

And that's where the scream came from.

*

The house was full of people. In the kitchen neighbours whispered to one another and made *you know what I'm talking about without saying anything* faces; the gardai were in the dining room, the table spread with papers and the girls' schoolbooks pushed to one side; their mother was in the sitting room, her hands clenched in her lap, staring into space. When Lizzie was called to talk to the gardai, everybody looked to see if their mother might get up and come with her but she was in trance so Patricia Whittle's mother rose. She was a short, plump woman with wiry hair and warm hands.

'I'll come with you, pet,' she whispered. 'Say as much as you want and don't worry about a thing.' She smiled as if that made everything all right.

Lizzie couldn't smile back. The sergeant was a big man from Cork with a face like John Wayne and a voice that rumbled up from the back of his throat and fell into your lap. You couldn't ignore or push it away without him noticing.

When Lizzie and Mrs Whittle sat opposite him, he cleared his throat so the questions could get out easily and joined his huge hands together as if praying.

'I need to ask you a few little questions, Elizabeth. Is that all right?'

Lizzie nodded.

He moved his chair around so that he was sitting nearer and when he leaned forward and rested his elbows on his knees his face was close to hers. She felt he could see right inside of her. She shut her eyes tight. Mrs Whittle was squeezing her right hand but her left was still clenched in a fist.

'Was there anyone in the barn before you went there?' he said.

She shook her head.

'So you were the first?'

Lizzie's eyes shot open. That was a lie. She'd answered the first question and it was already a lie. She was the second; Anne was the first. Sergeant Murphy's dark eyes were boring into hers. He knew already.

'We had to find our Da,' she said, 'Mam wanted him. She said to find him and we looked there.' His expression didn't change. 'And that's the truth because we looked everywhere else and he wasn't there because he was in the barn and... ' the scream was coming up from the bottom of her stomach again and it was shaking her voice as it came. Where the words should have sounded like normal speaking, they were climbing to the top of her mouth and wobbling there, squeaky and thin. If she didn't get them out, the scream would get there first and she wouldn't be able to talk at all. She swallowed.

Sergeant Murphy reached out and rested his giant hand on her hands. 'That's all right, you don't have to say any more if you don't want to.' He motioned to the papers on the table behind him. 'I have to get all the details so that we know exactly what happened.' His hand on hers was heavy and dry and she wished she could shake it off. She squeezed tighter and in her palm the edges of the penknife dug into her skin. If she ever opened that hand again there would be deep ridges along the sides. She doubted if they would ever go away.

As if he could read her thoughts, Sergeant Murphy looked down at her hands. Following his gaze, she could see a glimmer where the end of the knife protruded. Her forehead went cold as he opened his mouth to ask her what she was holding. Instead he looked up again and smiled. 'Do you want to show me that?' he said.

She didn't but her head nodded anyway. Her fingers opened and when she looked down she could see she was right. Angry welts ran the length of her hand, and her palm was a pool of sweat. The knife felt warm and slimy but the sergeant pinched his fingers together and lifting it up, held it to his face.

'That's a dangerous thing for a little girl to be carrying,' he said. 'Is it yours?'

She shook her head. The scream was right up to her neck now.

'Is it your father's?'

*Yes.*

He turned it over and examined the back of it, and then he slid his hand along the side. 'You have to be careful with a thing like this. You shouldn't have it really. You could cut yourself.' He looked as if he was going to open the blade. 'It's very sharp... you could easily have an accident.'

Lizzie shut her eyes. He was going to open the blade and she knew what would happen then. All Da's blood that Anne hadn't wiped off in the loft would drip out of it onto the sergeant's lap...

*You could cut yourself.*

He was opening it and soon he would see how thin the blade was and how dangerous and how, like he said, she shouldn't have it. And she shouldn't lose it. And she especially shouldn't lose it on the floor of the loft where her father would go in the morning and find the place in a mess...

*You could have an accident.*

And trip over on the loosened bales where she had slept the day before and fall onto the floor and not see the open knife as he fell and not realise what was happening till the blade of it sliced through the back of his head...

It was too late. Before the picture of her father came clear in her head the scream was out and the room was full of it. Mrs Whittle's arms were around her, holding on tight and the sergeant had fallen to his knees and was holding her hands. Someone was coming in the door.

Through the haze of terror, Sergeant Murphy's voice ordered the doctor to come and then Lizzie was bundled in a rug and taken back to the kitchen. Soft worried voices poked through the screaming in her head till it began to break up and turned into sobs instead. Gentle hands stroked her and she wanted to melt into each one of them. Eventually she calmed and the voices died down. Mrs Whittle's was the last to leave.

'It's all right, pet.' Her face was rosy and kind. She smiled and nodded. 'Better to let it out.'

She looked over Lizzie's head to where the sergeant was standing in the doorway. 'You don't need to ask her any more questions, do you?' She had the voice grown ups have when they are telling you something they don't want you to argue with them about.

Sergeant Murphy came over and patted Lizzie on the head. 'Not at all. Poor little mite, but I have to follow procedure.' He stood watching her for a minute then he turned his attention to Anne who was sitting at the table staring into space. As if she felt his gaze, she looked up.

'I'm the one you need to talk to.'

'Yes,' his voice was gentle.

Anne glared at him. 'You don't need to bother my little sister or my mother any more.'

'You're the one who found him.'

Anne put the mug she was holding down and rose slowly. 'That's it.' she said. She looked at Lizzie and her face was red. Like it had been up at the barn when Lizzie had told her the dreadful thing she had done and asked her to keep it a secret. And she said she would. And then they had gone in to the barn and discovered the terrible accident. Their father was dead.

The horror of it was pushing the backs of her eyes out and Lizzie blinked hard so that she could see her sister properly. There were no tears in Anne's eyes – just expressions that were impossible to understand. They moved across her face until she looked so sad that Lizzie started to cry again. She held her arms out. 'Anne?'

Anne paused a minute at the door as if she might come over and comfort her. Lizzie would have stood but her legs felt heavy and she knew that if she tried, she would just fall.

Even if Anne took a step towards her, she could lean over and whisper to her. *It was an accident. I never meant this to happen.*

But Anne turned away. She motioned the sergeant to go ahead of her out of the room. 'I can answer your questions.' She said and she looked sorrowfully back at Lizzie again. 'I'm the one who knows everything.'

## Rathshannan
### 2006

'LIZZIE! ARE YOU IN THERE?'

Lizzie forced her eyes open and looked around the room, unsure where she was. It wasn't her bedroom.

The doorbell rang again. 'Lizzie!'

'Coming, hold your horses.' She struggled out of the chair and padded stiffly to the front door. Anne's face was pressed to the glass.

'What in the name of God have you been doing to yourself – are you all right?' As Anne bustled past, a gust of cold air followed her into the hallway. 'Were you in bed?'

Lizzie rubbed her hands up and down her arms and shivered. 'I woke up and couldn't get back to sleep so I came down to the study. I must have fallen asleep in front of the fire. What time is it?'

'Ten.'

'For goodness sake! I'm dead late.' Lizzie made to go up the stairs. 'Put the kettle on – I'll get dressed.'

Anne put a hand out to stop her. 'Just get a dressing gown on for the minute. You're as pale as a sheet. I don't think you should go into the shop today.'

Lizzie said nothing. Her brain was muffled from lack of sleep and there was something she was supposed to remember but she didn't know what it was. She went upstairs and came back with her dressing gown.

'Come on, the town will survive without you for one morning.' Anne was standing by the kettle in the kitchen, regarding her sister suspiciously. When the kettle boiled she dropped two teabags into a pot and pressed them against the sides as she frowned and considered her question. Twice she opened her mouth and shut it again.

'Why don't you just come straight out with it?' Lizzie said eventually. 'You could say, *Lizzie, you look like shit, what on earth's the matter with you.*'

Anne dropped the spoon in the sink and carried the pot over to the table. As she went back for mugs and milk, she was smiling. 'Sensitively expressed – did I ever tell you that you have a way with words?' She put the mugs on the table and started to pour the tea.

Neither wanting to try her patience nor knowing where to start, Lizzie took a sip before she spoke again. 'I woke up in a sweat,' she said eventually.

'A nightmare?'

She shook her head. 'No,' she said, 'a bloody hot flush.'

Anne smiled. 'Is that all?'

'You mean it could be worse?'

Anne held a spoon of sugar over her tea and let the grains fall slowly into the mug. 'Nothing wrong with it at all.' She shrugged. 'Welcome to the inevitable.' She looked at Lizzie. 'It doesn't bother you, does it?'

'Not in the cold light of day, it doesn't.' She felt her nightdress inside her dressing gown. 'But it was awful last night. I didn't know what was happening to me. I thought I must have caught a chill or something then I passed the mirror in the hall and realised.'

Anne stifled a snigger. 'Did it steam up when you passed or what?'

'Worse. I caught sight of my reflection and it wasn't me.' Her sombre tone made Anne look up. 'It was our mother.'

A dark shadow passed over Anne's face. 'That's rough. You hadn't been drinking, had you?'

Lizzie banged the mug down on the table. 'No, I certainly hadn't!'

Anne's voice was soft when she spoke. 'It's not a silly question. You look nothing like Mam, as you know. I'm only asking what was it you recognised – and we both know how she most often looked. I wasn't suggesting you were going the same way.'

Lizzie hung her head, blinking to fight back tears. 'Oh Anne, I think I'm going crazy. It wasn't drink I saw – it was anguish. Sheer bloody anguish. It's as if every emotion I possess has a match lit under it and I flare up at the least thing. It's the way she used to be – volatile.'

Anne reached across the table and held her hand. 'Don't worry. Mam's volatility was down to alcohol, yours is completely different – it's not abnormal – it's ages and stages. If you're menopausal, you're bound to be all over the place. Things will settle down.'

Lizzie pulled her hand away. 'Maybe. At the minute I'm in the air.'

Anne topped up their mugs. 'Was there something else?' she asked without looking up. 'I mean something else that brought this on?'

Lizzie said nothing.

'It's not to do with your jigsaw man, is it?' She must have seen the blush. 'You've been tense since he arrived.'

She was right. Lizzie thought back to the first day and how he had seemed to herald a new beginning. She had jumped at his suggestions and started to overhaul her shop straight away. And he had put a spring in her step. And now she had discovered he was a fly-by-night and not worth investing emotion in. She shrugged. 'Around then, I suppose.' She took another sip of tea. Opposite her Anne was sitting calmly but still watching with that intense expression as if she could read right inside Lizzie's head – the same expression she'd had the night Sergeant Murphy led her out of the kitchen to tell it all – because she was the one who knew everything.

'Jim Nealon doesn't upset me,' she said eventually. 'Why should he? He's just passing through, making his jigsaws.'

Anne didn't look convinced. Her expression was inscrutable but she was thinking *I don't believe you*. Lizzie took a deep breath. 'Actually. It was you who upset me.'

Bull's-eye. Anne looked as if she had been slapped.

'You came into my shop and very condescendingly pointed out that my stock was old-fashioned and I, too, was past my sell-by date. When Jim came in proposing his new line, I didn't react to him by taking him up on it – he *was* the reaction. To you.'

Very carefully, Anne put her mug back on the table and sat forward. 'What I said was right and I said it for your own good.'

'Of course. You only ever say things for my own good.'

'Oh for God's sake, Lizzie! What's the matter with you? You are spoiling for a fight and I can tell you for nothing that you're wasting your time. I don't know what the problem is, but I do know that it's not me. If there's something on your mind, spit it out and clear the air. I'm not prepared to sit here and have accusations spat at me as if we're a pair of vindictive children.'

Lizzie was furious. 'Vindictive! You can call me vindictive!' The memory of Anne's back as she left the kitchen forty years ago was so clear in her mind that she could reach out and touch it. 'You were supposed to be on my side.'

Anne's shoulders sagged. 'I don't have the slightest clue what you're talking about. Your stock is dated, I point it out, and you call that vindictive.'

Lizzie shook her head. 'That's not what it's about though, is it?' She pulled her dressing gown closer over her chest and smoothed it flat. 'You have always been contemptuous of me, boring Lizzie, in her boring shop with her boring life.' Before Anne could protest, Lizzie held her hand up. 'Don't deny it. Lots of people see me that way and I don't mind. Boring's fine. It's non-eventful and can't harm anyone. And it's the way I am because it's the way I choose to be.'

Anne looked totally bemused. 'Good for you.'

'And if I don't have the exciting adventures other people have that make them so interesting, that's fine. I'll be the way I am and that doesn't harm anyone.'

Anne stood up. 'Lizzie, I'm not sure where all this is leading, or where it's coming from but I'm going to go now. If there's something you have an issue about, you know where I am. I'm not spending any more time listening to this. Something has got you going and if you don't want to tell me what it is, then there's nothing I can do to resolve it. In the meantime, I think you should get some rest. I'll call you later.' She turned to leave but Lizzie needed to stop her.

She grabbed Anne's arm. 'Wait! Stay there – I need to show you something.' She went into the study and came back with a pile of photographs. She placed them on the table – all except the last one. 'Look at these.' she said.

Anne picked up the photos and smiled. 'They're lovely. They're the photos your jigsaw maker is using, aren't they?' She traced a finger around the outline of the one with the bus. 'I remember this so well.' She picked up another. 'And this. It's a good thing he got the school now. If he'd arrived a few weeks down the line the developers would already have put their scaffolding up and he wouldn't be able to have that nostalgic look – it'll be all sanitised when they're finished it. The ivy will be off for a start.'

Lizzie held the barn photo close to her chest. 'Is that all you see?' she said. 'Ivy and an old bus?'

Anne nodded. 'What else am I supposed to see?'

Lizzie sat down. 'He asked me to make it real.' Her voice was soft, almost dreamy. 'And the only way I could do that was to go back there. Right back into that time and revisit everything I saw then, everything that happened.'

Anne was studying the photos again and Lizzie could see colour creeping up her neck.

'It was like being thrown back to a time in my past I'd really rather not visit.'

Anne nodded.

'It didn't bother me. These I could have coped with fine.' She pointed to the photos of the well and the old church. 'But he has an uncanny knack of finding places that are more than just the usual childhood memories. It's as if he is making me take the pieces of my past apart and then he will go and I will be left shattered by the memories.'

Anne came over and put her arms around Lizzie's shoulders. 'But you were happy in school, weren't you? And I know you were fond of Sister Cillian but I didn't realise you were so affected by her leaving.'

Lizzie shook her off. 'It's not that! Look at me!' She stood and held her arms out. 'What do you see, Anne?'

'Just you?'

'You see a middle-aged woman who by virtue of her middle age had retreated in greyness, anonymity. Past her sell-by date and perfectly happy with it. First you come along and tell me that's not acceptable, even though it affects nobody else and it's how I choose to be. Then he comes along and takes me back to a time when it looked as if it might all be different. Bit by bit I am being dismantled. And I don't like it.'

There was a faint smile playing on Anne's mouth. 'Is it the change of life that's worrying you?'

Lizzie wanted to bang the table in frustration. 'No, dammit! It's the upheaval. I don't want to delve into the past. I don't want to have to go there. I don't want to face my demons.'

'You, Lizzie? What demons could you possibly have?' The kindness in Anne's face cut Lizzie in two. How could she stand there and pretend not to understand?

'You really don't know what I'm talking about, do you?' Anne shook her head.

Lizzie held the barn photo away from her chest and studied it a moment. The edges were curled where she had clutched it in the night and there were smears on the surface where tears fell on it.

'You know my demons, Anne, better than anyone.' She held out the picture for her sister to see. 'Don't you remember? You're the one who knew everything.'

For a long time, Anne held the photo in shaking hands and stared at it. Tears welled in her eyes, slid down her face onto her lap. When she could no longer see, she shut her eyes and held the photo out for Lizzie to take from her. Then she pulled a large flowery handkerchief from her pocket and buried her face in it.

All the while, Lizzie watched. On the top of Anne's head, auburn hair mingled with silver and golden so that she could be any age. She wiped each eye carefully and blew her nose hard. Lizzie waited. The photo had certainly affected her but Lizzie would not have been the least bit surprised if Anne's wiped face reappeared and suddenly changed the conversation. That's the way Anne was. First sign of an awkward situation and she was off. Well, not this time. Lizzie wanted answers.

'Did you hate me for it?' she asked.

Anne lifted her face and blinked as if she had just woken from a long sleep. 'Why would I hate you?'

Lizzie took the photo from her and held it up. 'Don't pretend. You were there.'

Anne looked from Lizzie to the photo and back again but she didn't seem any the wiser.

Lizzie pulled open the drawer of her desk. Rummaging around the back of it, she pulled out a small suede purse. She unzipped it and let the contents fall into her palm. It was a penknife. She held it out. 'Now tell me you don't know what I'm talking about.'

Gingerly, Anne picked up the knife and the tears started flowing again. She blinked them away. 'I didn't know you still had this.'

'Well, I do. I know it seems ghoulish but I don't know where to put it. Throwing it in the bin hardly seems appropriate.'

Anne looked surprised. 'Why would you get rid of it, Lizzie? Da loved that knife – it was in our family for years. I suppose he hoped we'd pass it on to our children – if we ever had any.' Her cheeks were bright pink and for the first time, Lizzie wondered if she might be crazy. There she was, beaming at the penknife as if it was a treasured family heirloom.

Lizzie snatched it from her. 'And even if we had, he didn't live to see them, did he? Because he had a terrible accident that wasn't an accident at all.'

Anne paled. 'I didn't realise you knew.' She shook her head. 'How foolish of me. Of course someone must have told you.' She stood up and put her hand gently on Lizzie's shoulder. 'When did you find out? Why didn't you ever tell me?'

She *was* crazy. Stark staring, raving mad. She was looking at Lizzie as if cream was about to pour from her mouth. She, who knew exactly what happened, told the sergeant exactly what happened and then, after their father's funeral she got straight into Aunty Margie's car and headed up to Dublin – to her new, exciting life. Over the years she'd made brief visits to their mother – which always ended in tears and empty gin bottles – and only came back to stay when Lizzie made the final phone call. *Come home Anne, the coast is clear.* She never resented the fact that everything was left to Lizzie, and only after much persuading agreed to move into the old house to start up her confectionery business, while Lizzie moved into the village to carry on a life of her own.

'You don't need anyone to tell you anything, Anne.' She slid her fingers into the grooves along the blade's side and slowly eased it open. Even though it had been shut since that night when the sergeant opened it and declared it dangerous, it slid open as if recently oiled. Now it lay in her palm, glinting sharp in the light. 'And don't pretend you forget, either. You were the one who found it. You were the one who wiped the blood onto your skirt, remember?' She held the knife close to Anne's face. 'How could either of us pretend we don't know how our father died?'

She expected Anne to recoil with so menacing a weapon close but she didn't. She looked at the knife, frowning and then at Lizzie. Her eyes swept Lizzie's face and then she shook her head. 'Oh, my God!' she whispered. She picked the knife off Lizzie's palm and folded it shut again. Slipping it into the purse, she dropped onto the table. 'Are you telling me that you think this knife had something to do with our father's death?'

'I know it did.' Lizzie flinched as Anne lifted her hand and rested her cool palm against her cheek. 'I saw you, in the loft, just before I reached you. You were wiping the blood off the blade.'

Anne lifted her other hand and held Lizzie's face steady. 'Elizabeth Flynn, listen to me. Have you really, for all these years, thought that Da's death had anything to do with you?'

Lizzie nodded. 'I killed him,' she whispered. Forty years of guilt rode on that short statement and hearing it leave her mouth was like opening a floodgate. 'I killed him.' As Anne started to shake her head, the relief Lizzie felt was overwhelming. 'I took his knife and lost it and then he slipped and fell on it and cut his head open and it was all my fault. I killed him.' It was out and she didn't have to carry it around any more. Jim was right – regrets weighed heavy and guilt does too and now it was out she felt so light that she would have left the ground and floated upwards if Anne had not been holding her face, keeping her earthbound.

'You did not kill our father. Lizzie. I can't believe you ever thought you did.' Anne hands were shaking and her face was white. 'It was nothing to do with you.'

'It was, and there's no point in saying otherwise. I saw him. He was lying where the knife had been and there was blood everywhere and his face was gone. I killed him.'

Very slowly, Anne reached down and picked the knife up again. She unfolded the blade and laid it out on her hand. 'Look at this penknife, Lizzie.'

Lizzie looked. She ran her finger lightly along its length. 'It's very sharp,' she whispered.

'It's not.' Anne said. 'It's quite sharp but not as sharp as a father would have his eleven-year-old daughter believe if he didn't want her to play with it. It's only fairly sharp, good enough for peeling chestnuts but not much good if you're planning to cut someone's face off with it... '

Lizzie winced.

'And it's also very small.'

Lizzie looked at the knife again. Anne was right. The knife was small – much smaller than her memory recalled. She closed her eyes. She couldn't have got it wrong. She remembered everything: the rain hammering on the barn roof; the creak of the pitchforks in the breeze from the door; the touch of drops on her shoulders as their father's blood dripped onto her from the loft above.

'I thought you didn't want me there because you didn't want me to see what I'd done.'

Anne's hands dropped to Lizzie's shoulders. 'Wake up and see things as they really are, will you! I didn't want you coming up because you were eleven years old. Because you were too young – not to see what you had done but what he had.' She shook Lizzie hard. 'Have you really gone all these years and not understood what happened that night? Can't you remember what a palaver there was trying to convince Sergeant Murphy that it was an accident?' She wrapped her arms around Lizzie and held her tight. 'You didn't kill him, sweetheart; it was nothing to do with you, none of it. Our father put a gun to his chin and blew his face off himself.' In her embrace, Lizzie stiffened. 'That's what I thought you had realised.' She pushed Lizzie away and looked long and hard into her eyes. 'It was suicide, Lizzie. He killed himself.'

## The Churchyard
## 1969

ALL HER LIFE LIZZIE KNEW WHO SHE WAS. She had a certain place in the world and certain people around her and she knew exactly how she fitted in. Everything was familiar. Today, with a sharp autumn sun glinting through the scraggy branches of leylandii trees around the graveyard, that world had disappeared. And there was no Lizzie. Because Lizzie didn't live there any more.

Instead, Lizzie lived on an uneven mound of earth at the side of a rectangular hole in the ground. All around her people were crowded, looking into the hole so that they wouldn't have to look into one another's faces. On one side of her, her mother was heaving huge gulps of pain and swaying into the arms of whoever was there to catch her. Twice, there hadn't been anyone and she stumbled blindly onto her knees. Lizzie caught the looks of those nearby: some pitying and tearful, others contemptuous and angry until their eyes caught those of the child at her side and they turned away in shame. *Drunk... imagine... today of all days.* She caught the whispers too.

On the other side of her Anne stood stiffly. She must be cross with Mam as well because they hadn't looked at one another since the night Sergeant Murphy took Anne into the dining room for the chat. Maybe she hadn't just told him what Lizzie did with the knife; maybe she'd told him that the bottles of water Mam kept in the pantry weren't water at all but gin – a strange peppery drink that made Mam soft and sloppy at first, then sad until she took some more.

Lizzie kept her fists in her pockets. Once or twice, people like Patricia Whittle's mother tried to prise her arm out and hold her hand but she held firm. She had to keep them there, had to keep them tightly clenched so that nobody would see what she was holding, so that she wouldn't accidentally loosen her grasp and have to stand and watch as the little knife flew in nightmarish slow motion and the blade opened and glistened in the sun, cutting onlookers down as it fell. Then their blood would spurt out and splash on people's coats and they'd have to wait till it dried black before they could pick it off. Like the blood on the shoulder of her cardigan.

A gust of wind rattled a fresh harvest of leaves onto the mourners and Lizzie lifted her face to it. If a leaf fell on you before it touched the ground it meant you were going to have good luck for a year. From an oak tree by the gate, the little leaves like hands rushed towards her, but the curve of the wall made the breeze change direction so that they fell onto the path beyond. Lizzie squinted to see if any landed on a person.

It didn't look like it. All those people with their heads bowed and sadness etched deep into their faces and not one of them in line for a happy year – that was so unlucky. Lizzie squeezed her eyes together to try and stop herself crying.

*Look into the distance, Lizzie pet.* Her father's voice brushed her cheek. *Look at something far away and then you won't cry.*

'Da!' Her voice sounded strange above the priest's words and everyone turned away from him to look at her.

The touch of his words were on her cheek still.

'Da?'

Her mother bent down and with her pink face close to Lizzie's, whispered, 'Daddy's dead, Lizzie. Don't be calling him now. Let him rest in peace.' And she started to wail in a high keening voice.

Everybody shuffled uncomfortably. The priest cleared his throat and began praying again but now he speeded up a little. On either side of the grave, men in black suits with wide collars picked up corded strips that lay on the ground under the coffin. As they lifted the strips the coffin rose and they carried it till it was suspended over the hole. They fed the strips slowly through their hands till the coffin lowered out of sight. When it disappeared from view completely they whipped the strips back up but the coffin stayed where it was. Lizzie looked at them in surprise. They bowed stiffly and turned to walk away. They were rolling the strips of cord around their hands as if they hadn't noticed that the coffin wasn't there any more. They had left her Da behind!

'Don't go!' she called after them. 'Don't leave him!'

'Hush, pet.' Mrs Whittle moved in close behind her and was holding her by the shoulders. It wasn't a do-you-need-a-cuddle hold; it was a don't-move. Lizzie turned to look at her.

'They have to come back!' she whispered urgently. 'Tell them!'

Mrs Whittle shook her head sadly. She had huge tears rolling down her face. She must be very sad about Da too.

Maybe she thought he was a great fellow and was going to miss him terribly like everyone else. Like all the other people who were crying openly now. Lizzie felt a surge of affection for all of them. She watched two tears gain momentum over the spidery red vein marks on Mrs Whittle's cheeks and land on her coat where they soaked in, leaving dark stains that spread. Lizzie recoiled.

'*In the name of the Father and of the Son and of the Holy Ghost.*' The priest sang the blessing and the crowd muttered '*Amen.*' He closed his prayer book and looked around as if he had just remembered where he was. From the folds of his vestments he pulled out a silver container like a microphone and handed it to their mother. She took it with shaky hands and flicked it at the hole. Lizzie could hear the drops fall onto the wood beneath. Then Mam picked up some soil and threw that in as well. She turned and beckoned the girls to do the same. Lizzie didn't want to but Mam looked so desperate standing there, tottering on the edge as if at any minute she might fall in and disappear too that Lizzie went up to her. Anne didn't move. Lizzie lifted her empty hand slowly out of her pocket and took the container and shook it. Drops of Holy Water spattered on her face and she brushed them crossly away. Someone took the container from her and handed her a rose. It was red. Lizzie wasn't sure what she was meant to do with it. Some people were dropping flowers into the grave but Lizzie didn't want to. She put the petals to her nose and when she inhaled the memory rushed at her like a slap.

*She was in her parents' bedroom and it was Mam's birthday and she and Da had made her breakfast in bed. As they were about to carry the tray upstairs, Anne stopped them.*

*'Hang on. Da – ' she held out her hand, 'Give me your penknife for a minute.'*

*She took the knife and nodding at his warning to be careful, disappeared. When she came back, she had a rose stem. She put it on the tray. 'There,' she said, 'perfect!'*

*And it was. Mam was sitting up in bed as if she knew what was coming. She was smiling and when she saw the rose she blinked a couple of times and said, 'Thank you' in such a quiet voice that it felt like a kiss.*

Now Mam was standing beside her, waiting. She was looking at the rose and Lizzie wonder if she was remembering too. If she was, then Lizzie wanted her to keep remembering. She held the rose out to her mother. Her mother's hand shook as she took it, kissed its petalled head as if it was a baby that she didn't want to wake and then, turning to the grave, let it drop.

All the other people stopped, their hands in mid-air. Then, as if someone had given a signal, everyone turned and started to walk away from the grave. Anne was still where they left her, staring into space. As they passed her, some ladies took Mam by the arms and led her off the uneven grass to the safety of the path. Mrs Whittle put her arms around the girls and ushered them along.

\*

At the graveyard gates, all the neighbours were gathered muttering their condolences to the family. People who would normally just drive past without even a second glance looked deep into their faces as if they wanted to say something important, something that really mattered. Mostly they didn't manage it. They just mumbled, *I'm so sorry* or *what a sad day for you*. Some who were friends started to say *If there's anything...* but then their voices cracked and they left the rest unsaid. Mam patted them on the arm and said things like *of course* and *you're very kind*. Lizzie watched them and wondered at it all. It was a secret code that everybody understood.

Beside her, Anne was silent. People brushed her arm as she went but she didn't look at them. She passed slowly through the crowd, which parted in front of her, and when she reached the verge outside she stopped suddenly and looked around, as if she was searching for someone. Lizzie followed her gaze.

The entire village seemed to have turned up for the funeral. Back at the gate, Mam was keening again and the women were holding her. Their husbands, looking embarrassed, moved away. Further along, some of the nuns were standing, keeping a beady eye on the children who had taken a day off to attend the funeral. A couple of the boys had a stick and were poking it into a clump of grass by the wall. Sister Cillian moved quickly and caught them by the ears.

Distracted by the ensuing commotion, Lizzie did not realise that Anne was not at her side any more. When she turned around, Anne had broken almost into a run and was heading up the road to where a car had started up and was beginning to pull away. It was familiar but Lizzie couldn't remember whose it was. When she reached the car, Anne stopped, as if she was going to knock on the window. The car jerked to a halt but nobody got out for a minute. Then a door opened on the passenger side and Lizzie moved forward to see.

As if in slow motion, a girl uncurled herself from where she had been crouching behind the seat. She straightened as she climbed out and stood in front of Anne.

It was Bernie Healey. Although she was a bit younger, she was tall and the two girls were eye to eye. Lizzie gasped. If that was what having your tonsils out did to you, she was going to gargle TCP every night for the rest of her life. Bernie's face was so pale that she didn't seem to have any blood in it at all. There were lines, thick and dark, under her eyes as if someone had started to give her a clown mask and then changed their minds once they had drawn the outlines. She looked cold too, even though she was wearing a thick coat and had her arms wrapped tightly around her body. For a minute she stood perfectly still, unblinking, then a gust of wind threw a wave of leaves in their direction and the two girls swayed. All the leaves landed on the ground at their feet.

Bernie opened her mouth. If there were words in it, they didn't come out. Even from a distance away, Lizzie heard the choking sound and then watched as Anne's hand shot up towards Bernie's face. For a minute it looked as if she might hit her but when it was just an inch away, it stopped and instead of a slap, she laid her hand gently on Bernie's cheek. Bernie leant her head to one side to rest in the warmth of Anne's palm then she gave a weak smile and turned away. Anne stood perfectly still, her hand still in mid-air as the other girl folded herself slowly into the car, shut the door and then she was gone.

As the car came towards her, Lizzie watched. Bernie was in the back seat. She had her head down so that her hair hung on either side and her face was hidden. Even in the shadow of the car's smeared windows it was obvious that she was crying.

When the car was gone, Lizzie turned to find Anne behind her. She was crying too and Lizzie felt an over-whelming relief. It seemed like such a normal thing to do. She put her arms out but Anne shook her head. Sister Cillian, who had been standing with the nuns, broke away and came towards them. She put an arm around each shoulder and walked them to where their mother was now sobbing in Mrs Whittle's arms.

'If you look after Mrs Flynn, I'll take the girls back with me.'

Anne sniffed and looked as if she might protest but Sister Cillian held her hand up.

'It's best,' she said and the other women looked from the girls to where their mother was fumbling in her bag.

'Back at the house then?' Sister Cillian said.

The women nodded.

As the girls sat in the convent car and Sister Cillian and Mother Clement got in the front, Lizzie huddled as far as she could into the corner. With the seat at her back and her fists tightly clenched, she felt almost safe. She watched the top of the graveyard wall slide by and disappear and then they were on the road home again. Only it wasn't home now. Da's greatcoat wasn't on the back door hook because he wouldn't be wearing it now and his slippers weren't by the mat. He couldn't trail mud into the house any more because he wouldn't be there. She shut her eyes and tried to block out the sound of the earth as it fell pattering timidly on the coffin lid.

Deep in her pocket, the sides of a closed penknife cut deep grooves into her palm. When she opened her hand tonight it would hurt like hell.

And she was glad of that.

*

For a week after the funeral, everything was strange. Mam's sister came down from Dublin to stay and they were up late into the night talking. Visitors popped in with trays of cakes and dishes of food and Lizzie wondered why everybody thought they should be so hungry now. It was Da who ate the biggest dinners and now that he was gone, the food went to waste. Mam piled their plates high and urged them to tuck in but there was always plenty left in the pot – Da's portion. Long after the meal was over and the plates washed and put away, it stayed on the stove, growing cold. It would still be there when she was going to bed, almost as if there was a chance, a tiny, wonderful, hopeful chance that it had all been a terrible mistake and any minute now Da would come through the door demanding his dinner.

But he didn't. As she lay in bed, Lizzie heard Mam stumble out into the yard and scrape the pot into the big steel dishes they kept there for the dogs.

'Lizzie, pet, off you go to bed now,' Auntie Margie said on Sunday night.

'But I want to watch the telly!' Lizzie looked to her mother for support.

Her mother didn't take her eyes off the screen.

'Mam?'

Mam sighed. 'Do as you're told, Lizzie. Bed now – you have school in the morning.'

School? How could she go to school? Everybody would be looking at her and asking questions and she'd have to tell them what happened and the pictures would come into her head again. She stuffed her hands into her pocket and held the knife tightly. 'I don't want to.'

Auntie Margie stood up slowly and Lizzie waited for the onslaught. She was Mam's older sister and very protective of her. None came. Her aunt just smiled and nodded. 'I don't blame you one little bit. It's the hardest thing in the world to get back to normal after a sad time like this. I remember when your granddad died. But you have to – you won't start to get better till you do.'

'I don't want to get better.' Lizzie watched Auntie Margie's sympathetic face and knew she was disappointing her. Lizzie had always been her favourite. She pursed her lips and wondered who would give in first.

For a minute Auntie Margie watched her then she jerked her head towards the kitchen, beckoning Lizzie to follow her. When they were out of earshot, her aunt sat her at the table.

'Lizzie, I need you to do me a favour.'

Lizzie watched her suspiciously.

Aunty Margie spread her hands out on the table and fiddled with her watchstrap. 'I'm a bit worried about your Mam.'

Lizzie nodded.

'She's not concentrating on the real world and the things she has to do now and as long as I stay here, she won't. Does that make sense?'

It did a bit.

'So I need to go back to Dublin. I need to leave your Mam to pull herself together and start living again. If you go back to school, she won't be able to leave it to you to do things for her – she'll have to start doing them for herself.'

That made sense too. 'So you want me to go back to school so that Mam will go back to normal?' She wondered if Auntie Margie realised how odd normal sometimes was.

'That's right,' Margie said.

Lizzie thought for a minute. If that was the way to help her mother then there really wasn't a choice – she had to go back. She owed Mam that much. 'But what about Anne?' she said. 'Is she going back to school too?'

Auntie Margie stopped fiddling with her strap and her expression changed. She looked guarded. 'Poor Anne,' she said.

Poor Anne. Lizzie caught her aunt's hand and squeezed it tight. If her mother's behaviour worried her, Anne's was terrifying. She got into bed as soon as they came home from the funeral and she only got up to go to the toilet or when Auntie Margie forced her to come to the kitchen and eat. She hadn't spoken a word to anyone. Lizzie blinked back tears. 'She's very cross with me,' she whispered.

Margie looked surprised. 'She isn't, pet. She's just very sad about your father, that's all. What would she be cross with you for?'

Lizzie wondered if she could tell her. She wondered if she could open her mouth and let the whole secret come tumbling out of it into the darkness of the kitchen. She could imagine how it would be, every sentence trapped in a little speech bubble that floated around the room until it came to rest near her aunt's face. Lizzie could sit back, free, her horrible secret out in the open. Her aunt was watching her fondly, the way she always did and suddenly Lizzie realised that she could never tell. If she did, the bubbles would float closer and closer till they pinged open in sharp stinging flicks on her aunt's cheeks and then there would be no more fond looks – only pain and shame. 'There's no reason for Anne to be cross with me,' she whispered.

Margie smiled. 'Of course not. But she's very sad anyway and I think it might be a good idea if she came up to Dublin with me for a while. The sea air will be good for her.'

Lizzie was shocked. Anne was leaving too? She looked wildly around the room. No Anne and no Da – what sort of a home was that. 'But we'll be so lonely.'

'Not if you're back at school and busy with your lessons, you won't.' She started to get up. 'I've already had a word with your teacher and she's spoken to the other children. You don't have to worry about talking about it if you don't want to.' She put her hands on Lizzie's shoulders. 'So you need to get yourself off to bed now because it's an early day tomorrow.'

Lizzie stood up slowly. She had the idea she was being fobbed off somehow but she couldn't see how. At the door she turned but her aunt didn't give her time to think. She held out her arms and wrapped Lizzie tightly in them. 'You don't worry about a thing, Lizzie pet. Your Auntie Margie will look after Anne for you and when she's better she will be home and you'll have learned lots and you can tell her all about it.' She smiled sadly. 'Okay?'

Lizzie nodded. She called 'goodnight' to her mother who didn't even seem to hear and went to bed. Anne was curled into a ball with the covers over her head and didn't answer when Lizzie called her. Lizzie undressed and got into bed. She lay watching the shadows playing on the ceiling for a few minutes thinking about what her aunt had said. If someone had told her two weeks ago that her precious sister was going away it would have broken her heart. She turned over to where the outline of her sister's body was barely visible in the darkness.

'Annie? Are you there?'

No answer. The bump didn't move but Lizzie knew she wasn't asleep – she just wasn't going to answer.

Lizzie rolled onto her back again and let the tears fall over the sides of her face onto the pillow. So Anne was off to Dublin? It didn't really matter, did it?

She was already gone.

## Rathshannon
## 2006

A HALF-EATEN LOAF AND A BUTTER-SMEARED KNIFE was evidence that she had eaten lunch but Lizzie had no recollection of it. She stood up from the table and washed her plate and Anne's and put them away mechanically. Then she hung up the tea towel and without bothering to check her face or her hair, slipped on her coat and left the house. All the way down the road, voices in her head jostled for a front row position and an opportunity to be heard. *You weren't responsible for Da's death. Mam was an alcoholic long before Da died and you hadn't noticed because you were too young – there were other people there to distract you. It wasn't because she knew what you'd done and was so disgusted with you that sober, she couldn't bear to look at you.*

As she crossed the road past the butchers she caught her reflection – Lizzie again, tall and straight-backed and proper, as everybody else saw her. Good old dependable Lizzie, straight as a die. If they only knew what was going on in her head: how she had carried her dreadful secret around for forty years and had only just discovered that she was wrong. That she was innocent. She reached the front door of her shop and was about to open up when she stopped and checked her watch. She didn't have deliveries today and the order for school that Sister Marion sent could be made up at home if she collected the bits on the way. She looked around the street. There weren't many people about. She looked over to where the blackened remains of Matt's garage had been flattened and cleared away. Nobody was there.

Then she heard a noise. Two men were coming out of Reardons further up the street. They wore suits, slightly dishevelled and each carried an impressive case – salesmen. Rathshannan was a good midway point for these chaps en route to Kilkenny city and she often benefited from proximity to Reardons' wholesome lunches when the travellers, having satisfied their need for nourishment, suddenly realised that tomorrow was Valentine's Day, or their wives' birthday and they wouldn't be back in Dublin in time to buy a card. How convenient to pop over the road to Lizzie's shop and make a quick purchase there – emotional insurance, all paid up.

'Give you a call at the end of the month!' one of the men shouted as he got into his car.

'Righto! See you!'

Lizzie watched as they drove off, no big events to be catered for, just another day in their busy lives. Absentmindedly, her hand strayed to the edge of an envelope sticking out of her bag. No ordinary day in hers. Today was the day she discovered that she had not killed her father. The implications were huge. Because she had not killed him, she did not need to spend her life doing penance; she did not need to keep a low profile and hope she would not be found out. She did not have anything to hide. Her father, on the other hand, had something so terrible to contend with that he had put a gun under his chin and blown his head away.

*Why?* She'd asked Anne. *Why would he do something like that?*

Anne's face was a tumult of emotions and she could not reply.

*I though it was Mam who had the problems, Da was always the steady one.*

Anne shrugged, still choked.

*Maybe it was all too much for him. Do you think that was it, Anne, Mam's drinking and craziness got too much and he couldn't take it any more?* She had started to cry then and Anne wrapped her arms around her and held her tight and they both cried long and hard. When they ran out of tears, they wiped their faces dry and Anne had left without another word. Lizzie watched her walk away. Poor Da, poor, poor Da. That things could have got to him so much and nobody knew. And now they were both gone.

But none of it was her fault. The gratitude that she felt for that fact alone was overwhelming. In all the welter of emotions, that one was the strongest, the most immediate. All the others could wait till later. For now she had a life to get on with and the photographs were the place to start.

Crossing the road, she headed towards Reardons. There was no reason why Jim should be there in the middle of the day – except for seeing Teresa, of course – and she wanted to find him so that she did not need to be angry with him still. She did not want this day marred by being angry with anyone. She pushed open the door and peered to where a group of people were laughing by the counter. Jim was on the far side of them, waiting for change. He turned and waved.

'Hey, Lizzie! How are you today? You still look peaky.'

'Thanks,' she laughed. 'That makes me feel good, all right.'

He smiled. 'Only saying it straight.' He leaned over and kissed her cheek. 'Your eyes are puffy.'

'Oh, for goodness sake – what do you expect? This place is so crowded. I don't know how you can bear it.' She turned and made for the door with Jim on her heels.

He held the door for her and they came out into the sunshine. Jim slung his satchel over his shoulder. 'I was coming in to see you later. I have a few more of the school jigsaws done – that should see to the orders – and a few spare.'

'Great.' Her hand strayed to the envelope in her bag. 'I was going to talk to you about the jigsaws actually.'

He raised an eyebrow.

They crossed the road to her shop and Lizzie waited till they were inside before she pulled the envelope out. 'These are lovely, they really are. I can write some lovely memories for them except – ' she pulled the last one and handed it to him, 'this one. I'm sorry, this is out of bounds.'

Jim glanced over and frowned. 'No use eh? Shame, I thought that one particularly evocative.'

Lizzie took her coat off, avoiding his eye. 'It is, that's the problem.' She took a deep breath and turned around. 'It was my father's barn. All the land along that lane belongs to my family – to me – I let it out.' She smiled. 'That's why I can afford to indulge my sentimentality by running a shop stocked with pretty, if useless trinkets.'

Jim smirked. If he noticed the piece of broken pottery on the shelf beside the postcard, he didn't pretend.

'But the barn field, I don't let out. Nobody would go there.'

He raised an eyebrow.

'They're superstitious around here.' She made a meal of smoothing her coat on the back of the chair so that she did not have to meet his eye. 'I can't rent out that barn because that is where my father died.'

There was a sharp intake of breath.

'That's where he killed himself one dark night when I was eleven years old.' She handed him the photo.

Jim took it and hung his head. 'Lizzie, I am so sorry, I had no idea.'

'Neither did I.' Lizzie surprised herself with how calm she felt. The shock of today's revelations made the intensity of her feelings for Jim, for everything, over the last few days seem foolish, exaggerated. She motioned him to sit down. 'I found out myself this morning. Sit and I'll tell you the story I couldn't put on paper. Then you'll understand why this jigsaw shouldn't be made.'

Jim sat and Lizzie stood leaning against the side of the table, staring into space as she recounted the events of those two days nearly forty years ago. She told him how she had stayed home afterwards to look after their mother, trying in some way to compensate for the pain she had caused by depriving her of a good husband. She told him how Anne had crumbled into a heap as she walked out of the dining room and refused to talk to anyone so that when Aunty

Margie suggested she take her up to Dublin, their mother had agreed.

'I think Bernie and Aunty Margie were the only people who could get through to Anne in those days.'

'So Bernie and your sister were friends even then?'

Lizzie frowned. 'They weren't as kids but they became friends afterwards. Bernie turned up to my father's funeral, which was nice of her.'

Seeing Jim didn't understand she continued. 'She had not been seen in Rathshannan since the famous tonsil departure – ' Lizzie smiled and blushed. 'What an innocent I was – she was pregnant of course, but she still turned up. They kept in touch after that.'

'Bernie sounds nice.'

'She is,' Lizzie smiled. 'You met her.'

Jim shook his head. 'I don't think so. I have a head for names and faces and I'm sure I haven't been introduced.'

'You weren't – but she was there the other night.'

He looked blank.

'After the fire? In Reardons? She gave you a sandwich?'

Jim screwed up his face as he replayed the scenes in his head. 'I don't think you're right, Lizzie. The only person I recall feeding me that night – apart from Teresa – was her formidable mother.'

'I know.' Lizzie swept some bits of fluff off the top of her table. 'That's who I'm talking about – Teresa Callaghan's mother is Bernie Collins nee Healey – '

Before she could say another word, Jim had pushed back his chair and was standing. His face was white and as he turned to Lizzie she couldn't tell if he was shocked or angry. 'I didn't know.'

Lizzie shrugged. 'Does it matter?'

He was standing with his face in his hands, rubbing his skin so hard that she could hear the rustle of palm on bristle. 'Mam, Gran? The twins called her Gran and Teresa referred to her only as Mam. I had no idea she was Bernie Healey.' He lifted his head. 'Christ, Lizzie – why didn't you tell me?' He rummaged in his satchel and pulled out a jigsaw box. Tearing the wrapping off, he emptied the contents on the table. Small wooden pieces fell onto the floor but it was the paper he was after. He unfolded it and smoothed it flat on the table. Then, running his finger down the page, he muttered to himself as he read through. When he was finished, he held it out to her. 'See? There's nothing here about all that.'

Lizzie looked from the page to him.

'You don't tell about Bernie – you just tell how it was, generally. There's no way anyone could know what happened, specifically.'

'I thought that was the idea. Black and white and shades of grey – nothing that ties these memories down to the specific – they're for everyone.'

And then it struck her.

*The memories I'm looking for aren't yours – they're mine.*

He wasn't talking about creating memories at all; he was talking about finding them. Nor had he picked 1969 at random.

'How old are you, Jim?' she asked him gently.

'Thirty-six.'

She smiled and nodded. 'You look older.'

He shrugged. 'Thanks.'

'So you were born in 1969?'

He took his wallet from his back pocket and slid a piece of paper from it. He handed it to her. *James Arthur Farrelly, 7lb 6oz, born 27ᵗʰ April 1970, St Bertrand's Home, Navan Road, Dublin.* Art Farrelly's son!

The paper shook in Lizzie's hand. Of course he was Art Farrelly's son – he looked familiar the first day he walked in here. He was taller than Art, or what Lizzie could remember of him, and his hair was darker, but he had the same easy manner with women. She remembered Art's swagger as he stood astride Anne's bike outside the church. While poor Bernie was above in Dublin carrying his child. She flushed angrily. 'Your father was a fly-by-night,' she said, handing the paper back to him.

Jim folded the page into his wallet and started to tidy the jigsaw back into the box. 'I met him,' he said. 'He's a potter – very good too.'

Lizzie sniffed in disapproval.

'He's married but he knew who I was straight away. When I went into the workshop, he slowed his wheel till the jug he was making drooped like splayed candle wax and when it stopped moving, he looked up and said "hello". He's a good guy – I like him.'

There was so much bile collected in Lizzie's throat that she wanted to spit. A good guy? A guy who gets his girlfriend pregnant and forgets her when she's packed off in her shame. Who then runs away, leaving poor Bernie to pick up the pieces? A destroyer of lives. She watched Jim's face and felt sorry for him; the father who abandoned him and his mother turns out to be a good guy? He destroys people's lives and lets Jim come here to make them relive it. 'Oh my God!' Her hand shot to her mouth as she realised the implications of what happened next – Jim and Teresa. She tried to steady her voice. 'So now you know Teresa Callaghan is your half-sister.'

He nodded. 'It's so obvious – can't think how I didn't see it sooner.'

'And what are you going to do about it?'

Jim shrugged. 'I'll have to go and see Bernie – tell her who I am. It's up to her what she wants to tell Teresa.'

*You came here looking for the love of a good woman,* Teresa said as she beamed into Jim's face. And he'd agreed. And now he would leave it to her mother to tell her? To pick up the pieces? Maybe he was more like his father than she thought. She turned her back on him.

Jim reached out and caught her arm. 'I'm sorry, Lizzie. I should have told you before but I wasn't sure how close I was to the truth. I didn't want to commit to finding it and then have the trail run cold.'

'How could it?' she rounded on him angrily. 'Your father sent you here and you came. You didn't need me to fill in the gaps. You didn't even need to make this lot up.' With a swipe she sent the jigsaw box and everything else on the table flying.

Jim surveyed the mess and then reached into his bag. 'It's what I do. Lizzie. I'm an artist. I turn wood and I take pictures – here.' He handed her a brochure.

On the front, his face stared back at her, shades of sepia against a dark background. Inside, it was laid out like a catalogue – beautiful wooden sculptures on bare floors against a wall covered in photographs. Nothing was cluttered yet it teemed with life. She flicked through to the end. 'You're very good,' she said eventually.

'Thanks. The jigsaws are a new venture. I decided to make them when I realised that I was not going to get all the answers by myself. I found my father easily enough. My mother had left me a photograph of him, which I was given when I turned eighteen. I never felt the need to follow it up and probably wouldn't have if his face hadn't turned up on a catalogue for a crafts exhibition. I couldn't be sure he was the same man – the one in the photo was only a boy. So I looked him up and I like him.'

'Despite what he did to your mother?'

Jim gritted his teeth. 'I don't know what he did to my mother, Lizzie – he wouldn't talk about her. All I know is that he loved her but she wouldn't have him. He tried to see her but she turned him away. He wanted to marry her.'

What! *And he with the wheel of another girl's bike pinned between his legs.* How could a grown man fall for that? So much for disdaining sentimentality.

'Did he really?' she asked, her voice cold.

Jim raised an eyebrow. 'You obviously don't believe him,' he said. 'I do.'

'So why didn't she let him make an honest woman of her then? The scandal of her pregnancy would have been forgotten if they married quickly.'

'I don't know.' Jim ran a hand through his hair. 'I really don't know, Lizzie. That's what I'm trying to find out. My father wouldn't tell me because he said it was my mother's story to tell – her choice and I was to respect it. He told me that she might not want to know me so I was to tread lightly. He didn't want her hurt. That's why I've been pussyfooting around looking for answers.'

Lizzie's shoulders slumped. 'Maybe your father's right.' She was thinking of Teresa. 'You could be opening Pandora's box.'

'My father wants to know me,' he said, 'but not my mother and I want to know why.'

'You can't be sure.' Teresa with her shining face and laughing eyes. 'Maybe you should leave now. Go before she finds out. She obviously wants to forget so what good can come of you bringing it all back?' She pointed to the jigsaw. 'I don't think you have any idea of the pain you can cause people when you start to dismantle their memories, Jim. In the last few weeks you have unwittingly taken apart the pieces of my life and I'm not even involved.'

'But you are,' he said. 'You're the one I needed to find.'

Lizzie looked at him, astonished. 'What's it got to do with me?'

'I don't know.' Jim looked like a lost boy. 'My father would tell me nothing – I had to find where he was from on my own and when I challenged him, he advised me to leave it be. When he realised I wouldn't he asked, for my mother's sake that I tread gently and be careful not to barge in. I pointed out that I couldn't be careful where I stepped if he wasn't going to tell me where I needed to avoid so in the end he said. "Find the younger Flynn sister. She's local and she'll know the stories that are to be known. Ask her."'

Lizzie's forehead went cold. Art Farrelly sent Jim Nealon to Rathshannan to find her so that she could tell him about his mother? She shook her head. 'I don't understand, Jim. None of this has anything to do with me. Bernie Healey got pregnant and went to Dublin to have a baby – you – and give him away. Then she came back a year later and now she works locally and has a daughter and grandchildren. Sorry if I'm raining on your parade but on the face of it, there's no mystery. It happens. Her life is settled and you are not part of it. End of story. You father was right – leave it.'

Jim was rummaging in his wallet again. This time it was folded pieces of foil, sweet papers. 'I got some of this every year on my birthday. Mum never said who it was from – only that I was loved and never to forget it.' He unfolded the paper and held it under Lizzie's nose. She could smell fudge.

'So?'

'So my mother stayed loving me for years – enough to do this. Yet she didn't keep me and didn't marry my father. It doesn't make sense.'

'So all this is to satisfy your curiousity?'

Jim leaned close to her, his face angry. 'I'm the jigsaw maker, Lizzie. I put the pieces together. Don't stop me now –

it's nearly done.' And he picked up his satchel and turned and left the shop.

Lizzie watched his back as he marched away – the jigsaw maker who had taken the picture that was her life and thrown it in the air and when it fell back into place she found that it was a different picture altogether. Her real picture was smaller, no recriminations, no guilt. The pieces left over belonged to her father and his anguish; to her mother and her madness. They were not Lizzie's. At the far end of the street, Jim was barely visible now – without her distance glasses. At least he was not headed for Anne's where she and Bernie would be busy, stirring and setting. She hoped he wouldn't go there too soon, throw Bernie and Teresa's lives into the air before she had a chance to talk to Anne – ask her what should be done next.

She got a sweeping brush from the cupboard and began to sweep all the things she had flung across the floor into a pile in the middle to pick them up.

*

And because she was crouched down, Jason and Kylie didn't see her when they peeped in the window hoping to catch her eye so that they could tell her the news. No wonder Reardons was so crowded at lunchtime with all those people celebrating the great news.

Teresa Callaghan had just gotten engaged.

*

255

In the end, Lizzie stayed in the shop to pack her order and drop it around to the school on her way home. The house was quiet when she entered but its stillness didn't calm her as it usually did. She went from room to room, removing the odd flower that was past its best, the odd leaf that was drooping. She changed her duvet cover and sheet, bundled up the washing and went out to the utility room to pack it into the machine. As the sound of gushing water filled the room she tapped her fingers on the sideboard and looked around for what she could usefully do next. The house was tidy, the fridge was full and there was a humming in her ears. All the revelations of the day jostled with the excitement and tiredness of the previous ones till she felt that her head would burst. She turned on her heel, grabbed her coat from the hook and left the house.

Driving along the road with the radio blaring, Lizzie tried to clear her head. Too much was happening in her life and yet, on the face of it, everything was just the same. Poor Da. The memory of his great coat swinging out from the door and catching her in its warm embrace hit hard and there were tears rolling down her face. She swerved to avoid a car coming in the opposite direction and pulled up on the side, sweating and crying. Where had her life gone? Had that come up and nearly hit her too and she stumbling blindly along, keeping her head down for fear of anyone finding out that she was there. Lizzie Flynn, you are a fool. She opened the door and easing an unsteady leg on to the grass, looked around.

The spindly iron gates of the graveyard loomed up in front of her. On either side of them, dark blackthorn bushes stood guard and Lizzie shivered. She hated this place. Looking through the gate she could see over to the far corner where her parents were buried, their graves close together surrounded by a neat low border of stones and on top of them gravel – low maintenance and insurance against weeds. She sniffed. Even the job of looking after their parents after their deaths had fallen to her. Just as Anne disappeared and left Mam for Lizzie to look after in life, so she had left her grave for Lizzie to look after in death. Lizzie had seen her mother decently buried and then paid the churchwarden a small stipend to keep the grave tidy. She visited it herself for All Souls' Day every November but that was it – no need to wallow any further in the guilt she associated with her parents.

She lifted the latch and pushed the gate away from her. It wobbled as it swung, creaking in protest at this early evening intrusion. When it ground to a halt against some pebbles, Lizzie picked her way over to the far side where her parents lay. A modest headstone nestled in the centre of the plot.

Lizzie stood starting at the gravestone as if she was seeing it for the first time. It was the first time she had stood at this spot without a trickle of fear running the length of her spine as she read that inscription and heard the question people asked as they read it too.

'Only 41? Poor fellow, and he with young children. What did he die of, I wonder?'

And she would stand there and pretend she hadn't heard it because if she did, she might have to lift her head and meet their eyes and say, he was killed – I did it. Now she felt none of that. Now she was the one to ask.

She knelt on the stone border and laid a hand on the cold earth.

'Da,' she whispered, 'why did you do it? Mam wasn't bad. She couldn't help it. All her demons were her own and you should have tried to help her. You shouldn't have run off and taken the coward's way out.' For the first time since Anne told her, she recognised the emotion that was coursing through her – anger, pure white freezing anger. Her whole body was shaking with it. She thought of the two young girls standing in the barn loft, with a watery morning light coming through the window, rigid with horror at the blood-spattered body they had just found. She thought of their mother's face when they came down the lane hand in hand and stood in front of her. She hadn't even asked them what was wrong. She held Lizzie's cardigan a while but when she came back into the house she looked more sober than she ever had before.

'Daddy won't be home, will he?' Her face was set.

Anne shook her head.

Their mother nodded and then turned on her heel and picked up the phone. 'I need Sergeant Murphy to come here now.' And then she dropped the receiver and headed straight to the larder where she got out a bottle of gin and put it to her head.

Lizzie crumbled the cold earth and watched it fall between her fingers. Poor Mam – you were never sober again. Did you think it was your fault? Is that why you stayed in your twilight world? Did you hate Anne because you were afraid she blamed you and did you think I was too young to matter? The soil made a mound and she pressed her finger into the centre of it until it was shaped like a bowl. Then she picked a tiny yellow flower from a clump of weed that was growing by the graveside and stuck it in the middle.

'I don't blame you, Mam,' she said. 'You were ill, not wicked, and none of what you did was intentional.' She remembered her mother's gratitude for every kindness Lizzie showed her in later years and how she would slur her praise for her daughter to whoever would listen. All Mam's venom was saved for Anne.

'And you, Da,' she said as she stood and wiped the grit from her knees, 'you shouldn't have done that. You took the easy way out and left the rest of us to pick up the pieces and put them back together. And do you know what?' Her voice shook with anger. 'We haven't been able to, because you can't put something together when there are pieces missing!' She flung her arms wide. 'Look at me, wherever you are, you should have been one of the pieces but you, you bloody coward – you weren't here. I was – every agonising step of the way. Look at me! I'm not your little Lizzie any more. I'm a middle-aged woman, given to mood swings and hot flushes and do you know what I've done with my life? Sweet feck all!' She kicked the gravel. 'Damn you for leaving us like that. Damn you for making me spend my whole life feeling guilty.'

She stormed back to the gate. I've paid my dues, I've given you my whole life and none of it was my fault. Each of you, in your weakness, tied me to this place and I don't want to be here any more. In the car the radio blared into life. The slot was the 'golden oldies' and when the gritty strains of *Take me home, country road*, squeezed through the speakers and filled the air around her, she laughed out loud.

I don't even know where home is, she thought as she drove. The fields and hedges around Rathshannan that she had looked at all her life seemed alien to her now because she had lived there under false pretences. And she didn't want to any more. Now she was free she could do anything, go anywhere she liked. She pulled up in front of her house. It was a nice place, modern and convenient for the village and the main road. It wouldn't be too hard to let out while Lizzie took off and made up for lost time. Rathshannan could get along fine without her.

*

By the time she had taken her coat off, her plans were made. Jim would have to reveal himself to Bernie and God knows what floodgates that would open. Teresa was bound to be heartbroken but Lizzie reckoned, if she chose her time carefully and asked Teresa to take over the shop in her absence, she would at least be set up financially for the time being and that would ease the blow. Once the story of Bernie's long-lost son reached the high street there'd be no stopping it. Everybody would want to claim a bit of it, touch the excitement, and the recollections and reminiscences would be everywhere. And people would be bound to remember that was the year everything happened: that Bill Healey beat hell out of Art Farrelly for what he did to his daughter; that Jack Flynn put a gun to his head; that Maureen Flynn put a bottle to hers; and young Anne broke down and went away. And Lizzie inherited the rest.

And then all the memories would be in the air like so many colourful jigsaws, the pieces embellished with the personalities of those who caught them and slotted them into place. Lizzie would have no part of any of it. She had relived the nightmares; she had no need to relive the memories. She went up to her room and pulled a heavy suitcase from the top of the wardrobe. She opened the catches and sneezed as it sprang open and years of imprisoned dust flew out.

She started to pack.

*

Dublin was a million miles from Rathshannan. It took ages to reach the small hotel she'd booked and work out how to find the car park. The receptionist was efficient, indifferent, and handed over the keys without apparently making eye contact at all. Lizzie felt anonymous for the first time in her life. It was like freefalling. She had flown the nest and hadn't a clue where she was headed or where she might land. She looped the keys over her finger as she walked the corridor looking for her room number. Outside, the city streets teemed with life and she wondered how people coped with the noise.

Anne's voice was fraught with worry when Lizzie eventually called her.

'It's like the opposite of a mid-life crisis,' Lizzie kept her voice light, confident. 'I just wanted to spread my wings and there was no point in hanging around. If I'd waited, I'd have had cold feet and it might never have happened.'

Anne didn't sound convinced. She'd been round to the house but there was nobody there. She wasn't happy about Jim having keys. 'For God's sake, Liz, you don't even know him. He could be anyone.'

Lizzie smiled. 'He's someone all right. Go talk to him for yourself. He's okay.' At the other end of the line, Anne was holding her breath. 'Don't worry – really. I just needed a holiday. I'll send you a contact address when I decide where to next.'

'Don't you even know where you're going?'

'I intended to plan that once I got here.'

'Oh, for – ' Anne tutted in disapproval.

There was a knock on the hotel room door.

'Anne, I have to go – I'll call you. Bye.' Lizzie put the phone down. Outside, the maid had left a tray with afternoon tea and as Lizzie ate she wondered what she would do next. Despite the rumble of traffic outside and the steady throb of city life beyond it she felt she could sleep for a week. The sounds of cars crossing the speed ramps outside the hotel set up a rhythm in time to the beating of her heart. When the lights further down the road turned red it slowed and she could feel the tension of the day's travelling seeping out of her. Back home it would all be happening but none of it was happening to her. She was on her own adventure. She folded her hands on her lap and as she drifted off she could feel the touch of another hand in hers, pulling her upwards, and she was a little girl again, standing in Dublin Zoo watching the elephant pacing backwards and forwards. As she watched he suddenly turned and looked at her and it appeared that there was a smile on his face. From either side of his dusty body, two huge wings sprouted and then he was in the air, high over the enclosure, heading for freedom.

And Lizzie was on his back.

*

It felt like a week later when she opened her eyes. The room was in semi-darkness and outside there was an intermittent rumble as the city woke. Lizzie squinted at the bedside radio – ten past six. She had slept for thirteen hours! She pulled the cover off and looked out. The lights of another world blinked back at her.

On the table there was a folder with suggestions for excursions and places to shop in it. Lizzie made herself a pot of tea and sat down to see what she might do with her day. There were historical tours, seaside tours, literary tours. She shut the folder and sighed. Already the noise outside the window was louder and she couldn't think. She needed somewhere quieter.

By afternoon, she had found her bearings and checked out of that hotel heading for a cheaper one on the city outskirts. The owner of a guesthouse she stopped at greeted her like a long-lost friend and showed her to a bright room overlooking the sea.

'You'll be comfortable here,' she said. 'How long are you staying?'

Lizzie shrugged. 'Until I'm ready to go home.'

The woman's eyes darted to Lizzie's ring finger. 'As long as it takes.' Then she patted the already smooth pillows. 'You'll be comfortable here. The bathroom's across the landing and there's a phone in the foyer if you need to make any calls.'

Lizzie indicated her bag. 'I have a mobile, don't worry.'

'Grand so.' The woman held out a hand. 'I'm Geraldine by the way, call if you need anything.'

'Thanks.' Lizzie fought the temptation to laugh out loud. Geraldine was fizzing with curiosity, dying to know why a middle-aged woman would turn up in the middle of the day, looking for a room to stay in indefinitely. She was about to leave when a thought struck Lizzie.

'Geraldine, is the Zoo far from here?'

Geraldine frowned. 'Long enough as the crow flies but it's a bit of a palaver in a car, all right.' She shut her eyes and drew a map in the air with her index finger. Eventually, a smile broke out and she looked at Lizzie. 'No, actually, it's not hard at all. You just have to drive towards the city and turn west at the right time. I'll get you a map.'

*

The Navan Road was busy as Lizzie drove along it the following day. She watched the houses crawl by, pausing at some to see if they had been there forty years ago – if they sparked off that shiver of recollection in her spine, and

264

annoying the other drivers queued behind her, keen to be free of the city. At the big church she stopped a while for pedestrian lights and watched the people cross. If her memory served her right, the Home wasn't too far now. Her thought was to go there – stick her head inside the door and get a feel of the place. Maybe get a feel of how young Bernie Healey might have felt at fourteen when she arrived there alone, pregnant, in disgrace. And how she might have felt when she left it six months later, heart and womb emptied out. The lights turned green and Lizzie eased the car forward.

Three minutes later she spotted a stone wall on her right. From a distance it looked newer than it ought to be but it was in the right place with a bus shelter outside where once there was a stop. Where she had seen Bernie in the yellow light. She slowed as she came to it and ignoring the beeping of a motorist behind her, turned to look.

The Home wasn't there. Instead, a semi-circle of modern town houses faced her. There wasn't a trace of the older building. Lizzie tutted and speeded up. Silly old woman – what did she expect? This wasn't prudish Ireland of the 1960's – it was the twenty-first century, for God's sake. Girls didn't have to be locked away any more, their shame hidden. They didn't need a wedding band on their fingers to qualify to hold a baby in their arms. Poor Bernie. Lizzie pressed on the accelerator and sped away.

When she reached the roundabout at the end of the road, she swung left without thinking about it. Signs directed her to the Zoo and she shrugged. Might as well cover all of memory lane while she was at it; lay all the ghosts to rest. She joined the queue outside the Zoo's car park.

*

The Zoo wasn't as she remembered it either. Modern ticket booths and a smart shop lined the entrance and visitors were directed to one side with information boards everywhere. Signs urged them not to feed the animals, not to aggravate them. Lizzie smiled – that was an improvement. At the gorilla enclosure there was nothing to be seen. The female had just given birth and wasn't on show while she nursed her baby. All the enclosures and spaces seemed so much bigger. Lizzie relaxed and let her mind wander. Nothing was like it was when she was a child.

Until she reached the elephants.

Around the circular elephant enclosure a crowd was waiting expectantly. Inside, a young bull elephant pawed the ground as he watched the keeper come towards him with a bucket. The keeper was lecturing the crowd on eating habits and warning them against throwing plastic wrappers on the ground that might blow in and end up being ingested by his charge. Most eyes were on him as he dipped his hands into the bucket and took out fistfuls of stalks, which he dropped on the ground for the elephant to pick up. The crowd 'oohed' and 'aahed' as the huge creature lumbered around, sweeping the stalks under his trunk and snorting up dust and grit, seemingly oblivious to the onlookers. The space he had now seemed bigger than the tiny one of her childhood but it still only took a couple of minutes to walk all the way around the edge. As he passed Lizzie she tried to catch his eye, willing him to look at her so that he would know she didn't think this was clever, didn't think it was kind. That if she could, she would give him wings.

'Excuse me, are you okay?'

Lizzie turned to see a young woman with a pushchair beside her. The child in it had broken off watching the elephant and was now studying Lizzie instead.

The woman waited for her to answer. When Lizzie said nothing she fumbled in a large baby sack and took out a box of tissues. 'Here,' she said, pulling out a fistful. 'I have to travel prepared.' She jerked her head towards the child, his face smeared in snot and ice cream.

Lizzie took the wad from her and putting a tentative hand to her cheek was surprised to find that it was soaked with tears.

The young woman smiled. 'You get days like that, don't you?'

'Do you?'

The woman nodded. 'I do. It's not that I'm sad or anything – just tired and overwhelmed. I need a good cry and then I feel better.' She reached down and wiped the smears from her son's mouth. 'Chocolate works just as well, of course, but that's fattening and I'm still trying to shift the weight after this fellow.'

'You look as if you've managed it okay.'

'Bless you, that's what I like to hear.' She stuffed dirty tissues into her bag and straightened. 'You don't fancy a coffee, do you?'

Lizzie blinked back another wave that threatened to spill down her face at the suggestion. The woman was right. She wasn't sad, not consciously anyway, but all of a sudden, the intensity of emotion that bombarded her in the last few weeks was completely overwhelming. It washed over her and she was sure that if she flapped her arms fast enough she would actually take off. All around her the crowd stirred and she turned to see the elephant squat and dump a large foul-smelling faeces in the middle of his enclosure. It lay there steaming while the children squealed in delight and the adults turned away in disgust.

The child in the pushchair grabbed Lizzie's coat. 'A poo! A poo!'

'Oh Lord.' His mother sighed. 'That'll be the highlight of his day now.'

The little boy arched back in the chair, straining at the harness and kicked his legs. Bits of ice cream cone went flying and Lizzie bent to brush them off her coat.

'You need the coffee as much as I do,' she said. 'I'm Lizzie.'

'Avril.' The young woman held out her hand momentarily then retracted it. 'Actually no, most of the ice cream landed here. Take the handshake as read.' She reached into the pushchair and brushed her son's fringe out of his eyes. 'Say bye to Nellie, Sean.'

'Bye Nellie, bye poo!' He waved enthusiastically.

Lizzie turned to follow them to the café. A quick glance over her shoulder as she left found the elephant standing defiantly over his production while the keeper went to get a shovel. She paused a minute watching him, lifting her hand in farewell.

Avril stopped and waited for her. 'That's the answer to the age old question, you know,' she said.

'What is?' Lizzie fell into line.

'That steaming mountain of "poo" as my son so politely calls it – it's the answer to an age old question...' She smiled at Lizzie expectantly.

Lizzie raised an eyebrow. 'Which is?

Avril stopped and pointed to where the keeper was now loading the shovel while the onlookers muttered their delighted disgust. 'Why elephants don't fly!'

Lizzie looked from the keeper to the young woman in front of her and back.

Avril looked uncomfortable. 'I mean, pigeons are bad enough.'

Lizzie exploded. She clutched her sides as the tide of laughter rose and filled the air around her. Her stomach clenched and tears poured down her face. All around, people stopped and smiled. A man touched Avril's arm. 'Must have been a funny one.'

Avril shook her head. 'It wasn't that great.' She looked as if she wanted to walk away.

Lizzie reached to stop her. 'I'm not crazy,' she said, wiping her eyes. 'Oh dear, I needed that.' Suppressing the hiccups, she took a deep breath and tried to calm herself. 'It's not easy to explain but I came here today to find something – a memory, a solution, an explanation. I'm not even sure what, to be honest. I think I was even looking for the elephants – hoping they wouldn't be there.'

Avril shrugged. 'I have the same relationship with the flesh on my thighs.'

Lizzie tried to laugh but managed only a hiccup. 'Now I really need that coffee. You still on?'

Avril nodded. 'Why not? I don't get a reaction like that every day.'

\*

As Avril drank her coffee, Lizzie told her story. By the time she was finished Avril was holding a sandwich limp in her hand, staring.

'Sweet Mother of God, Lizzie! What a story!'

Lizzie smiled. 'Did I do the right thing?' she asked. 'Running away?'

Avril shook her head. 'No! The fat's in the fire now and there'll be sparks all over Kilkenny. I would have stayed for the grand finale. I mean, when Bernie finds her son – or he finds her – and Teresa realises he's her long-lost brother.' She stuffed the escaping lettuce into her sandwich and took a bite. 'I hate loose ends. I'd want to see how it all turns out. So my advice is to get back there and see the story played out. It's Rathshannan you need to make peace with, not Dublin Zoo.'

'Aren't you the wise one?' Lizzie made a face. 'Though you're probably right.' In his chair, Sean stirred and Lizzie smiled at him. 'In any case, I am very pleased that I came here and met the two of you. You are good to listen to my ramblings and I think maybe you're right – I should go home. Oh! I forgot!' She reached over and caught Avril's arm. 'I completely left out something. I should explain why it was that your joke was so funny. It's not relevant to the Bernie/Jim story but it will explain why I am forever beholden to you for earth-bound elephants. D'you remember I mentioned Sister Cillian at the beginning? Well, she had a story of her own... ' and she related that as well.

'Poor Lizzie. Were you hoping to fly too?'

'I think I probably was.'

Avril smiled. She reached over and patted Lizzie's hand as if it were Sean's. 'And now do you understand why it's much better for you and everyone else to keep your feet firmly on the ground?'

Lizzie laughed. 'I do – though if you're suggesting I might be a threat to the general public, airborne, I can assure you that is categorically not the case. I'm still perfectly in control of my functions, thank you!' She turned to get her coat from the back of the chair.

*

Outside, the sun was high and Lizzie's spirits lifted with it. The two women parted company still smiling.

'Thank you for letting me offload all my ramblings on you,' Lizzie said.

'Hey, I was glad of the company.' Avril wrapped Lizzie in a warm hug. 'Will you go home now?'

'Probably. I don't think there's anything more for me to do here.'

Avril held her at arm's length and studied her face a minute.

'What? What are you looking at me like that for? A minute ago you were advising me to go home and watch the last jigsaw piece fall into place and now you've got that quizzical face that suggests I've missed the point. My sister does that – it's the "poor Lizzie" face.'

Avril dropped her arms and shrugged. 'Poor nothing. You're free as a bird. I was just wondering, if you were planning to stay on another couple of days... '

'Well?'

'Don't you want to find out the end of the runaway nun story?' Before Lizzie could object, she raised a hand. 'I know you think it ended. They fell in love and ran away but I'm a sucker for a romance. Don't you ever wonder what happened? If they were happy, if they had kids, if they stayed in the bus business?'

Lizzie shrugged, 'Not really.'

Avril's eyes were sparkling. 'Oh, go on, Miss Marple, see if Barrett's Buses still exists. If it does, follow it up; if not, you haven't lost anything.'

Lizzie shrugged. She wasn't particularly interested about finding Sister Cillian, or Mrs Barrett again. She had probably died by now anyway.

'Come on,' Avril jigged her arm, 'I can see you're weakening.'

Lizzie smiled.

'And as I can't follow you home to see what happens when Jim meets Bernie – I can at least help you to find where your flying elephant landed. Why don't you ask your landlady?'

Lizzie held out her hand. 'Why not?'

'Or get a hold of the Golden Pages and have a look in there. Oops, here's my bus.' Avril swung the pushchair around and ran off towards where a bus was just pulling up in the distance. 'Bye!'

'Bye!' Lizzie called after her. She waited till Avril was safely boarded before she set off for the car park. As she joined the traffic on the Navan Road, she felt more relaxed than she had for years. She passed the gates where St Bertrand's used to be without even a second glance. Everything that had happened there had happened to other people and wasn't anything to do with her at all. She was just an onlooker. Avril was right. She wasn't a flying elephant heading to freedom at all. She wasn't even running away to; she was running away from. And she didn't have to.

Forty-five minutes later when she pulled up outside the guesthouse she was still smiling. She'd ask the landlady about bus companies and maybe they'd turn up something and she could find out the end of Cillian's story. She hoped it was a happy one. Either way, it wouldn't affect her. It was just another jigsaw to be pieced together and then Lizzie could put it back in its box.

Nothing to do with her.

*

Lizzie rang Anne that evening. Avril's confidence that she should be there rubbed off and she decided to give Dublin one week of sightseeing before setting off home. Anne took ages to answer the phone and when she did, her voice was hoarse.

'Your timing's perfect, Lizzie. I've been in bed with a stinking head cold all day – everyone has it.'

'Absolutely everyone?'

'That I know of. I got it from Bernie who reckons she got a chill the night of the fire. The twins, Teresa, Matt... '

'Jim?'

'Haven't seen him around. How are you anyway?'

Lizzie told her she'd been at the Zoo.

Anne laughed. 'Revisiting your childhood?'

'You'd better believe it.' Lizzie marvelled at her sister's ability to be close to the truth yet completely fail to see it. 'Actually, talking of childhood, did you ever wonder what happened to Sister Cillian and Mr Barrett – afterwards, I mean, like how their lives turned out?'

'Who? That nun you had in sixth class? Never.'

'But you met them in Dublin.'

'Oh yea, well, too long ago.'

'What do you remember about them?'

'Very little. He had a small bus company which they both worked in, they were married, that's it.' Even through a telephone wire, Lizzie could sense her sister losing interest.

'Do you recall where?'

'Oh Lizzie, I dunno, somewhere by the sea, I can't remember.'

'North or south of the Liffey?'

Anne sounded annoyed now. 'North, I think, like I said – I don't remember. Look, I feel rough; I need to rest. You take care of yourself and come home soon.' She put the phone down and Lizzie was left with her mobile crackling in her hand.

She looked at it in amazement. Must be a bad dose to have Anne contrary. Oh well. If everybody was laid up, Jim wouldn't have had a chance to introduce himself to Bernie yet so that picture was still in the air. She might as well find the last piece of the runaway nun story.

*

The following morning Lizzie woke to the smell of cooked bacon wafting up the stairs. Geraldine, who appeared to be on a one-woman crusade to fatten up culchies, would be piling a plate for her if she didn't get down and stop her. She dressed quickly and headed for the small dining room overlooking the sea. Geraldine came in and out with dishes laden with food.

'Geraldine?' Lizzie said, in a vain attempt to stop herself eating the biggest breakfast of her life, 'Are there any bus companies in Howth?'

Geraldine paused, spatula in hand. 'I don't think so. More scrambled?'

Lizzie held her hands up in protest. 'Not another bite, I'm begging you. This is delicious.'

'There's plenty of buses that go all the way up to Malahide and into the city – is that what you were asking about.'

275

Lizzie shook her head. 'Not really. I wanted to look up... an old friend. She married a fellow and they set up a small bus company in Dublin – at least I think they did. They lived by the coast, north side.'

Geraldine shook her head. 'That could be anywhere. Is this recently or what?'

'What.' Lizzie smiled. 'Forty years ago, more like.'

Geraldine put her hand on her knee and lowered herself slowly onto the chair opposite. 'Let me think. So this was before? Called what?'

'He was a Mr Barrett.'

Geraldine's eyes lit up. 'Barrett! Bill Barrett! Sure of course I know him.' She looked so pleased that Lizzie's gut wrenched. It could hardly be the same man.

'Do you know where he lives?'

'He doesn't – he died, oh, must be ten, fifteen years ago now.' She shut her eyes to clarify the memory. 'But he'd stopped the buses long before that.'

'Oh dear, so I haven't much hope of tracking him down then.'

Geraldine got up. 'Afraid not. Anyway the Dart's taken most of the city traffic so there's not much call for a small bus company in Howth.' She piled the plates for the other guests into the oven to warm them and turned to leave the room. 'Though to be perfectly honest,' she said as she left, 'I wouldn't get on that train myself in the night. You wouldn't know what gurriers you'd find on it. I always give young Barrett a ring and go with him.'

'Young Barrett?'

'The son.' Geraldine looked at her as if it was obvious. 'I told you. They gave up the buses and started in the taxi business.'

'And they're still there? Is it far?'

'A couple of miles up the road and I hope they're still there,' she chuckled, 'otherwise I'm stuck for a lift to bingo on Friday.' She pulled a small business card off a notice board by the doorway. 'They're reasonable too. You should give them a try.'

'Thanks – I'll write down the details and put this back.'

'Don't worry.' Geraldine pointed to a small pot heaped with cards. 'There are plenty more.'

Lizzie shoved the card into her pocket, her heart racing. What a small world – what a hoot! Geraldine was already greeting a sleepy American couple who'd arrived late last night so she wouldn't interrupt and ask if Mrs Barrett was alive. She'd take a trip up to Howth anyway and have a wander around. If she found the place, well and good; if, not, no matter. Cillian had children and they were carrying on the family business.

A happy ever after ending.

*

'Can I help you?' Even if he had appeared at the far ends of the earth, Lizzie would have recognised Mr Barrett's son. He was a clone of his father, same ruddy complexion, same broad smile.

Lizzie reddened. 'Maybe,' she said, 'I was looking for – em.'

'A taxi maybe?' He was smiling.

'Oh, yes, of course,' Lizzie grinned. 'It's an age thing.'

He rubbed the top of his head where his hair was thinning. 'Tell me about it. ' He motioned her to sit down.

'I came up on the Dart,' she said, 'but I fancied a less crowded trip home. The lady in the guesthouse where I'm staying gave me this.' She held out the card.

Young Mr Barrett smiled. 'They're my best customers, the guesthouse ladies, but... ' he scanned the computer monitor in front of him. 'I'm afraid all my fellows are out at the minute. Do you want to hang on? There's a nice coffee shop around the corner you could go to or you can try some of our fearsome brew.'

Lizzie smiled. 'I'm sure yours will be fine, white, no sugar, thanks.' She took the scalding beaker from him and put it on the desk while he turned his attention to the radio receiver in the corner from which garbled messages were being issued. To Lizzie they were unintelligible but after a lengthy exchange with one he turned and smiled at her. 'If it's only to Sutton, I can get a fellow back here for you in ten minutes. How's the coffee?'

'Hot.' Lizzie leaned back in the chair and looked at the hundreds of photos covering the walls. Some were quite old and even at a distance, one looked familiar. She went over to examine it more closely. Her heart jumped. 'Good Lord! I don't believe it!' It was the photograph that Sister Cillian took on the day of that school outing back in '69. They'd lined up outside the bus with Mr Barrett standing on the step while Cillian fussed around trying to get a shot. The excitement at the prospect of the adventure ahead was evident on their faces. She scanned the photo to find herself, whispering. *Patricia Whittle and Kathleen Mullen and Frances Meredith...*

'Sorry?'

Lizzie turned around. 'I was talking to myself.' She pointed to the picture. I'm in that.' She ran her finger along the front row. 'Look, the skinny one with the desperate haircut.'

'You don't say!'

'Really, I can remember it being taken.'

He looked momentarily uncomfortable then smiled. 'A momentous day – my father loved that picture.'

Lizzie smiled. She turned away from him again. 'You wouldn't believe the excitement of those outings.'

'Ah, the old buses were great – coaches we have to call them nowadays.'

'You know that one existed till a couple of weeks ago, then it was destroyed in a fire. A fellow was renovating it and one of the kids helping him had an accident with a cigarette and that was the end of that.'

'Bloody kids. I have three myself, and they're all divils.' He smiled affectionately at a photograph on the desk. The middle child, a girl, had the look of her grandmother about her. Lizzie decided to go for it.

'I can't believe that,' she said. 'Your mother was a stickler for discipline.' She smiled at him. 'I learned more from her than from any of the others.'

'That's good to hear.'

No point in coming this far and not seeing it through. 'Is she – ?'

'Still around?' He laughed. 'She is, the tough old bird. My father's dead thirteen years now but my mother – we'll have to have her put down!' A young man came through the door and they both turned to him. 'James, could you do a quick run down to Geraldine Brady's on the coast road with Mrs... ?

'Flynn, Miss Flynn.' Lizzie stood up and held out her hand. 'Well, it was good to meet you anyway. Please give my regards to your mother. Tell her I remember her fondly and can still draw the Irish coastline freehand.'

'I will,' he said, smiling.

The driver chatted to Lizzie on the short journey home and when he dropped her off, refused payment. 'Mr B said it was on the house, seeing as you're an old friend of his ma's.'

'That's very kind,' Lizzie handed him a five-euro note. 'And that's for you – as I don't know your mother at all.'

'Neither did my father!' the fellow said, stuffing the note into his top pocket. 'Thanks! Call us again if you need a lift.' And he drove off leaving Lizzie laughing on the pavement.

*

Lizzie was snoozing when Geraldine knocked on the door later that afternoon. 'Call for you!'

She leapt off the bed in a panic. There must be something wrong for her to be contacted here. She was halfway down the stairs before she realised that it couldn't be from Rathshannan. People there had her mobile number, they wouldn't know where she was staying. She picked up the receiver. 'Hello?'

'Annie, is that you?' The woman's voice was shaky.

'No, I think you have a wrong number.'

'Oh, I'm sorry. I was looking for Miss Flynn.'

'I'm Miss Flynn, Lizzie Flynn.'

'Elizabeth! What a surprise!' The voice cracked into focus as the years rolled back. Sister Cillian. Lizzie found herself checking that her collar was neat and her hair tidy. As her mouth opened and closed a few times she found she really wasn't sure what to say. Cillian came to the rescue.

'When Dermot told me that a Miss Flynn was asking after me I thought he meant your sister. Well! Little Elizabeth. I should have guessed when he said about the outline of Ireland. You were always a neat girl.'

'You never mentioned,' Lizzie was smiling.

'Doesn't do to give girls notions.' There was a pause. 'Are you in Dublin for a while?' and before Lizzie had a chance to answer. 'Are you busy tomorrow teatime?'

When she admitted to no plans, Cillian invited her to tea – a good opportunity to catch up on old times. Lizzie accepted and put the phone down, her cheeks burning. What a hoot! Tea with Sister Cillian. She rushed back upstairs to call Anne but she was out. Lizzie frowned. She hadn't sounded well enough to be gallivanting. She thought to ring Teresa but there was no point really. She was starting to miss home already and decided not to bother waiting the week. After seeing Cillian there'd be little point in hanging on. Sightseeing alone might be a lonely business. She'd get her packing done now and tell Geraldine that she would leave tomorrow. As she placed her neatly folded clothes back into the case she found herself smiling. Some runaway you are, Lizzie Flynn. You haven't managed a week out of the place. She laid a fresh outfit for the evening on the bed and started to get ready for her shower. There was a fizz of excitement in her chest as she washed. It was less than a week on the outside but she was a million years forward on the inside. No need to run away at all. Tea and a chat with Sister Cillian – Mrs Barrett – and then she was going home.

\*

If forty years had been tough on Lizzie they were kind to Sister Cillian. When the taxi pulled up outside a small bungalow, Lizzie found herself being greeted by a little old lady with white hair and rosy cheeks. Although she was wearing glasses now it wasn't that which made her look so different. She turned to usher Lizzie into the house, as straight-backed as ever, and Lizzie could see what it was. All the tension, the intensity that Sister Cillian had always carried with her was gone and in its place, a serene grandmother.

'In here, sit yourself down.' She indicated a chair by the fire with a glass of port on a small table beside it. 'It's good for your digestion.' She picked up her own glass and sipped.

Lizzie followed suit, fighting the temptation to laugh. Crusty old Cillian feeding her alcohol at five in the afternoon!

As if she could read her thoughts, Cillian leaned forward. 'You must call me Kitty,' she said. 'Your sister always did.'

'Did she?'

Kitty took another sip. 'When she was in Dublin, she did.'

'I hadn't realised you saw so much of her. Did she study near here?'

Kitty paused and looked at Lizzie closely. She rolled the port around her mouth a couple of times before swallowing it. She put her glass down and then smiled brightly. 'But it is Elizabeth who has come to visit me.' She rested both hands in her lap. 'Tell me all about your life, my dear. What did you go on to do? What brings you to Dublin now?'

If it struck Lizzie that the conversation had been veered off in a different direction, she wasn't being given time to think about it. She shrugged. 'I stayed at home and looked after my mother after my father died.' Kitty clucked sympathetically. 'And I ran the farm.'

'On your own?'

Lizzie explained how most of the fields and some of the outbuildings, except for the barn, were let out – a steady income sufficient for an alcoholic widow and her unambitious spinster daughter. Kitty shut her eyes at the description but she didn't interrupt. Then Lizzie told her about their mother's death and how Anne came back and Lizzie moved out. When she finished she was smiling. 'You must come and visit it some day.'

Kitty shook her head. 'Oh, I don't know if I could. Even if nobody knew who I was, I don't think I could go back. Too much water under that bridge.'

'Was it so awful for you?'

Kitty nodded. 'If you're not in the right place, Elizabeth, even if it's fine for everyone else, it's the wrong place.'

Lizzie nodded. 'I know what you mean.' She looked around the cosy family room. 'That's what I'm doing in Dublin. I thought Rathshannan wasn't going to be the right place for me for a while so I ran away.' She drained the glass. 'It was a good move. I've found out a lot about myself.' She reached into her bag. Wedged in the pocket was a postcard. She passed it over. 'I needed the break away, however short, to discover that I am not a flying elephant nor was meant to be.'

Kitty looked at the picture and her eyes were bright. 'Well, goodness me.'

For a few minutes the two women sat in companionable silence. Lizzie studied the face of the old woman opposite her. Sister Cillian, in her day, was a formidable figure – guardian of morality and possessor of all facts known to man and some known only to women. She managed classrooms full of girls with ages varying by up to three years and experiences varying by a lifetime and had managed to speak to them all.

Eventually, Kitty eased herself out of the chair and beckoned Lizzie to follow her to the kitchen where a feast was waiting for them. As they ate, Kitty told her all about her life, her children and grandchildren and the fun she'd had. 'Don't regret a minute of it.' She wiped her mouth with a serviette. 'And do you know when I realised that I had to escape?'

Lizzie nodded. 'The day of the outing of the Zoo?'

'That's right!' She leaned over and rested her hand on Lizzie's. 'When we were standing looking at that poor creature I was feeling unbearably sad and then a little hand found its way into mine and that was all the strength I needed.' She smiled at Lizzie's surprise. 'You were my spur.'

'I never found that strength for myself.' Lizzie said.

'Did you want to leave Rathshannan?'

Lizzie shrugged and then, for the second time in two days, recounted her story; only this time she admitted how she'd felt about it – the guilt and the secrets. Kitty listened patiently, occasionally looking puzzled but she said nothing till Lizzie was finished. Then she poured another cup of tea and tutted. 'So you blamed yourself for your father's death? You poor child.'

'I thought I had to stay there – to make amends.'

'What a terrible thing shame is.' Kitty shook her head. 'Are you free of it now?'

'Absolutely!'

Kitty put the pot down slowly and deliberately. She had the same expression she wore years ago when she about to ask them the hardest spelling of all. 'So why have you left?'

'It's just a holiday. Some big news is about to break out in Rathshannan and I didn't want to be there when it happened.'

'What's that?'

'Well, do you remember Bernie Healey?'

Kitty nodded, her face clouding over.

'She had her "tonsils" out when we were in sixth class. Well,' she took a sup of her tea, 'they've turned up again.'

Kitty's cup clattered in her saucer. 'What do you mean?'

'Bernie had a child back in '69 and now that child's turned up and they are about to be reunited.'

Kitty shook her head vigorously. 'That's not possible, Elizabeth.'

'It is, honestly. He's been in the village for a few weeks now making sure he has all the facts straight and he's about to reveal himself to Bernie. That's bound to spark off a million reminiscences and I'm afraid I'm not emotionally prepared to go back to those days just yet. Or at least I thought I wasn't. And anyway, it might get messy.'

In response to Kitty's raised eyebrow, Lizzie told her about Teresa, and how she had seen her eyes shine for the first time since her useless husband ran off with another woman and now she was about to be crushed again. 'I just couldn't bear to be there to witness it. It's too soon after finding out about Da; I need to get my own head straight first. I don't think I could take the excitement.'

Kitty took a slice of cake and was cutting it into small pieces on her plate. She lined the pieces up and popped them into her mouth one by one, chewing slowly and thoughtfully. When she finished the last piece she sighed and pushed the plate away. 'Oh dear,' she said. 'I think you do need to go home, Elizabeth.'

Lizzie shook her head. 'Not yet, maybe. Bernie, Teresa and the twins are close knit – they'll manage to cope with the new addition to the family without me.'

Kitty shook her head. 'I'm afraid they won't.' She sounded so certain.

Lizzie leaned forward and looked into her face. Her eyes were shiny with tears. 'I don't understand.'

Kitty looked her in the eye and she had the same expression she'd had the day Mr Healey came to the school and shouted up at May standing in the window. It was her *pull yourself together and be strong* face. 'You must go back. Stop him before it's too late.'

'But why? He's a grown man and he wants to find his mother.'

'Yes but he can't be sure that Bernie is the one.'

'He is,' Lizzie smiled, 'honestly. He's met his father and found out where his mother was and everything I've been able to tell him confirmed that. He even knows his name – James Arthur Farrelly. Are you okay?'

Kitty was holding the side of the table and her face was white. Lizzie knelt beside her. 'What's wrong, Kitty? What am I missing?'

'Stop him, Elizabeth.' She forced the words through clenched teeth. 'Go home and stop him. He isn't Bernie Healey's son!'

'How can you be so sure?'

Kitty took her hands and held them tightly. 'There was so much going on at that time; you probably don't remember all of it. And that's as it should be – the past is best laid to rest. Nobody should be reminded – not Bernie especially. Not after what happened.'

'What? Why can't she meet her son?'

Kitty stood up and she was Sister Cillian once again, her face set and her voice stern. 'Because,' she said, 'Bernie

Healey's baby didn't live. It was premature, it was stillborn and, Elizabeth,' she leaned down, her face close to Lizzie's, 'it was a girl.'

*

After the initial shock of Kitty's revelations, Lizzie thought to rush home straight away. Instead, Kitty urged her to ring Anne. She would know if Jim had been to Bernie's yet.

'Use my phone, dear. Those mobiles are extortionate.' Lizzie went into the hallway and dialled Anne's number

Bernie wasn't around, Anne told her. She and Teresa went into Kilkenny to do some pre-wedding shopping and had decided to stay overnight.

'So the shop hasn't been open either. The fire damaged the lines and they've had to turn the power off on Main Street. Everybody's out. They said it'll be back in action by Monday.' Anne sounded hoarse but light-hearted. 'Why'd you want to know if your jigsaw man was up in Bernie's anyway – are you jealous?'

'As if – I'm too old for him, I told you that,' Lizzie said, pleased that Anne was on form again. 'Whose wedding are Teresa and Bernie catering for this time?'

'Don't you know?'

Lizzie waited. She couldn't think who was due to get married in Rathshannan.

'Teresa.'

'What about her?'

'It's her wedding. I tried to tell you the other day but you put the phone down too quickly.'

Lizzie's forehead ran cold. What on earth was that man playing at? He thought she was his sister; he knew she was in love with him; he planned to leave her behind. And he had asked her to marry him?

'Bastard.' She spat into the phone.

'What was that?'

Lizzie bit her lip. Anne was suspicious of the jigsaw man from the beginning – and Lizzie had hotly defended him. 'When did this happen?'

'Last week. The day after the fire... '

The day Jim stood in her shop and confessed that he had only ever come looking for his mother. A wife wasn't in the equation. He didn't do commitment.

'When Matt realised that Teresa was awash with guilt over what those brats did, he decided to get in there quickly and ask her.'

Matt? Teresa was engaged to Matt? In a flash, Lizzie had a picture in her head. She and Teresa were standing outside Reardons watching the garage burn.

*Damn it*, Teresa said, *I've gotten used to having him around... it'd be a shame to go back to the way we were. I don't think I could bear it...*

*Me neither.*

In front of them the village men were fighting the blaze with Jim and Matt in the centre of them. Lizzie had been looking at Jim. But it was Matt Teresa was watching.

Then all the other pieces fell into place as well: Bernie feeding Matt samples of fudge; Matt saying the fire might help his cause; even Teresa's easy manner with Jim, the laughing eyes, the glow in her cheeks. It wasn't because she was in love with him – it was because she wasn't.

'Lizzie? Are you still there?'

Lizzie was smiling so broadly she could hardly speak. 'And there I was thinking I had it all put together so cleverly – I am so stupid, Anne, you wouldn't believe it.'

'Try me.'

'I thought it was Jim she liked.'

'She does – but she loves Matt.'

'Tell her congratulations from me – no, in fact, I'll tell her myself. I'll be home tomorrow.'

'Great.' There was a shuffle as Anne prepared to put the phone down. 'Lizzie?'

Lizzie didn't wait. Now Anne would want to know why she had asked about Bernie. She'd tell her tomorrow. 'Bye!' she called and put the receiver down. Kitty was standing at the door watching her.

'Everything okay?'

Lizzie beamed. She told her the news. 'So if I can get to Jim before they get back he will leave and they will be none the wiser.'

Kitty didn't look as pleased as she expected. 'And Jim?'

Lizzie shook her head. 'Jim? I don't know. He's come a long way to find himself up a blind alley. Poor fellow. There must have been another child with the same surname born in St Bertrand's at that time and somehow the two of them got mixed up. Farrelly's quite a common name, I suppose. Poor Art – all those years thinking he had a son.'

Kitty nodded. She was leaning against the doorframe and with her shoulders slumped like that she looked old, tired.

Lizzie pulled out her purse. Kitty stopped her. 'Don't you dare,' she said. 'The phone call's on me. I owe you, remember?' She flapped her hands and smiled.

Lizzie smiled back. 'Anyway, I've taken up enough of your time.' She wrapped her arms around the old lady's shoulders. 'Thank you so much for phoning me and for the tea. It was lovely to see you again.' She gestured to the photographs lining the walls. 'And I'm chuffed it all turned out so well for you.'

Kitty hugged her back. 'Thank you, my dear. I've been very lucky.' She pulled away and held Lizzie at arm's length. 'And what are you going to do next?'

Lizzie slung her bag over her shoulder. 'I'm going home,' she said. 'I'm going back to my lovely house in my lovely village to work in my lovely shop till I don't want to work any more. Then I'm going to retire – and be content.' She nodded as if that was the end of that.

Kitty's smile was wistful. 'It's a good ambition. I wish you the very best of luck, Lizzie Flynn.'

'Well, bye then and I hope we meet again.'

Kitty said nothing.

Lizzie got in to her car and drove slowly away, watching the tiny figure grow even smaller in the rear-view mirror. She had the radio on and was humming to herself. Another hour and she'd be on the road – home.

\*

Kitty Barrett waited till the car rounded the corner onto the coast road before she went inside and shut the door. On the table, the remains of tea were testament to a fine feast. She smiled. Lizzie Flynn had turned out all right but how awful that it had taken till now for her to make peace with herself. What a waste. As she passed the phone she noticed something on the floor. It was the elephant postcard. She had a flash memory of Lizzie pulling her purse out. Bother. She picked it up and wondered if she should just stick it in the post – she knew the address. She turned the card over and over in her hand, knowing with dread what she had to do.

'Oh blast!' she said picking up the phone, 'I can't leave her to find out on her own now.'

Then she pressed redial.

# The Last Jigsaw Piece
## 2006

LIZZIE ARRIVED HOME IN THE EARLY HOURS, surprised to find a note from Anne.

*Come for lunch. 12-ish. Ax*

Lizzie turned it over. Canny old psychic or what? She dumped her bag on her bedroom floor and climbed straight into bed.

She left the house next morning at a quarter past eleven. After the long drive her legs were stiff and Geraldine's meals left her heavy and sluggish. Halfway to Anne's the wind picked up and it started to rain. She pulled her collar closer and picked up speed, trying to suppress a sense of uneasiness that had been growing through the night. *Come for lunch. 12-ish* was a welcome invitation after a long night-time drive. In the cold light of day it sounded more like a summons.

She rounded the corner by the gate and stopped. Bernie's car was huddled beside Anne's. As she scrunched over the gravel to the back door, the uneasiness reached her throat. She coughed to clear it as she put her hand out to lift the latch then stopped dead. The quiet of the yard, the patter of the rain on the sheds' roofs, the sense that there was something unpleasant waiting for her was overwhelming.

In the kitchen, Anne and Bernie were sitting at the table. In front of them they had a tray of toffee and they were cutting it. Anne looked up and smiled. 'Hello stranger! Glad you're home.'

'What's wrong?' Lizzie looked around the kitchen. On the stove a large pot of soup was heating and there was a smell of fresh bread. Crockery and cutlery were stacked on the dresser ready to be set once the table was cleared. Everything looked so very normal.

'Nothing's wrong.'

Anne continued her cutting but Lizzie caught the glance that flashed between her and Bernie. She looked from the top of one head to the other. She'd often seen them like this before, carefully cutting the slabs of creamy toffee and lifting the pieces onto waxed paper to cool before being weighed and bagged. They were masters of the art of steady hand-cutting and usually flew through the job but today the knife slid slowly around the confection. Lizzie moved closer to the table.

That was different too. Instead of neat rows of equal pieces, Bernie was holding the tray while Anne cut swirls and curves and wonderful fluid shapes into the sweet. She prised her knife under one and easing it slowly off the tray, put it to one side. It looked like a little female.

'It's called a whimsy,' Anne said, without looking up. 'Victorian jigsaw makers used to cut them on a whim and they helped to tell the story behind the jigsaw.' As she spoke, she cut and lifted, lining the little figures up on the table. Lizzie watched. There was a woman and a man, a woman and a man, a little boy and then she stopped. She looked at Bernie then and slowly turning the knife around, offered it to her. Bernie tried to smile but her eyes were bright. She cut a man too, bigger than the others and then bending close to the tray, held her hand steady as she pressed into the sweet toffee and cut a tiny rectangle, or almost a rectangle. She prised it out and laid it on the table beside one of the couples. Then the two women sat back and motioned Lizzie to sit.

'Aren't we having lunch?'

'Not yet,' Anne said. 'We have a jigsaw to complete first.'

Lizzie sat. All the little figures faced her as she waited for the other jigsaw pieces to be cut. When they were finished, Anne jumbled them together. Then she put the whimsies back into the middle. She looked across at Bernie who nodded in support.

'Right, Lizzie,' she said, 'No more secrets.'

The air was full of the smell of toffee, sweet and sickly. Lizzie looked from one woman to the other. They were watching her calmly but there was a buzzing in Lizzie's ears. She stood up.

'I don't want to hear this,' she said. 'I'm just managing to get my head together and I don't need any more.'

They raised their hands in protest.

'I'm serious. The past is done and I don't want to go there again.' She turned to leave. As she reached the kitchen door a draught blew in as Lizzie screamed. A man came through the back door, his head bent, his great coat blowing behind him. He slid the coat off his shoulders and hung it on the hook. Everything about him, the hunch of his shoulders, the way his dark hair fell over his forehead, the smell of the outdoors in the folds of his coat as it swept past her was familiar.

'Da?'

The man shook the rain from his head and lifted his face to her. It was Jim.

Lizzie froze. Her hand was on her throat and she knew that if she didn't keep it there, the scream would come out. 'Why are you here?' The buzzing in the air around her was breaking up into images that crackled and spat as they swirled in the air around her head – Anne's pale face the night Lizzie fell asleep in the barn, the funny smell off her when they stood looking out the window, the understanding between two pale girls outside the graveyard... Lizzie held her hand out to Jim.

'You're not Bernie's son.'

He shook his head. Now that he was standing in the better light of the kitchen she could see what it was that made him so familiar when he turned up that first day. It wasn't that he looked like Art Farrelly at all.

'You're Anne's.'

'That's right.' He moved towards her and placing his hand gently under her elbow, led her back to the table. 'Sit down here with us, Lizzie, and help us to put this jigsaw together.'

Lizzie sat. Anne was watching her son as he took his place at the other end of the table. When he was sitting too, she reached out and covered his hand with hers. 'It's so good to see you,' she said breathlessly.

'When did you find out?' Lizzie's words were clipped.

'Last night. After Jim went to Bernie's they came here.'

Lizzie looked at the three of them. 'One big happy family – how nice for you!' She spat the words across the table at him. 'And did nobody think to tell me?'

'You weren't there. You had already left the guesthouse and when Kitty phoned, she said you were already on the way home.'

Lizzie was so angry she couldn't speak. The name tripped off Anne's tongue as if she was talking about an old friend, someone she spoke to every day. *I dunno, I can't remember, north side, I think.*

'She pressed redial, Lizzie. She told me you knew Bernie's baby was a girl and she warned me that it was time you knew the whole truth.' She reached across the table and squeezed Bernie's hand. 'D'you want to start?'

Bernie leaned forward and picked the rectangular piece from the jumble on the table. 'This is my baby,' she said, 'In her little coffin.' She put it to one side. 'I was thirty weeks pregnant. My father – ' she reached out and took the largest man piece and put it beside the coffin, 'he came up to Dublin to find me.' She paused, unable to continue. Then she took a deep breath.

All the time she was talking, Anne had been picking the irregular pieces and fitting the outline of their jigsaw together. Bernie's baby was in the middle. She picked up the two female shapes and slid them, sticky, on either side. 'That's us,' she said. 'When I reached St Bertrand's Bernie was there already. Aunty Margie had already made contact with her and so we were given a room together.'

Aunty Margie knew? *I think it would be a good idea if she came to Dublin with me for a while.*

'Have I been lied to my entire life!' She looked from one to the other. 'Have I?' She banged the table. 'I thought you were grieving, Anne. I thought you were so consumed with grief at our father's death – a death for which, by the way, I blamed myself – that you had to go away to rest.' Anne hung her head. 'And then I thought you stayed away because you were angry with me!'

Anne held her arms out. 'Oh, Lizzie, I had no idea you thought it was your fault. I thought it was mine! The night before Da died I had told them both that I was pregnant. They were in shock – '

*'Oh Annie, Why? How could you let this happen?' Her parents looked through her as if they hadn't been worried about Lizzie at all, as if they hadn't noticed she was missing...* They hadn't.

'And the next day our father put a gun to his head.'

'Oh God.' With shaking hands, Lizzie reached out and picked up one of the little men. She stuck him beside the women. Art Farrelly straddling Lizzie's bike; Art Farrelly telling Jim his mother loved the child but would give no reason for not marrying his father. Anne had Art Farrelly's baby. 'And that's why you wouldn't have anything to do with him – because of Da?'

Bernie held her father's piece hovering over the rest. 'He found out. Even though Art denied it, my father was convinced Art was the father of my child and he followed me to St Bertrand's and saw Anne there, pregnant. He waited for me one night when I was coming home from the cinema and he came marching out of the shadows, demanding the whole story. When I wouldn't tell him he grew angry, threatened to kill me, and Anne too, if I didn't tell. Said we were whores sharing the same man. And then he started to slap me, slowly at first and I knew he would do it. All the time his voice was growing quieter and he described how he would be waiting for us and so I told him – I had to. Then he hit me hard – first on the face and then in the stomach.' She was holding the piece so tightly now that it distorted in her hot palm and she flicked her hand to be free of it. 'He hit me till my face bled, till my body bled – ' she gulped and the pain cut filled the room, 'till my baby bled.' She pressed the distorted shape in to its position in the jigsaw. 'And so I lost that baby, Lizzie. Sister Cillian was well on the way to being Kitty Barrett by then and she helped me through the worst of it. Then your Aunty Margie took me home and nursed me and when Anne – after Anne's baby was born and given up for adoption – the two of us signed up for college together. We'd had enough of the sour and nasty – we decided to devote our lives to sweets.' She gave a sad smile. 'I wasn't as smart – I dropped out eventually and came home.'

Lizzie was staring at her in amazement. Strong tough Bernie Collins beaten to a pulp by her own father till her baby was dead! 'But why *you*, Bernie? When he thought it was Art, he went for him. Why didn't he go for the real father? Why you?'

Bernie shook her head. 'He couldn't. It wasn't possible. It was too late.'

For a while nobody said any more. The four of them picked the pieces up one by one, turning them this way and that to see where they fitted. By now the toffee was cooled and brittle and some pieces began to chip as they were pushed into place. Hands grew sticky and Anne got up and offered them all protective gloves. Lizzie and Bernie shook their heads.

'We'll see this through without protection, thanks,' Lizzie said. Jim's baby piece slid in easily between his parents and the spaces filled in slowly. Eventually the jigsaw was almost complete. Only one whimsy remained on the table. It was the third man. Anne and Bernie both reached out for him at the same time, hesitated and sat there, their hands in mid-air.

'Well?' Lizzie said. 'Aren't you going to finish it? Aren't you going to put the last piece in?'

Bernie's hand clenched into a fist and Anne put hers back on the table. They sat staring at one another seemingly unable to move.

The humming Lizzie felt in the air before started up again. It was thick and muffled but she knew there was a scream waiting somewhere behind it. Anne and Bernie were watching her and the look in their eyes was so sad that she knew she shouldn't press on. At the other end of the table, Jim had his head in his hands. He knew too and on the table between them Lizzie had the impression that the little figure had started to shift. Icy fingers crept up her forehead and spread out over her scalp. Shimmering at the edge of her vision the figure was trying to get up. He was going to walk over to her and tell her himself. Only that he had lain there so long and was stuck to the table, he'd have reached her by now. She could hear him calling to her.

Without thinking about it, Lizzie's hand slid off the table, onto her lap and back to her bag hanging on the back of her chair. She felt around till she found what she was looking for. She clasped the penknife tightly in her hand and brought it back to the table. The little figure was waiting.

'Lizzie, don't look!' Anne's voice came from somewhere far above her, high up in the loft. 'Go back... stay there.'

But it was too late. Lizzie reached out and slid the blade under the little figure to prise him off the table. He was stuck fast and she had to push the blade hard against his side to release him. Hands shaking, she pushed the blade further in until the figure sprang free and slid across the table. His head splintered and remained where it was as the rest of him came to a halt in front of Bernie.

'Is that why your father took it out on you, Bernie?' she didn't take her eyes off the table. 'Is it because he couldn't do anything to the baby's father – '

Bernie was nodding and sobbing at the same time.

'Because he was already dead?'

Lizzie picked the body up and dropped it into place in the jigsaw. Then she picked up the shards and dropped them into the last space, pressing them down with the handle of the penknife.

She looked from Anne to Bernie and back again. So that explained everything. The last piece of the jigsaw.

Da.

## Rathshannon
## 2006

THE LANE WAS DARK AS IT HAD ALWAYS BEEN. Once she was past the chestnut tree at the gate, there was no trace of light. Heavy clouds that had hung over all day were breaking up and Lizzie prayed they'd let enough moonlight through to guide her safely to the top. As she stumbled along, bushes on either side closed in on her. Nobody used this lane any more; nobody drove his tractor up it, knocking off overhanging branches as he went so that by the time she reached the corner at the top, she had to keep her arms over her face to stop it from being scratched.

As soon as she reached the gate, the clouds parted and the hillside was bathed in blue-silver light. The grass was fringed in frost and for a second, Lizzie wished she had asked Jim to come with her. It looked beautiful – ghostly and shimmering. She put her hand out to lift the latch but it wasn't there. Over years it had rusted and hung useless on an old nail. Lizzie pushed the gate open.

As she walked across the grass to the barn, the freezing wet stalks and weeds stuck to her legs – she barely noticed. Inside the barn it would be dry. The doors were bolted and it took all her strength to force the bolts so that she could pull them open. She eased each one back over the weeds until they were splayed like a pair of huge curtains on either side of a gigantic stage. Then she went inside.

Her audience was there already. Pot-bellied sacks lined up on either side barely muffled the scuttling of field mice as she walked the length of the barn. When she reached the far end, she turned and looked up at the loft. With the light from the little window shining through, it looked spot-lit. The bales had come loose and flattened and now lay scattered on the floor. It looked empty but she knew it wasn't. If she put her feet on the one remaining ladder and climbed to the top, there would be plenty to see. Anne would be there, aged fifteen, lying in the arms of young Art Farrelly, his dark hair falling over his face as he whispered in her ear; or maybe her father would be there. She wondered if he'd had to whisper anything to young Bernie Healey or would the excitement of being with a man who didn't shout at her and hit her be enough? A man who would stroke her face and smile so that she didn't need sweet words to lift her skirts and part her legs for him.

No wonder the barn was out of bounds. *It's not safe for you to be there on your own*, Da warned, time after time. *You could have an accident and get hurt*.

Lizzie thought of Bernie's face as she watched Jim and Anne wave the happy couple off after Teresa's wedding. She thought of her mother's face as she stood swaying over an open grave after the funeral.

'People got very hurt, Da. It wasn't an accident!'

Then she took her bag off her shoulder and laid it on the ground. The moon was behind clouds again and she had to fumble in the darkness. Eventually she found them – a small leather pouch and a box of matches. With shaking hands she lit the matches, cursing as the draught from the open doors blew them out. When there was only one left, she stopped.

'I need to do this,' she said. 'I need to finish it.' Then she turned her back to the loft and hunching over the match, struck it. The tiny flame flickered a moment then grew, steady and strong. She held it against the side of the pouch till the leather caught fire and the smell of burning skin stung her nostrils. The match had now burned down and the tips of her fingers scorched. She swung around and flung the pouch as high as she could, onto the loft floor.

For a moment there was nothing, no rustling, no light. Then it came – a steady orange glow as the remains of scattered bales caught light and spread crackling around the timbers. They licked up the handles of a pair of old pitchforks and flowed orange down the rungs of the ladder. Soon the whole entrance was aflame, lit up like the bulbs on an actor's mirror. Framed by the light, a young Lizzie stood on her loft stage, a picket fence guitar in her hand. She was strumming the air wildly and with her head thrown back, giving the performance of her life. Below her, her father stood watching. He waited till she was finished and then clapped enthusiastically.

*That's my girl*, he said. *Wait till the world gets to hear you! You'll be dead famous, so you will – and I'll be dead proud.*

But it didn't turn out like that. I'm still here, still giving my best performances in my own head and you? You're just dead.

She kicked a pile of straw and watched as it caught the front of one of the pot-bellied audience and burst into flame. The smell of fire was everywhere now and the crackling loud in her ears. Unlike the night of the bus blaze when the air

304

was acrid with smoke, this fire burned cleanly. Through the burning frame of the doorway, she could see the lights of Rathshannan in the distance. Nobody was waiting up for her there. Nobody would be angry if she was late. Nobody would look up in relief when she came rushing through the door and say, *Lizzie! Thank God! Where have you been?* Nobody ever had.

Above her head there was a thunderous cracking as one of the huge roof beams splintered in the heat and started to come away. In a moment, Lizzie thought, it will come crashing down on my head and that will be the end of it.

On both sides of the barn the fire was spreading towards her, urging her into its heated embrace. Only the middle of the floor was still clear, like a walkway. Her audience of flame cracked and clapped, waiting for her decision. It could be the end. Beyond the door, the twinkling lights of the village waited too.

As the huge beam cracked impatiently over her head, Lizzie understood what she wanted. She lifted her head proudly and without looking back, walked towards the door. As she reached it, the clouds parted again and she stepped out into the blue-silver light and breathed deeply.

Then she went home.

*Toppling Miss April*
Adrienne Dines

*'Monica Moran was not the woman she used to be. Or rather she was not just the woman she used to be. She was at least one other woman as well and their combined weight sat heavily on her overburdened bones. Where her breasts had been generous twenty years ago, they were now magnanimous, munificent... If that cleavage was any closer to the ground you could stand a bicycle in it.'*

Twenty years ago, when Father Barry ruled the Tullabeg roost, Bernadette Teegan and Monica Moran vied for his attention. Life was a maelstrom of mixed emotions and misplaced extremities – two young girls with plenty to learn. Then Monica went away and life settled down.

Now Monica is back.

And Bernadette has no intention of making hers a happy visit. She has plans – to snare the most eligible bachelor in town, Cormac Hegarty, Estate Agent, and keep nephew Michael's soul (and overalls) spotless.

But Monica has plans too.

A comedy of errors, misdirection and cross-wired agendas, *Toppling Miss April* is a triumph of flesh over fantasy, when menopause is just a pause between men and experience counts for everything.

*'A laugh-out-loud screwball comedy. This is humour sized 44FF ... uncontainably funny.'* Meg Gardiner

ISBN 1 905175 12 4